CRESCENT CITY
CHRISTMAS CHAOS

Also by Ellen Byron

The Vintage Cookbook Mysteries
BAYOU BOOK THIEF
WINED AND DIED IN NEW ORLEANS
FRENCH QUARTER FRIGHT NIGHT *

The Cajun Country Mysteries
PLANTATION SHUDDERS
BODY ON THE BAYOU
A CAJUN CHRISTMAS KILLING
MARDI GRAS MURDER
FATAL CAJUN FESTIVAL
MURDER IN THE BAYOU BONEYARD
CAJUN KISS OF DEATH

The Golden Motel Mysteries
A VERY WOODSY MURDER
SOLID GOLD MURDER

** available from Severn House*

CRESCENT CITY CHRISTMAS CHAOS

Ellen Byron

First world edition published in Great Britain and the USA in 2025
by Severn House, an imprint of Canongate Books Ltd,
14 High Street, Edinburgh EH1 1TE.

Paperback edition first published in Great Britain and the USA in 2026
by Severn House, an imprint of Canongate Books Ltd.

severnhouse.com

British Library Cataloguing-in-Publication Data
A CIP catalogue record for this title is available from the British Library.

ISBN-13: 978-1-4483-1318-1 (cased)
ISBN-13: 978-1-4483-1872-8 (paper)
ISBN-13: 978-1-4483-1685-4 (e-book)

Typeset by Palimpsest Book Production Ltd., Falkirk, Stirlingshire, Scotland.
Printed and bound in Great Britain by CPI Group (UK) Ltd,
Croydon CR0 4YY

The manufacturer's authorised representative in the EU for product safety is
BGC Sustainability & Compliance, 7 avenue du Général Leclerc, Paris 75014
(gpsr@baldwinglobalconsulting.com)

Praise for the Vintage Cookbook Mysteries

"Byron's heroine navigates a bumpy road with grace
and panache"
Kirkus Reviews on *French Quarter Fright Night*

"Byron, author of the award-winning 'Cajun Country'
mysteries, combines setting, vintage cookbooks, recipes,
and family drama in another delectable cozy"
Library Journal on *Wined and Died in New Orleans*

"The characters feel like old friends. Everything about this
story keeps the reader invested . . . you won't be
disappointed. This book will keep fans excited and looking
forward to the next installment"
thecozyreview.com on *Wined and Died in New Orleans*

"Fans of Byron's award-winning 'Cajun Country' mysteries
will enjoy her return to New Orleans with an engaging,
fun cast of characters"
Library Journal on *Bayou Book Thief*

"Cozy fare served up Crescent City style"
Kirkus Reviews on *Bayou Book Thief*

About the author

Ellen Byron is an Anthony Award nominee, bestselling author, and recipient of multiple Agatha and Lefty awards for her Cajun Country Mysteries, Vintage Cookbook Mysteries, and Catering Hall Mysteries (as Maria DiRico). She is also an award-winning playwright and non-award-winning writer of TV hits like *Wings*, *Just Shoot Me!*, and *Fairly OddParents*, but considers her most impressive achievement working as a cater-waiter for Martha Stewart.

A native New Yorker, Ellen is a graduate of Tulane University and lives in the Los Angeles area with her husband, daughter, and a rotating crew of rescue pups.

www.ellenbyron.com

This book is dedicated to the Friends of the Studio City Branch Library (Los Angeles) and the Friends of the New Orleans Public Library (Milton H. Latter Memorial Library Branch). I've found some of my favorite vintage cookbooks at your amazing fundraiser sales. It's also dedicated to libraries and librarians everywhere. You are rock stars!

CAST OF CHARACTERS

At Bon Vee Culinary House Museum:

Miracle "Ricki" Fleur de Lis James-Diaz—Proprietor, Miss Vee's Vintage Cookbook and Kitchenware Shop at Bon Vee

Zellah Batiste—artist and café manager; also works at Peli Deli, her family's business

Eugenia Charbonnet Felice—President of the Bon Vee Foundation board; niece of the late owner of Bon Vee, Genevieve Charbonnet

Olivia Felice—Eugenia's granddaughter and Ricki's intern

Theo Charbonnet—Eugenia's nephew and self-titled Director of Community Relations

Cookie Yanover—"Recovering children's librarian" now working at Bon Vee as the Director of Educational Programming

Virgil Morel—former executive chef at Charbonnet's restaurant; current cooking world hottie; co-owner of the Bayou Backyard, a popular hangout

Mordant—haunted history tour guide and Bon Vee handyman

Ruth, Jennifer, Larry, Edgar—caroling tour guides

Beth Norris—a customer

Various community cookbook wannabes

Law Enforcement:

Nina Rodriguez—detective

Samuel Girard—detective

Peony Place residents:

Phyllis Gibbs—a sketchy woman from Josepha's past

David and Melissa Sachs—her neighbors on one side; they don't get along

Arthur and Brenda Broussard—her neighbors on the other side; they do get along

Renate Rancourt—a gorgon of a grand dame

Tomas—house sitter/gig worker

Crescent City Concierge Care:

Dr. Rachel Vernon—dermatologist

Dr. Jeremy Mansieur—primary-care physician

Helene Mansieur—his mysterious wife

Delia Robbins—head office manager

Various office staff

Krewe of Gaia:

Lizette Rancourt—Olivia's friend, Renate Rancourt's grand-daughter, and a Gaia maid

Penelope Vogelspack—Olivia's non-friend, a maid

Owen Vogelspack—Penelope's father, an ambitious lawyer

And . . .

Josepha James-Diaz—Ricki's mother

Luis James-Diaz—Ricki's father

Kitty Kat Rousseau—Ricki's landlady and Josepha's friend

Ky Nyugen—co-owner with Virgil of the Bayou Backyard

Lady Smith-Foucault – manager of the Good Neighbor Thrift Store

Patrick Flynn—director of Virgil's show

Mateo—a college student

ONE

Ricki sipped her non-alcoholic Chardonnay and cast an affectionate glance around the Bon Vee Culinary House Museum's elegant dining room, where about two dozen guests were transitioning from the Thanksgiving buffet to seats at the table. She was already seated, having claimed the spot that her boyfriend Virgil Morel had saved for her.

The chef-turned-celebrity cooking show judge was still at the buffet, serving his delectable take on a sweet potato casserole. He'd found the recipe in one of the cookbooks Ricki sold in her gift shop at the NOLA Garden District estate-turned-house museum, Miss Vee's Vintage Cookbook and Kitchenware Shop. Ricki had named the shop in honor of Genevieve "Miss Vee" Charbonnet, the famed Big Easy restauranteur and owner of Bon Vee. The late Miss Vee had also recently been revealed to be Ricki's biological great-grandmother. Family history in New Orleans could be as complicated as a 1930s recipe for sweet potato casserole.

Virgil came to the table. He tapped his knife against one of the mansion's antique crystal goblets to get everyone's attention, then raised it. "First of all, a toast to our hostess who is always the mostest." He held his glass up to Eugenia. "To Eugenia."

"To Eugenia!" every guest echoed as they toasted.

Virgil lowered his glass. "And I have an announcement." He took a deep breath. "Wow. When I say this out loud, it's gonna make it real. Friends . . . I'm making my first solo TV cooking show special."

Everyone hooted and applauded, no one louder than Ricki. She jumped up and hugged the chef. "I'm so excited for you. And proud." She let go of him and pumped a fist. "Whoo-hoo!"

Virgil laughed. "Thanks, chère."

"What's the focus and would it help ratings if a short, cute blonde paraded through the show a few times?" Cookie, Bon Vee's educational programming director and the short, cute blonde in question, mimed fluffing her pixie cut.

"No to the second question but thanks for the offer," Virgil said, amused. "The focus will be on our special New Orleans Christmas tradition of Réveillon dinners." For the benefit of the out-of-towners at the table, he explained, "Réveillon means 'awakening'. The tradition dates back to the early 1800s when the Creoles celebrated the start of Christmas with a big family meal after returning home from midnight mass."

"Where will we be able to watch the show?" Eugenia asked.

"On Food Plus, a new streamer that's already got a lot of heat on it. They realized they were short a unique holiday special and reached out to me. Because it has to come together quickly, they agreed to let me executive produce—basically be in charge of the whole production—something I've always wanted to do. And thanks to this woman here . . ." he again raised his glass to Eugenia, "I'm shooting the whole show right here at Bon Vee."

This brought additional cheers from everyone, especially Ricki. For one thing, it would mean more time with Virgil, who was often on the road in his role as a judge on the TV show, *America's Top Southern Chef.* For another, it would draw positive attention to Bon Vee, a nice break from the notoriety brought upon it by a couple of murders that unwittingly involved the house museum.

"So much to give thanks for this Thanksgiving," Eugenia said with a beneficent smile.

Virgil held up his hand to reclaim everyone's attention. "I have one more announcement." Virgil's light-blue eyes, a sexy contrast to his deep brown complexion, twinkled. "The time between filming and airing the show is so tight that I decided I'd only make it if I could assemble the best crew possible. Which meant bringing a certain camera operator out of retirement." He leaned back and called into the hallway, "Your cue, friends."

"Ta-da!"

To Ricki's shock and delight, her parents Josepha and Luis

James-Diaz appeared in the doorway. They each struck a pose, then opened their arms to Ricki.

"Mom! Dad!" She ran to them.

"Ricki sandwich!" Luis declared. The three enveloped each other in a group hug with Ricki in the middle.

"This is the best surprise ever," Ricki said to Virgil over Josepha's shoulder. "Thank you."

Virgil shrugged. "I wish I could say I was being altruistic but it's as much for me as for you." He came to them and clapped Luis on the back. "The man knows where to put a camera."

The James-Diaz family broke apart and Ricki introduced her parents to everyone. Josepha motioned to her and Luis's matching burgundy track suits. "Sorry we're underdressed. We came straight from the airport."

"Like I care." Ricki hugged her mother. "Did you fly nonstop from PV?" she asked. After Luis retired, the couple had moved from Los Angeles to his hometown of Puerto Vallarta.

"We're staying in another shotgun Kitty Kat owns," Josepha said, referring to Kitty Kat Rousseau, who was Ricki's landlady by dint of being Josepha's best friend from their days working as nurses at the now-defunct Charity Hospital.

"How long will it take to shoot the show?" Ricki asked Luis, who had grabbed a plate and was loading it up with Virgil's sweet potato casserole.

"With preproduction and production, about two-and-a-half weeks. The show's set to air the weekend before Christmas, so it's a rough schedule. Since we won't have a chance to spend much time together while I'm in production, we thought we'd stay through Christmas and New Year's, if it's OK by you."

"OK?" Ricki practically bounced up and down with excitement. "It's the best Christmas present ever. The production shoot will sync up with holiday sales, which will keep me busy in the shop. Aside from that, things should be uneventful and we'll have plenty of time to relax and hang out."

In the coming weeks, Ricki would look back at this innocuous comment and wish with all her heart she'd been right.

TWO

Since Eugenia was possibly the last purist on the planet who refused to put up a single strand of Christmas lights before Thanksgiving, the day after turned into an all-hands-on deck day of decorating for the holidays instead of Black Friday. Ricki was grateful to landlady Kitty Kat for hosting her parents, freeing her up to turn Miss Vee's Vintage Cookbook and Kitchenware into a must-shop holiday destination.

Olivia Felice, Eugenia's granddaughter—which made her another of Ricki's newly discovered cousins—blew into the shop through its mullioned glass French doors. Miss Vee's was located in a lovely room formerly known as the nineteenth-century mansion's "Ladies Parlor." Pale green damask covered its walls and ornate molding painted white encircled the room. A glistening chandelier dangled from an intricately carved ceiling medallion. The instant Ricki had stepped foot in the parlor it felt like the perfect home for a gift shop dedicated to sharing the culinary past with fans of all things vintage.

"Ugh, I'm so glad to be here and out of the school library. Can I tell you how much I hate finals?" Olivia accompanied the statement with an eye roll and flip of her thick, dirty blonde ponytail. A junior at Tulane majoring in Communication, she'd added a minor in Psychology, motivated by a recent misjudgment of someone's character that had almost led to her death. She'd transitioned from intern to Ricki's sole part-time employee and lifetime young friend as well as relative.

"I'm glad you're here. I could use help decorating this." Ricki motioned to an artificial Christmas tree that exceeded her petite height by a foot. "I think I've bought up food-themed ornaments at every thrift shop in town. I thought we could fill in with smaller kitchenware items like these old measuring spoons." She held up a set of nesting tin spoons. "Every item on the tree will be for sale, so I'm going with white lights. Colored lights would be too busy."

"I'm on it." Olivia reached into one of two big boxes loaded with holiday paraphernalia. She pulled out a long strand of tiny white lights. "And no, I haven't heard anything from a krewe."

"I was afraid to ask."

While Ricki was born in the Big Easy, she'd moved to Los Angeles as a child when Josepha met and married Luis. She was still learning the ways of the quirky city she now called home. Olivia had educated her on the machinations of krewes, the organizations responsible for the city's elaborate Mardi Gras parades and balls. The krewes chose local young women, mostly debutantes, for their courts. While carnival season didn't officially kick off until January 6th—Twelfth Night—invitations to join the courts were delivered much earlier via a "court call" paid to the future queen and maids by representatives of the krewe. New Orleans might celebrate the winter holidays in a big way, but to Ricki, the local greeting of "Happy Almost Mardi Gras!" made the city's priorities clear.

Olivia threaded the lights through the tree's branches. "I honestly don't care if I get a court call or not. I might even say no if they ask me to be on one."

"Liar," Ricki teased.

A fierce squawking disrupted the conversation. Ricki and Olivia dropped what they were doing to peer outside the shop's bay window, where they saw Bon Vee's resident peacocks Gumbo and Jambalaya chasing co-worker Theo Charbonnet— Eugenia's nephew and yet another cousin to Ricki—across the mansion's verdant green side yard.

"You OK?" Ricki called to Theo.

"I read somewhere that the Victorians put stuffed peacocks on top of their trees instead of stars or angels," he called back. "Think about it."

He disappeared around the corner.

The women left the window and resumed decorating. "Have you noticed Cousin Theo's been acting more weird than usual?" Olivia asked as she added a second strand of lights to the tree.

"I wouldn't call it weird," Ricki said. "More like he's being squirrelly. Secretive. I think he's up to something."

"That's a scary thought."

Ricki nodded in agreement. While she and Theo had achieved a rapprochement, she still wasn't sure she could completely trust him.

"So, your parents are really nice," Olivia said, providing a change of subject.

"Oh, thanks. They're the best. I'm so glad you got to meet them."

"Are you going to do anything special while they're here? Like, a swamp tour or something?"

Ricki, who was about to hang a ceramic beignet ornament, paused. "Actually . . . since Dad will be busy on the TV shoot, I thought Mom and I could work together and dig up clues about my bio mom."

Ricki had been abandoned as an infant in New Orleans' infamous Charity Hospital, her teen mother disappearing after giving birth. She thanked the universe for Josepha, a NICU nurse who fell in love with the parentless baby and adopted her, parenting as a single mother until she met and fell in love with Luis, who happened to be in town working on a film.

Ricki adored her parents beyond belief, but questions about her past drove her to seek answers. So far, she'd learned that Genevieve Charbonnet had secretly given birth to a baby who would have been Ricki's grandparent. Her friend Mordant, who'd added private investigator to a list of occupations that included haunted tour guide and Bon Vee handyman, had tracked down the father of Genevieve's baby. Sadly, he'd died at the age of twenty-four of a rare heart condition.

Ricki resumed hanging ornaments. "Mordant hasn't been able to come up with any leads since he discovered my great-grandfather's grave. And I haven't come across any new connections on my genealogy sites. I thought I'd drive Mom around to some of the places from when we lived here and see if anything jogs a memory that might be useful."

"Sounds like a plan. I'm *starving*."

Ricki grinned, amused by Olivia's 180-degree turn to her own needs. "You keep decorating, I'll get us a snack."

She left the shop and headed down the mansion's capacious center hallway. Cookie waved from the beautifully appointed living room, which she was showing off to a group of tourists. Bon Vee was currently low on both tour guides, who were paid part-timers, and docents who volunteered their time, so Cookie and other staff members had been drafted to lead tours.

Ricki gestured to her and Cookie detached from her group. "I'm making a run to the café. You want anything?"

"An iced coffee would be great. It's on me." Cookie reached into the phone pocket of her leggings and extracted a twenty. She gave it to Ricki. "Plenty more where this came from," she said in a low voice. "This group's a mix of Houston and Dallas-ites, or whatever you call 'em. We just started the tour and they're already trying to out-tip each other to prove their city is better."

"Nice."

"I want to buy Nat the best Christmas present I can, so I need these groups to make it rain." Cookie rubbed her thumb to her index and middle finger, indicating money. She was dating the neighbor next door to Bon Vee and determined to make him the future Mr. Cookie Yanover. "Any idea what you're getting Virgil?"

"Not a clue," Ricki said. "I better get to the café before it closes."

Ricki continued down the hallway, embarrassed by her obvious change of subject and feeling guilty because she hadn't even thought about getting Virgil a gift. *It's because our relationship is so new*, she told herself, batting back the insecurity that led her to fear she and the handsome, successful chef weren't destined to go the distance.

By the time Olivia reluctantly left a few hours later to continue studying for finals, Miss Vee's was decorated to the point of kitschy. No shelf was left untouched by thrift shop Santas, nutcrackers, ornaments, and a variety of small artificial trees in materials ranging from silvery mylar to one made of oyster shells wired together as branches. Ricki's favorites were the items that were Louisiana-themed, like the alligator nutcracker wearing a Santa hat, which claimed a space next to a ceramic ornament of Santa riding an alligator.

"You could put together a whole display of gator items."

Ricki started, not realizing she had company. She turned to see Josepha. "Mom, hey." The women hugged.

"I thought your dad might wanna have dinner, but he and Virgil still have a lot to go over. He's taking a break, though."

Josepha indicated the bay window. Ricki glanced out of it and saw Luis doing a series of choreographed movements in slow motion. "Dad's still doing tai chi?"

"Yup. It relaxes him. And Lord knows that man could use some relaxing." Josepha delivered this in a droll but affectionate tone. "Anyhoo, I thought me and my darlin' daughter might go out for dinner."

"A giant yes to that." A thought occurred to Ricki. "I just want to make one stop on the way."

Ricki locked up the shop and led her mother to the small staff lot where she parked her Prius. They followed Washington Avenue past lovely historic homes swathed in holiday lights and garlands, eventually reaching Claiborne Avenue, a much less scenic thoroughfare of dollar stores, gas stations, and fast-food restaurants. Ricki made a right on Tulane Avenue, followed by two more right turns that placed them in front of what was once Charity Hospital, rendered uninhabitable after Hurricane Katrina and now on the cusp of a new life as Tulane University's downtown medical school. Scaffolding covered the center of the massive twenty-story edifice, but even at the tail end of twilight much of the building's 1930s structure was still evident and impressive despite years of decay.

Josepha stared out the car window, her expression unreadable. "Why are we here?"

"You haven't been to New Orleans in so long. I thought maybe seeing Charity again might bring back memories."

"About your bio mom."

Ricki nodded. Josepha clasped her hand and held it tight as she continued to stare out the window. She and Luis had been nothing but supportive in Ricki's quest for answers about her past but Ricki sensed her mother's pain as she took in the abandoned monolith where she'd once pursued a career she loved.

The two were silent for several minutes. "I wish I could remember something that would help," Josepha finally said in a husky voice. "All I keep seeing is your tiny body in the NICU and how my heart broke for you and how that turned into burning, all-consuming passion to be your mama."

"Oooh . . ." Ricki fought back tears. "I'm sorry, Mom. I shouldn't have brought you here."

"Nothing to be sorry about, baby girl." Josepha gave Ricki's hand another squeeze then released it. "I'm glad to see the old place and know it's gonna be brought back to do good things in this city. Hey, we're not too far from Mother's restaurant here. I could go for one of their oyster po'boys."

"Let's do it," Ricki said, knowing a change of subject when she heard one.

Ricki circled back to Tulane Avenue. As they drove, Josepha cheerfully recalled memories inspired by locations they passed. Ricki noted that none involved Charity or her experiences as a nurse. Ricki mused that perhaps it was too painful for Josepha to recall that time in her life. But another thought loomed larger: Josepha was hiding something.

And what she was hiding was tied to Ricki's birth.

THREE

Ricki had no time to ponder this thought over the next couple of days. As a follow-up to Black Friday, which she'd spent putting up holiday decorations, she'd designated the weekend Super Sale Saturday & Sunday. The sale attracted a steady stream of shoppers.

Olivia showed up late Sunday morning. She hopped back and forth impatiently as Ricki waited on a customer. "A wonderful choice," Ricki said as she finished gift-wrapping *The Pans 'N Pancakes Country Store Cookbook*, a popular mid-century cookbook by authors Maddie Day and Edith Maxwell. She placed the book in a reusable tote featuring the shop logo and handed the bag to her customer. "Merry Christmas and cooking."

"Cheesy," Olivia muttered under breath. Ricki shot her a look. Olivia continued her impatient dance until the customer exited, then threw her hands up in an exultant gesture. "I'm the Krewe of Gaia court queen!"

Ricki squealed and clapped her hands. "I'm so happy for you."

"I know I said I didn't care, but I really did want to be in a court," Olivia admitted.

"Yeah. I figured that out." Ricki picked up a few cookbooks that shoppers had pulled out and began reshelving them. Olivia joined her. "So what happens now?"

"I have to get fitted for my queen dress, cape, and collar. And go to a ton of parties between now and Mardi Gras. My friend Lizette is a maid in the court. She's meeting me here later and we're going shopping for stuff to wear to the parties."

"Sounds like fu—"

A four-part harmony drowned out Ricki's response. "*Angels we have heard on high, sweetly singing o'er the plains . . .*"

Olivia made a face. "What's that?" She spoke loudly to be heard over the caroling.

"Eugenia hired a quartet of carolers to do double duty as tour guides," Ricki responded, equally loudly.

"That's going to get old fast."

"It's festive. They dress like characters out of a Dickens novel. It's very Christmassy. I like it." The carolers finished, with the soprano hitting a high note that made Ricki's ears ring. "I think."

The afternoon flew by. By the end of the day, Ricki had a splitting headache, which she chalked up to a combination of no time for lunch and the constant fade-in and fade-out of the carolers. She was thrilled to get a text from Virgil inviting her and Bon Vee staff members to sample the trial run of a dish he hoped to replicate on his show.

Ricki shared the invitation with Olivia and her friend Lizette, who had shown up an hour earlier and was helping out by taking photos for the shop's social media accounts. Lizette was tiny and waiflike. She sported spiky hair dyed black, multiple ear piercings, and a nose ring. Having heard from Olivia that the krewes skewed traditional, Ricki figured that when it came to being anointed queen of the Gaia court, the nose ring was the deal-breaker for Lizette.

"My mom, grandmother, and great-grandmother were queens, so I broke the family streak." Lizette shared this with a grin as the three left the shop for the Bon Vee kitchen. She was clearly not bothered by the demotion. "This way, I get to be on the court and dress up and go to parties, but the pressure's not on me. It's all on Olivia." She patted Olivia on the back. "And I am *so* glad my friend here beat out Penelope Vogelspack. What a beeyotch."

"I think Penelope is really upset about it," Olivia said. "It won't be fun being on the court with her."

Ricki noted that her young cousin sounded worried.

They reached the kitchen. Unlike the rest of the home, it had been modernized and wasn't part of the Bon Vee tour. Given Genevieve Charbonnet's reputation as one of the city's most legendary hostesses, the kitchen was designed for entertaining, with gleaming stainless-steel appliances, a giant center island, and two professional stoves as well as a cooktop built into the island. It opened up to a spacious family room whose centerpiece was an enormous stone fireplace. Currently the room was crammed with the equipment needed to shoot Virgil's show. Cords, cameras, and lighting paraphernalia had turned the space into an obstacle course.

Ricki saw her father Luis in the middle of a conversation with a man who kept gesturing to the iPad he gripped in his hand. The man, who looked to be in his early thirties, had a wiry build. His hair, dark curls cut close to his scalp, could also be described as wiry. Ricki caught her father's eye and wiggled her fingers in a subtle wave. Luis responded with a small nod, then trained his eyes back on whoever he was talking to . . . or being berated by, if Ricki's assessment of the moment was correct.

She went to Virgil, who was ladling a creamy broth into a dozen soup bowls. "Hey." He kissed her cheek without a pause in his ladling. He wore a canvas apron with an image of a crawfish and the question "Who's your crawdaddy?" over a T-shirt and jeans.

"Hey yourself." She glanced at her father. "Who's my dad talking to? Or being talked to, is more like it."

Virgil looked in Luis's direction, still ladling. "That's Patrick. He's a last-minute fill-in for the director I hired. She can't do the show because she got a bad ear infection and the doctor won't let her fly. We'd lose too much time if she came by train, so I had to find a last-minute replacement."

Ricki watched as Patrick held up his iPad so close to Luis's face he had to take a step backward. "He seems really tense."

"The production company wouldn't up my budget so I had to go with a local hire. He's only worked on news shows here. He's trying too hard to prove himself. I'll talk to him."

Ricki, feeling protective of her father, glowered at the director. "Good."

Bon Vee staffers drifted into the kitchen. Ricki helped Virgil distribute his dish, along with thick slices of baguettes. "This would be the dinner's soup course," the chef explained. "It's a unique recipe for almond soup from 1933 that I found in one of Ricki's cookbooks." He gave her a warm smile and Ricki's heart rate sped up. She forced it back to normal. "I thought I'd add some vegetarian options to my Réveillon menu."

Everyone dug in and a flood of compliments ensued, including a harmonized "Delicious" from the carolers. Virgil took off his apron and relaxed into one of the family room's plaid-upholstered armchairs. Ricki parked herself on the arm of the chair. "If all your dishes are this good, which I know they will be, your show will be the hit of the holiday season."

"From your lips to God's ears," Virgil said with a sigh. He put his empty bowl on a side table. "Are you sure you don't mind me springing your folks on you?"

"Mind? Are you kidding? I'm thrilled." Ricki toyed with the soup left in her bowl. "The only thing is . . . I was hoping the visit might trigger memories for Mom that would help me move closer to finding my bio mom. I drove her by Charity Hospital but instead of generating memories it seemed to shut her down."

Virgil gave a nod. "You haven't been here long enough to know a visit to Charity will do that to someone. All they can think about is Katrina."

"Except we weren't living in New Orleans during Katrina. Mom and Dad had married and we'd moved to L.A. by then."

"You guys talking about Charity Hospital?" This came from Lizette, who happened to be standing behind Virgil's chair. "There's a lady named Phyllis Gibbs who lives on my grandma's block who used to work there. I remember because there was this weird story about her. An obituary ran in the paper about her and everyone thought she died but it turned out to be someone with the same name. Isn't that freaky?"

Something sparked for Ricki. "Very. Do you know how old this woman is? I'm wondering if she worked with my mom."

Lizette shrugged. "I dunno. Older than my mom but maybe not as old as my gram?"

Yikes. A wide age range but it could time out right, Ricki thought. "Excuse me. I have to call my mom about this."

She separated from the others and texted her mother: Did you know a Phyllis Gibbs?

Josepha quickly texted back, Yes. Worked at Charity. Medical Records. She passed away.

No, she didn't. It was a mistake.

WHAT?!

A second later, Ricki's cell rang. "What do you mean she didn't pass away? Are you telling me she's alive?" Josepha didn't sound happy about the news.

"It's a long story but she is, and she lives on . . ." Ricki called to Lizette. "What's your grandmother's street?"

"Peony Place," Lizette called back, projecting over the carolers, who'd broken into a spirited version of "God Rest Ye Merry Gentlemen."

"Peony Place," Ricki repeated into the phone. "Mom, she might know something about my birth. Especially if she worked in Medical Records. We have to see her."

"No." Josepha's forceful response took Ricki aback. "She wasn't—isn't—a good person. I have no desire to see her ever again."

Josepha ended the call. Ricki stared at her phone. Her parents had always been supportive of her quest to identify her birth parents and still seemed to be—except when it came to Josepha's past at Charity.

"What'd your mom say?" Lizette, curious, had wandered over.

"She said Phyllis wasn't a good person."

Lizette let out a chortle. "According to Grandmama, she's not. Gram's all about her rose garden. Someone's been stealing them and she's sure it's Phyllis. Gram says she's low-class, which is about the worst insult she can give anyone, and she's making my dad put in security cameras just to catch her stealing the roses."

Ricki took this in. "Do you know Phyllis's exact address?"

"I can figure it out." Lizette tapped on her phone. "I found it on my map app. I'll text it to you. What's your cell number?"

Ricki and Lizette exchanged numbers. "Thanks so much," Ricki said. "You get to pick out anything from my shop you want."

"Cool. I really liked the beignet ornament."

"It's yours."

Ricki searched the room until she spotted Mordant, who

was helping himself to a second bowl of soup. She hurried to him. "Do you have plans tonight?"

"Not until later. I'm going dancing with Zellah." A dreamy expression colored the tour guide's long face. It was the look he got every time he mentioned his girlfriend Zellah, the unconventional artist who ran Bon Vee's café and was Ricki's closest friend. "My favorite zydeco band is in town at Mulate's. I can't wait for her to hear them." Mordant's perpetually doleful expression belied his enthusiasm.

"Great. As soon as you finish your soup, I'm paying a visit to one of my mother's former co-workers, and I want you to come with me. I could use your P.I. instincts." Ricki pursed her lips, her expression determined. "Judging by Mom's reaction to the name Phyllis Gibbs, I have a feeling in my gut that this woman might hold the clue to my past."

FOUR

Peony Place lay on the Central City side of St. Charles Avenue. Like so many streets in the Garden District, lovely homes from the nineteenth century lined the block, interspersed with early twentieth-century abodes whose traditional architecture made them a seamless fit.

Ricki drove slowly while Mordant checked addresses, on the hunt for Phyllis's home. "It's a beautiful block," she said. "We've had the kind of weather that lets everything stay in bloom."

"It has been mild," Mordant agreed. He pointed to one of the newer homes across the street, newer probably being the 1930s. "There."

Ricki parked. She studied the house through her closed car window. Traditional in style, it was painted beige with white shutters. A solid oak front door gleamed with polish and a trim lawn separated the house from the street. A neat circle in the middle of the lawn contained a desultory mix of flowers that included roses, hydrangeas, and delphiniums, all in the same basic shade of white. Two lines of meticulously trimmed shrubs lined the walkway to the front door. "Huh. It's like Phyllis's place is the house version of the clothing trend 'quiet luxury.'"

"My mom would say it's lovely."

"So would mine. But she'd also say it's a little too lovely for a retiree who made a medical records salary. When I was little and Mom was still working as a nurse at Charity, she could barely afford our two-bedroom rental in the Lower Garden District."

"Charity went down in 2005," Mordant said. "This Phyllis person must've had other jobs since then. Maybe that's how she made her money."

"True."

Ricki rolled down the car window a few inches and squinted as she examined the home's surroundings. "There's what looks like a brand-new wall between her and her neighbor on the right. A tall one. But only trees between her and the neighbor on the left. Interesting."

"She must be home. There's a car in the driveway." Mordant lifted the small pair of binoculars he kept on hand for his P.I. cases to his eyes. "A new model Mercedes sedan."

"Another sign that whatever Phyllis has been doing since Charity pays well." Ricki closed the window. "Ready to ring her bell?"

"What's our plan of attack?"

"Very simple and honest. I'm going to tell Phyllis I'm Josepha's daughter, the one she adopted from Charity, and that I'm looking into my past and I'd love to talk to her. You can watch her and take mental notes on the way she reacts."

"Got it. Let's roll."

Ricki got out of the driver's side. It took Mordant longer to extract his tall, spindly body from the compact car. He unfolded himself into standing and the two crossed the street. They made their way up the path to Phyllis's front door. "That's not promising," Ricki said, noting a lawn sign that read in block letters: NO SOLICITORS. VIOLATORS WILL BE PROSECUTED TO THE FULLEST EXTENT OF THE LAW.

"Empty threat," Mordant said. "Don't worry about it."

Before ringing the bell, Ricki leaned left, then right, trying to peek into the bow windows symmetrically framing each side of the front door. Heavy curtains made seeing inside impossible. Ricki took a moment to center herself. "I am resilient, strong, and brave," she murmured.

"Good one," Mordant said, nodding approval of Ricki's affirmation.

"Thanks. You can borrow it anytime."

Ricki rang the doorbell. There was no response. She and Mordant waited a minute, then she rang again.

"I hear footsteps," Ricki whispered.

"So do I."

There was silence, then a woman's voice snapped from

behind the door, "Obey the sign on the front lawn or I'll call the police."

Heels clicked on a hardwood floor in the opposite direction of the front door. "Wait," Ricki cried out. "Don't go. We're not solicitors. My name is Miracle James-Diaz. My mother is Josepha. You worked together at Charity."

The front door opened the amount of space allowed by a chain lock. It was enough to allow Ricki a glimpse of Phyllis Gibbs. Cold gray eyes peered out from behind the door, their expression guarded. The woman's unnaturally smooth and pale complexion matched her platinum hair in an effect so ghostly Ricki wondered if the obituary's premature announcement of her demise might have been correct. Ricki could see how the question about Phyllis's age flummoxed Lizette. It was hard to tell whether Josepha's former co-worker was a well-preserved older woman or someone who'd started anti-aging procedures way too early.

The gray eyes appraised Ricki. "You must be the baby she adopted."

"Yes. That's me." Ricki released a nervous giggle. "I've been trying to learn more about my birth parents and I'd love to talk to you. And since Mom's in town—"

The woman's eyebrows shot up. "Josepha is here?" Phyllis interrupted. "In New Orleans? She's not . . . gone?"

"No," Ricki said, thrown by Phyllis's odd choice of words.

"That's wonderful news. We were in touch for years but then lost track of each other. I'd love to see her again. It's been way, way too long."

There was a calculating undertone to Phyllis's response that set off alarm bells for Ricki. She sensed Mordant stiffen, indicating he felt it too. "That's great," Ricki said, cringing as her voice cracked from an enthusiasm overreach. Unnerved, she backed off her original plan. "I'll let her know. Apologies for barging in on you like this but when I heard from a friend you lived on this street and used to work at Charity, I had to look you up. I'll let you go, and I'll tell Mom you'd like to get together. We'll be in touch. Thanks so much for your time and have a nice night."

Ricki plastered on a smile and waved as she navigated the two steps leading to Phyllis's front door backward. Mordant did likewise. They turned when they reached the front path and hurried to Ricki's car. "That was creepy," she said once they'd climbed into the car.

"A twelve outta ten on the creep scale," Mordant agreed. He frowned. "But I'm not sure you should have shut it down so fast. There's something going on with that woman. She gave me all the P.I. feels."

Ricki started the car. "I had to. From the vibe she gave off, I'm a hundred percent convinced Phyllis would jump at any chance to reconnect with Mom, but not in a good way. The question is, why? Do me a favor. Use my phone to text my parents that I need to speak to them urgently. It's time for a come-to-Jesus with my mama."

After dropping off Mordant back at Bon Vee so he could retrieve the reconstituted hearse that served as his car, Ricki raced home. She was greeted by a cacophony of barking, whining, and meows. The barks came from feisty chihuahua mix Thor, who was on a mission to defend Princess, a timid German shepherd mix, from kitten Red Beans. The kitten, a recent addition to the family, had discovered teasing the big dog was a great source of amusement.

"That's enough, Beans." Ricki picked up the kitten and scolded her affectionately. "If you're not nice to Princess you're going to find yourself living with Daddy."

"Daddy" happened to be Virgil. The couple's relationship had kicked off when they agreed to co-parent the canines adopted from New Pawlins Kritter Krewe, a rescue founded by the chef's mother who now lived in a memory care facility.

Moments after Ricki wrangled her own critter krewe, her parents showed up. She immediately noticed that her father seemed to have aged in the brief time he'd been in town. There was a gray pallor to his brown skin and the shadows under his eyes had darkened. "Dad, are you feeling all right?" Ricki asked, concerned enough to go off topic.

Luis waved off her worry. "I'm fine. Not used to working hard anymore."

"Too hard." Josepha glared at him. "You need to talk to that director Virgil dug up. He's not treating you like a professional, he's treating you like his manservant. If you don't talk to him, I will."

"You will *not*."

The edge to Luis's tone made Josepha back off. She turned her attention to Ricki. "What's going on, baby girl? Your text sounded urgent."

"We need to talk."

Ricki motioned to the front room's brightly colored couches, under a portrait of a masked celebrant painted in colors that were practically Day-Glo. Ricki's landlady Kitty Kat had leaned into a decorating theme that could best be described as Contemporary Mardi Gras Float.

"Why do I have a feeling this ain't good news?" Josepha said, nervously threading her fingers together.

Ricki took a seat opposite her parents. She got right to it. "Mom, what's the deal with you and Phyllis? You had a weird reaction when I brought her up. Mordant and I went to see her tonight—"

"You saw her?"

There was palpable fear in Josepha's response. "*Bombon*," Luis said, using his favorite term of endearment for his wife. "What's wrong? You have to tell us." His expression grew flinty. "Is this woman trouble? Do I need to set her straight?"

Josepha put a hand on her husband's knee. "Nothing for you to do here. Simmer down, mi alma." Her phone pinged with a text. Josepha read it. She pressed her lips together, then stood up. "We can finish this conversation tomorrow," she said to Ricki. "It's time to get your father home to bed." She gestured to Luis. He gave a helpless shrug and rose from the couch.

Not knowing what else to do, Ricki blocked the door. "Was that text from Phyllis? Mom, talk to us. Please. Tell us what's going on with you and this woman." Near tears, she pleaded this.

"Baby girl, relax." Josepha sounded calmer. "I'm tired too and I got way too emotional about all this. Phyllis is just an old friend I had a falling-out with."

Josepha kissed her daughter's cheek and ushered Luis out the door. Positive her mother was lying, Ricki let out a frustrated curse.

Josepha didn't respond to Ricki's texts in the morning. Ricki finally gave up trying to reach her and got ready for work. Rather than go with one of her cheery vintage outfits, Ricki opted for a simple look of black leggings and a purple tunic top. She used a black scrunchie to corral her mop of light brown curls into a ponytail, put on a touch of mascara and olive eyeliner that accentuated her hazel eyes, and took off for Miss Vee's.

Before opening the shop, she stopped for coffee at the Bon Vee café. She'd hardly seen co-worker besties Zellah and Cookie since her parents arrived, and she missed them. "Love the ornaments," she said, complimenting artist Zellah, who loved using herself as a canvas and often painted detailed images on various body parts. This morning, intricate painted ornaments adorned each of her dark cheeks.

"I'm thinking of doing a popcorn and cranberry strand that runs up my arm and neck to my face," Zellah said, adding a splash of milk to Ricki's coffee.

"That would be cool. Or a little freaky."

Zellah lifted a corner of her mouth in a half-smile. "Freaky's good. I like freaky."

Ricki shook her head, amused, then she and Zellah joined Cookie at a café table. Cookie hugged her coffee mug. "It's getting chillier every day. We may not be able to sit out here much longer." She gave her short blonde hair a tug. "I may have to grow out my hair to cover my neck and warm it up."

Zellah snorted. "Girl, you know you'll never do that as long as that boyfriend of yours likes it short."

"True dat. Ya gotta love a man who loves a girl who could play Peter Pan in a high school production." Cookie, who looked half her early thirty years, struck a pose as if flying and the others laughed.

"Hey, so what happened last night?" Zellah asked Cookie. "Mordant said he got bad vibes from wherever you two went but he wouldn't tell me more."

"We met a woman my mom once worked with. And yeah, bad vibes is right." Ricki filled her friends in on everything that had happened since her parents arrived. "It's not even about finding my birth parents right now. Mom and Dad have always been great about that. They've encouraged me. They've helped. Until now. When Mom got to New Orleans it set her off in some way, but I can't get her to talk about it."

"I think you need to let her share when she's ready to," Zellah said.

Cookie nodded in agreement. "Whatever's going on is emotional for your mom. If you pressure her, she may shut down completely."

"You're right." Ricki, who'd been staring at her mug with a disconsolate expression, raised her head. She released a sigh and smiled. "Thank you. I love you guys."

"We love you too," Zellah said.

Cookie jokingly shook a finger at Ricki. "And what do we say here in N'awlins?"

"*Y'all*, not 'you guys.'" Ricki delivered this in the sing-songy tone of a student responding to a teacher. She saw Theo hurrying across the side yard lawn. "There's Theo. Hey!" She waved to him. "Come join us for coffee."

"'Nuther time." Theo kept going until he disappeared into the former carriage house which contained the Bon Vee offices.

"That's another mystery no one's been able to solve," Zellah commented. "Theo's got something going on, for sure."

"A side hustle?" Cookie guessed. "Whatever it is, he's into it. He didn't even notice Gumbo and Jambalaya trying to nip at him."

The women finished their coffee and went off to their respective jobs. Ricki opened Miss Vee's. She hung a pine air freshener she'd bought on one of the artificial tree's branches. Her hope it would give off the scent of a live Christmas tree proved to be in vain.

"Ugh, why does it smell like a car wash in here?"

Olivia wrinkled her nose in distaste as she entered the shop and parked her backpack inside the mid-century desk repurposed as an ersatz checkout counter and gift-wrapping station.

"Epic fail on my part." Ricki removed the air freshener and dropped it into the shop trash can.

"OMG, I have to tell you the craziest thing." Olivia popped up, eager to share a bit of gossip. "You know how you and Lizette were talking about her grandma's neighbor, the one nobody liked, Frances or something?"

"Phyllis, and yes."

"Get this." Olivia took a dramatic pause. "She died last night."

FIVE

Ricki gaped at her young cousin. "No."

"It's true."

"*Deck the halls with boughs of holly!*" rang out from the hallway.

Ricki opened her mouth, then clapped it shut before yelling "Shut up!" at the carolers. Olivia released a groan and rolled her eyes simultaneously, a reaction from the twenty-year-old that Ricki had seen enough times to give it a facetious nickname: The Groll.

Ricki shut the shop door to drown out the singing. Considering she'd met Phyllis only the night before, the news of the woman's sudden death shook her. She couldn't help feeling there was something ominous about the timing of it. "What happened?"

"Nobody knows for sure. Lizette said the neighbors are all guessing it was a heart attack. Her cleaning lady showed up and Phyllis was still in bed. She thought she was asleep but she was really dead. Hey, that rhymed."

"Not appropriate," Ricki admonished.

Olivia responded with a shrug. "Sorry. But I didn't even know the lady. And from what Lizzie said, nobody on Peony Place is gonna miss her."

Having shared the shocking news, Olivia was done with it. She went behind the desk and tended to the task of uploading photos of new arrivals to the shop's website.

The carolers delivered a tour group to Miss Vee's and Ricki did her best not to appear distracted. She barely noticed the robust sales they generated. All she could think about was Josepha and how she might react to the news about Phyllis.

The tour group left and Ricki made a decision. "Liv, can you watch the store for a couple of hours?"

Olivia shook her head. "I can only stay an hour today. I have a group study session."

"Got it. Thanks anyway."

Determined to tell her mother about Phyllis's death in person, Ricki ran through the Bon Vee staff in her head, searching for someone who could keep an eye on the shop for her so she didn't have to lose a chunk of valuable holiday sales time. Her go-tos of Cookie and Zellah were busy with their own jobs. Theo was busy with whatever he was up to. Eugenia wasn't an option either. In addition to being head of the Bon Vee board, she was covering for Executive Director Lyla Brandt, who'd taken a leave of absence to focus on her teen daughter's traveling volleyball team schedule.

Having no other options, Ricki stepped into the hallway and flagged down the carolers. "Hi, you guys—y'all. Is there any chance one of you could cover the store for a couple of hours? I have to run an important errand."

Ruth, the soprano, a spritely woman in her fifties, raised a gloved hand. "I'd be happy to. It will give me a chance to rest my voice."

"Thank you so much."

The soprano left the others, her dark blue velvet nineteenth-century gown taking up much of the hallway as she came Ricki's way. She tilted her dress and hoop skirt undergarment sideways to fit through the shop doors. All the Bon Vee employees got a lesson in running Miss Vee's in case they were ever called upon to do so and Olivia promised to give Ruth a refresher course, so Ricki left the shop in their hands and took off.

She texted Josepha to meet at Peli Deli on Magazine. The deli belonged to Zellah's family and they greeted Ricki with love and joy, refusing to take a dime of her money for the coffee and beignets she ordered. Peli was the only eatery in the neighborhood that fried up the delicious pillows of dough and powdered sugar, and the line for them was long. While Ricki waited, she debated the best way to break the news about Phyllis to Josepha. By the time Zellah's dad handed her a plate of the piping hot sweet treats, she'd decided how.

Josepha had claimed one of the two-seater tables lining the sidewalk outside the deli. Ricki offered her mother a coffee and a beignet.

"You OK, sweetie?" Josepha took a bite of her beignet, which came with a cloud of powdered sugar that floated onto her lap. She brushed it off. "I never expect to hear from you in the middle of a workday."

Josepha took a sip of coffee. Ricki waited for her mother to swallow. "Phyllis Gibbs is dead." Josepha froze, much as Ricki expected when she chose to go with a direct approach. "So now you can tell me the truth about your relationship with her." Josepha pressed her lips together. Her eyes glistened with tears. Ricki felt horrible, but soldiered on. "Mom, you haven't been yourself since you got to New Orleans. I need to know why. It's the only way I can help. I'd do anything for you and dad. Anything. You two are my world."

"Sweet, sweet girl." Josepha extracted a napkin from the table's silver holder and wiped the tears slipping down her cheeks. "I'm not gonna lie. Phyllis being gone is a relief for me." She drew in a breath, then released it. "So . . . when the hospital figured out your birth mother had disappeared and abandoned you, they assigned your case to a social worker. I knew in every fiber and cell of my being that God wanted me to be your mother. But a single Black woman adopting a white baby? In Louisiana? Even New Orleans?" Josepha shook her head. "Wasn't gonna happen."

She paused. Ricki placed a hand over her mother's, offering support. Josepha closed her eyes briefly, then opened them and continued. "But a *widowed* Black woman . . . now *she* had a chance. I'd heard rumors Phyllis could help people with problems. Adjust a medical record. Change the order number for a prescription to hide a missing bottle of pills. I went to her and asked if she'd confirm I was widowed, not single, to the social worker. Which she did. All Phyllis wanted in return was a thank-you. In the form of a regular check I sent her every year to keep Child Services from finding out the truth and taking you away from me."

Ricki, speechless, tried to process this. It was difficult to comprehend the threat hanging over both of them for her entire life. Josepha could have been prosecuted for lying to a government official. Ricki would have been torn away and placed in foster care. And while Ricki had aged out of foster care long ago, there might not be a statute of limitations on the charge that could be brought against Josepha.

"You were right when you asked me last night if the text I got was from Phyllis," Josepha continued. "I kept the same cell number all these years on purpose. I was scared if I changed it and she couldn't reach me, she'd turn me in. Then I heard she passed away and I thought, finally, it's all over, so I stopped sending her checks. Phyllis didn't hunt me down for them. I was such a reliable mark that when she didn't get one for a few years, she probably thought *I* died."

"She did. Phyllis said she thought you were 'gone.' Now I know what she meant. But I showed up on her doorstep and let her know you were alive and well." Ricki cursed herself for the impulsive visit.

"Don't blame yourself, baby girl. There's a good chance she would've found out anyway. I'm not worried about what the law could do to me. I was afraid of what you might think of the lie I've been hiding." Josepha looked at Ricki with pleading eyes.

"*Mom . . .*"

Ricki leaped up from her chair, ran to Josepha, and threw her arms around her. The women wept in each other's arms. "Nothing to see here," Ricki said to a couple who were staring at them as they used the rest of the napkins in the holder to wipe up their tears. "Just a mother and daughter sharing a whole lotta love." The couple moved on.

Josepha leaned back in her seat. "I cannot tell you how much better I feel."

"I bet." Ricki returned to her chair, helping herself to a beignet on the way. "All these years, you've been carrying a weight as heavy as a Mardi Gras crown."

Josepha laughed. "That's a very nice New Orleans metaphor."

"I've picked up a few things from Olivia." Ricki studied Josepha, looking for signs her mother was still withholding something from her. "That's it? No other big reveals? If there are, now's the time to tell me."

Josepha waved her hand in a dismissive gesture but Ricki noted she didn't give a verbal no. "Dad knows about all this, right?"

Josepha shook her head. "I'll tell him now, of course. But I couldn't say anything before. I was afraid if I told him about Phyllis, he'd be so angry he'd track her down and do something he'd regret. At least I don't have to worry about that anymore."

For a reason Ricki couldn't explain, this sent a jolt of fear coursing through her body.

SIX

Ricki calmed herself and focused on enjoying a brief bit of quality time with her mother, something that had been in short supply, as in nonexistent, since her parents came to town. Having shared the secret she'd held for so long, Josepha's warmth and good humor returned. The native New Orleanian allowed the affection she'd always felt for her hometown to return and Ricki enjoyed the stories her mother shared of growing up in the Holy Cross neighborhood.

"See these?" Josepha showed Ricki an image on her phone of two turn-of-the-twentieth-century houses built to resemble steamboats. "They were built by real steamboat captains. One was a woman. My friends and I used to play on the levee by them. We'd pretend they were real steamboats and we were either piloting or crashing into each other." She grew nostalgic at the memory. "I'd love to show them to you."

"I'll put it on the list of things for us to do while you're here." Ricki noticed the time on her mother's phone. "Yikes, I've been gone longer than I planned. I better get back."

The women stood up. Josepha came to Ricki and affectionately pinch her daughter's cheeks. "You're the best thing that ever happened to me. You know that, don't you?"

"Me and Dad," Ricki said with a grin.

"Yeah, you and your dad. But in that order." Josepha released Ricki. "When I think about what an operator Phyllis was, there's a chance she knew more about your birth than she ever let on. And she might have shared what she knew with you . . . for the right price. Mad as that makes me, if it's true, I'm sorry you didn't get the chance to say ay or nay to her."

"I doubt that's the case, so don't worry about it."

Still, Ricki regretted she'd never have the opportunity to grill Phyllis and see if she did have any clues to her past.

* * *

Soprano Ruth greeted Ricki's return with a high-C hello, leading the shopkeeper to fear that if the caroler held the note much longer the vintage set of highball glasses she'd recently scored would shatter. Tours were light, so Ricki took the time to bid online for a set of 1960s books from a Time Life cooking series. She closed the shop at five p.m. and decided to drop in on Virgil and Luis to see how the show's preproduction was going.

Cookie, Zellah, Eugenia, and a few others were in the kitchen sampling another creation from Virgil. "Ricki, my friend, if a forkful of this crabmeat au gratin is the last thing you ever eat, you will die a happy woman," Zellah said, mouth full.

"Here, chère."

Virgil scooped a serving into a ramekin and passed it to Ricki. She inhaled its heavenly scent of fresh crab, herbs, and mushrooms, then took a bite. "Oooh." She mimed a faint. "This is so good my eyes practically rolled to the back of my head."

"So it's a yes to making this as the Réveillon dinner appetizer," the chef said with a broad smile.

"It's a hella yes." Ricki pumped the air with her free hand. She noticed the group was light on production staff, including her father. "Where's my dad?"

"Patrick had an appointment, so he sent everyone home."

Knowing Luis needed a break, the update made Ricki happy. She finished her au gratin and placed the empty ramekin in the dishwasher. Eugenia did the same, then picked up a cloth napkin and daintily dabbed at a piece of crab on the edge of her mouth. "Virgil, I'm curious. Will the viewing audience be able to access your recipes?"

"We haven't settled on specifically how but they should be able to."

Ricki gasped, startling the others. "Ricki, don't do that," Cookie scolded. "I almost dropped my crab."

"Sorry. But I just had a brainstorm. What if we put together our own Bon Vee community cookbook?" She clasped her hands together, excited. "As a fundraiser? There could be a special section with Virgil's recipes, but it would also include recipes from everyone involved with Bon Vee. Staffers, board members, volunteers. Even people from the neighborhood. What do you think?"

All eyes turned to Eugenia. In addition to her titles of Board President and Acting Executive Director, she owned Bon Vee. Genevieve Charbonnet had willed the estate to her niece. Turning Bon Vee into a culinary house museum honoring her beloved aunt's contributions to the city's culinary history had been Eugenia's idea and she protected its legacy with a ferocious passion. Ricki felt a flash of nerves as she waited for the grande dame's verdict.

"Brilliant," Eugenia declared.

Ricki sagged with relief while her friends hooted their agreement.

Eugenia fixed her eyes on Ricki. "How fast do you think you can pull this together?"

"How fast do you want it?" Despite her attempt to sound confident, Ricki's voice cracked from the fear Eugenia would say "next week" and Ricki would have to deliver.

"A few days prior to Christmas would be perfect. I think we should consider this Volume One and keep it relatively simple as it's our first go at it."

"I like that approach," Ricki said, her blood pressure lowering to a normal level. "We can call it *New Year, New Recipes from Bon Vee*. If you like," she added, making sure to give the house museum's boss of all bosses the final say.

"I do. I'll draft Theo into handling production of the cookbook. With all the self-publishing options these days, the timeline should be doable."

"I'll volunteer myself to do cover design," artist Zellah said.

"And if we want photographs of any dishes, I can do that," Cookie held up her cell phone. "It'll help me justify my impulse phone upgrade. I can also do the book layout. Not to brag, but I'm still a legend at my high school for my yearbook layout."

Eugenia gave a nod of approval. "Excellent. Project *New Year, New Recipes* is a go." Having given the green light, she departed to tend to other Bon Vee business.

The impromptu gathering broke up. Ricki went to Virgil. "Do you need help cleaning up?"

"Thanks, but I like doing it myself." He placed a large pot in the sink and ran water into it. "Mindless tasks let my mind wander. I've come up with some of my best recipe ideas while loading the dishwasher. Hey, I've been meaning to ask—can you keep custody of the pups until I finish filming?"

"Of course."

"I'll make up for it. Promise."

Virgil confirmed this with a kiss that sent Ricki floating out of Bon Vee on a romance high. She was about to get into the car when her cell rang. The caller's ID came as a surprise. Like most kids her age, Olivia using her phone as an actual phone was anathema. Worried, Ricki took the call. "Hey. What's going on? Is everything OK?"

"Yes, but I had to call you." Olivia sounded excited. "I'm at Lizette's and the police are all over that lady Phyllis's house. Hang up and we'll FaceTime so I can show you."

Ricki ended the call. A second later, her cell rang again. This time, Olivia's face popped up on the screen. "Look."

She pivoted the phone. A phalanx of police cars was parked in front of the bland beige house where Phyllis had lived. Their blinking lights flashed red against the dark night sky. A van Ricki recognized as belonging to the NOPD Crime Scene Unit took up most of the driveway. As if the ominous picture the police presence painted wasn't enough, she saw the backs of two plain-clothes officers she was sure she recognized. The woman turned around. Ricki's heat sank to see homicide detective Nina Rodriguez.

If Nina and partner Sam Girard were on the scene, it could only mean one thing. Phyllis Gibbs hadn't died by accident or from natural causes. Her cause of death had been moved into the category of "suspicious circumstances."

SEVEN

Ricki placed a hand over her rapidly beating heart. *I release fear and welcome peace . . . I release fear and welcome peace*, she repeated to herself. "Thanks for the update," she told Olivia, forcing herself to sound nonchalant. She ended the call.

She thought for a moment, then made a decision. Ricki turned and race-walked back to the house and the Bon Vee kitchen. "Oh, thank God, you're still here," she said to Virgil.

The expression on her face was enough to make Virgil drop the pot he was holding into the sink. He kicked the dishwasher door closed with his foot, took Ricki's hands, and led her to the family room sofa. "Talk to me."

She bit her lower lip, then released it. "I'm going to tell you something I swore I'd never tell a living soul." She shared the secret Josepha had kept for almost thirty years by sending monetary "gifts" to the one woman who could reveal it: Phyllis, now dead and very likely murdered. "I don't know if Mom could still get in trouble with the law for lying on official documents but I don't want to take the chance."

"I wouldn't worry about it. NOPD is understaffed and overworked. They got enough on their plate to keep from bringing an old charge against a woman who told a small lie that kept a baby out of the system and gave her a wonderful life."

"Stop, you're going to make me cry. Too late. I'm crying." Ricki wiped her eyes with the back of her hand. "What about everything else?"

"There is no everything else, at least not yet." Virgil tilted his head and eyed her. "But something tells me you think there might be."

"When I asked Mom if she was keeping anything else from me, she went like this . . ." Ricki imitated her mother's dismissive gesture. "But she didn't come out and say no."

"Hmm." Virgil rubbed his chin, thinking. "Could be something. Could be nothing. The police might be at this Phyllis woman's place for a different reason than murder. My pop used to say, 'worry is paying interest on a debt you may not owe.'"

"That's a bit of a thinker, but I get it."

"There's nothing you can do right now, so put it out of your mind. Put all that amazing energy of yours into your shop or better yet, the Bon Vee cookbook. Not sure you realize what you've taken on with that."

Ricki gulped. "I know. I'm starting to feel like I might have idea remorse."

"Too late, I'm afraid. You got Eugenia all hot and bothered about the cookbook. She's already spreading the word. Your shop inbox is gonna be busting at the e-seams."

Ricki gulped again.

"I'm sure everything's gonna be fine with your folks." He stood up and took Ricki in his arms for a reassuring hug. "I gotta finish up here. I'll see you tomorrow."

He resumed cleaning the kitchen and Ricki left for home. She prayed Virgil was right. But every instinct in her pushed back against the prayer.

When Ricki got to Bon Vee in the morning, the caroling quartet was waiting for her. "We heard about the Bon Vee cookbook and we're so excited!" Soprano Ruth trilled the last two words.

"My grandmama's gumbo recipe is the best in Louisiana," declared baritone Larry.

"Except for my grandmama's," alto Jennifer said, waving a teasing finger at him.

"Or mine," Ruth literally chimed in.

"Or *mine*," bass Edgar said, his deep voice vibrating like a car where someone had the bass turned up to eleven.

All four laughed. To Ricki's ear, it sounded forced. "I'm looking forward to all your recipes, although I recommend submitting non-gumbo options because I foresee a lot of those," she said, opting for a neutral but polite tone. "Thanks so much."

"Thank *you*," the four harmonized.

Ricki scooted past them and into the shop before they began singing their recipes to her.

Once inside, she took a moment to enjoy Miss Vee's festive atmosphere. She and Olivia had run strands of tiny white lights along the tops of all the bookcases and they twinkled merrily. Ricki called up a holiday playlist she'd curated on her phone and hummed along with the tunes as she opened her inbox. Virgil wasn't exaggerating when he predicted it would be packed with recipe submissions. Ricki stopped counting at fifty.

She'd weeded through the first ten of them when her cell rang. Ricki saw the caller was her mother and answered. "Mom, hi. What's up?"

"Someone is here who says she's a friend of yours."

The strange tone in Josepha's voice unnerved Ricki. "What's her name?"

"Nina. She's a detective. And she wants to talk to Luis and me about Phyllis."

No . . . Ricki groaned to herself. *Curse my instincts for being right!* "Mom, can you hear me?" She spoke in a low, intense whisper

"Yes," Josepha whispered back.

"I'm on my way to you. One word: *stall*. Make small talk. Ask a lot of questions. It doesn't matter if Nina thinks you're ditzy. I don't want you talking about Phyllis without me there."

Ricki ran into the hallway. She saw the carolers had split up to lead different tour groups. None were free to run the store for her. And with four potential groups of customers in the house, closing the store to deal with the fire alarm of Nina descending on her parents was a nonstarter.

Theo came through the front door, shutting it on his squawking peacock nemeses. His thinning sandy hair was wind-blown, exposing more scalp than he'd like. He patted it down. "I hope you're giving serious consideration to turning those flipping peacocks into tree toppers."

"Tabling that. Theo, I have a huge favor to ask you. My parents have a problem and I need to get to them, but I can't close the store and lose customers. Can you cover for me? Only for an hour or two. Please? I'll pay you back."

The doubt on Theo's face made her fear he was going to say no. Then his expression changed. "Are any of the groups locals?"

"Yes. One of them is a gardening club from Uptown."

Theo's eyes lit up. "Uptowners? They'd be good ones. I'll do it."

"I have no idea what you're talking about. But lucky for you, I also don't have time to be nosy. Thanks so much. I'll text when I'm on my way back."

Ricki raced to her car. She drove as fast as possible on the city's deteriorating, potholed streets, ignoring New Orleans' notorious school speed zones. She zipped into the first available parking space on her parents' block.

Ricki jumped out of the car and ran to her parents' rental. She bounded up the front steps and into the house. Josepha had followed Ricki's instructions to leave the door open so Ricki could make an unexpected entrance, hopefully startling Nina and throwing her off balance.

"Hi there, everyone!" Ricki smiled broadly, doing her best to hide the fact she was out of breath.

"Well, hey there, girlfriend." Nina grinned back at Ricki, unfazed by her entrance. "I'm having a nice chat with your mom and dad. Did you know that more than three cruise ships dock in Puerto Vallarta a day during the height of tourist season? I didn't."

The detective crossed one of her long jean-clad legs over the other and casually swung it back and forth. As always, she wore a black blazer over a white T-shirt, and her thick hair, also black, was pulled back in tight bun. And as always, Ricki was the one off balance. Her relationship with the detective stubbornly defied definition. Sometimes Ricki felt like they were genuine friends. But more often—like now—the feeling was the exact opposite.

Ricki dropped onto the bright yellow sofa between her parents. The room's cheery décor was in sharp contrast to the tension in the air—all emanating from Josepha and Luis, and none from Nina. "I was looking forward to introducing you to my parents," she said, "but you beat me to it."

"I kinda had to. Now that you're here, I'm assuming we can stop talking about the wonders of P.V. and get down to business, n'est ce pas?"

"I took Spanish in high school."

"So she could talk with my family," Luis interjected. He patted her shoulder. "She's a good girl."

Ricki noticed the sweat stains on her father's cotton guayabera shirt. She sympathized. Nerves were generating perspiration under her own arms, portending stains she wasn't sure would come out of the 1950s tomato-red cardigan she wore. She took a side trip from the current drama to muse, *Note to self: buy old-timey dress shields for old-timey outfits.*

"I'm happy to discuss Ricki's wonderful characteristics at another time," Nina said. "Right now, I'm more interested in why the two of you were caught on Phyllis Gibbs' security camera the night preceding her death . . . but at different times."

With this revelation coming as a shock to each of the three James-Diazes, the family exchanged a round of mixed reactions. Nina focused her penetrating dark eyes on Josepha. "Let's start with you."

Josepha opened her mouth to speak but Ricki placed a warning hand on her knee and she stayed silent. Ricki summoned up the courage to push back on Nina. "Has Ms. Gibbs' death officially been classified as a homicide? If so, my parents won't be talking to you without a lawyer."

Nina raised an eyebrow. The small gesture gave Ricki a thrill, knowing it was Nina's way of saying touché. "No," she admitted. "Not officially. But there are enough questions about her death to warrant interviews with anyone who was in her vicinity in the time period prior to her death. No one is a suspect at this point in time. We're just gathering information."

Noting the ominous phrase "at this point in time," Ricki was about to end the interview when Josepha blurted, "I didn't do anything except try to protect my family. Phyllis had been making me send her money 'gifts' for years so she wouldn't reveal something from my past I'd rather not tell you about. I thought she'd died but when I found out she hadn't, I went to her and said I'd give her anything to leave us alone."

"Mom—" Ricki interrupted, desperate to shut her up.

Luis cut Ricki off. "My wife told me everything, which I can't tell you either. I followed her to this Phyllis woman's house and after Josepha left, I told Phyllis to stay away from my family or else. Then I left. Eso es todo. That's it. I didn't do nothing else."

Ricki let out the frustrated groan she'd struggled to suppress. She dropped her head in her hands, then raised it. "I was going to point out that security camera images can be grainy and unreliable, so you can't say for sure the people on Phyllis's security camera footage were my parents."

"A nosy neighbor who lives across the street from Phyllis also ID'd your mom and dad's visits." Nina delivered this with sympathy to Ricki's plight. If—or more likely, when—Phyllis's death was officially declared a murder, her parents had done a bang-up job of incriminating themselves.

"Did Phyllis have cameras on the sides of her house or in the back?" Ricki asked, hunting for alternatives.

"No," Nina said. "Not on either location."

"Then someone could have visited her from another direction and you wouldn't know it. There's a wall between Phyllis and her neighbor on the one side, but only bushes on the other. Even a nosy neighbor would miss someone sneaking onto the property, unlike my parents, who marched right up to the front door."

"And could have snuck back later."

"We didn't!" Josepha and Luis chorused. The panic in their voices telegraphed their simultaneous realization they were potentially in trouble.

Nina's phone buzzed with a message. She uncrossed her legs and read it. She rubbed her eyes as if tired and Ricki noticed a pallor to her olive skin. "The department is down a third of the officers we need to maintain a semblance of order in this crazy city. This means every investigation is proceeding slowly. I'd love to know the thing from your past Phyllis was holding over you, Mrs. James-Diaz, but it'll have to wait. I just got called to a drug deal gone bad. The number of killings around here could go head-to-head with the number of cruise ships dropping anchor in P.V." The detective stood up. "I'll be in touch. In the meantime, I recommend a visit to Mardi Gras World, where they make the parade floats. Locals think it's a tourist trap, but it's actually a lot of fun."

With that, the detective departed.

No one spoke for a moment. "So . . ." Josepha finally said. "Either of you up for making a coffee and beignet run? I know I am."

"Sounds good to me." Luis struggled to lift his heavy frame off the old sofa.

"I need to get back to work," Ricki said, adding to herself, *and figure out how to get you two out of this disaster. Because I sure can't count on Nina and NOPD to do it.*

EIGHT

Ricki found it tough to sleep that night. Her parents had sworn they weren't hiding anything else from her. It didn't matter. Phyllis's nefarious and illegal hold over Josepha and Luis's reaction to it was enough to make even Ricki see them as suspects. *Not really*, she thought, turning in bed for the hundredth time and bumping into Thor, who grunted his annoyance, *but I can see how NOPD would*.

At dawn, Ricki gave up trying to catch a modicum of rest and traded shut-eye for strong black coffee. She pulled on leggings and a zip-up fleece hoodie to take Thor and Princess for an extra-long walk. First, she had to extricate the German shepherd from the closet, where she and her favorite stuffed toy Lamby had sought refuge from Red Beans. "We don't tolerate bullies in this house," Ricki scolded, lifting the kitten up and placing her on top of the cat tree she'd picked up at a yard sale. Princess scampered to the door with Lamby in her mouth, eager for an escape.

Ricki leashed up the dogs and the three headed out. She glanced across the street at Virgil's house as they exited her place. It was dark, indicating the chef was either still in bed after a long night or already at Bon Vee getting a head start on the workday. She and the dogs continued on, passing her favorite hangout, the Bayou Backyard, an indoor-outdoor bar co-owned by Virgil and his friend Ky Nyugen. Unlike Ricki, the bar was sound asleep. It wouldn't come to life until mid-afternoon at the earliest.

The trio strolled past rows of the nineteenth-century shotgun cottages that populated Ricki's Irish Channel neighborhood. All were decked out for the holidays with lights and outdoor displays. On one lawn, a blow-up Santa piloted a sled led by reindeer. Giant colored ornaments hung from the oak tree fronting the house next door. Ricki longed for a bit of holiday spirit but all she could think about was her parents' predicament.

A mist deposited dew on the lush green foliage. Ricki shivered. The Big Easy's temperature might rarely drop below the forties but its humidity could be bone-chilling. She piloted the pooches back home, where they devoured their breakfast, then jumped on the bed to go back to sleep. "Lucky you," Ricki said. It wasn't the first time she envied her pets. *Food, walks, and love; would my life was this simple,* she thought.

In an effort to shake off the gloomy attitude, Ricki pulled her yoga mat from the closet. The meditative exercise did the trick of at least calming her down. She dressed and left for work with a much more positive attitude, ready to handle whatever might be heading her parents' way. Much as she hoped she was overreacting to Nina's visit, her instincts kept setting off alarm bells, which were born out when she got to Miss Vee's.

She arrived an hour before opening and found Olivia and her friend Lizette waiting for her, buzzing with impatience. "You're here early," she said to the girls as she unlocked the shop's French doors. "I'm guessing there's a reason for it."

Olivia locked the doors behind them. "We have news," she declared, then dropped her voice. "Big development on Peony Place."

Lizette picked up the story. "Word on the street is that Phyllis OD'd on some heart medicine. Digi something. And it may not have been an accident."

"By 'word on the street,' you mean gossip. And that would be digitoxin."

Olivia hoisted herself onto the shop desk, dangling her legs over it. "All the neighbors have been telling the police how much the other neighbors hated Phyllis. Everyone is pointing the finger at someone else."

"If I ever have enough money to buy a house, Peony Place won't be on my list. It's coming off as a nasty place to live."

Lizette helped herself to a mini chocolate bar from a bowl Ricki left out for shoppers. She unwrapped it and popped the chocolate in her mouth. "I'm sure someone offed Ms. Gibbs.

Once the police are gone, Olivia and I want to figure out a way to get into her house and look for clues."

"No! That's a terrible idea!" *At least for you. Banking it for me, though*. "No amateur sleuthing. If I encouraged you in any way, my bad. Finish your finals. Do whatever you have to do for your krewe courts. Leave investigating to the police."

"And you," Olivia said with a wink.

"To the police," Ricki repeated more forcefully. *And me*, she added to herself.

After the girls left, Ricki pondered what they'd told her. Were Phyllis's neighbors guessing that the unpleasant woman's death was no accident or was the assumption based on insider knowledge of the block's dynamics?

Knowing nothing about digitoxin except its name, she went to her computer and entered a search for it. Articles detailing the side effects of a possible overdose populated the left side of the page. But two images on the right side caught Ricki's eye: one of a foxglove, the other showing the vibrant blue blooms of delphiniums. Coming from bone-dry Los Angeles, where native plants and succulents dominated the landscape, she didn't know enough about either flower to tell the difference between them but she knew she'd seen either—or both—in several Peony Place front yards.

She read on. Foxglove fell under the genus of digitalis while delphinium landed in a different category. But the two plants shared one thing in common: if ingested, they could be fatal. And symptoms could lead to "cardiac arrest, seizures, and death."

Raised voices in the hallway distracted Ricki. She stepped out of the shop to find Virgil and his director Patrick in the middle of a heated conversation. "I'll keep saying it until you hear me," Virgil delivered this to Patrick through gritted teeth. "*I am not firing him*."

"He's a murder suspect," Patrick shot back. He glanced around to see if anyone could hear him, missing Ricki, who had stepped back to hide behind her door yet still hear the argument. "When the show airs, it's all anyone's gonna talk about," he hissed.

"It's B.S.," Virgil shot back at him. "Gossip. He's not a suspect because as of now, there is no official murder. And even if there were, Luis would be last on my list of *anyone's* killer."

Ricki tensed, hearing what she suspected fully verbalized: the "suspect" in question was her father.

"Luis James-Diaz has a résumé most camera operators can only dream of," Virgil continued. He kept his voice low but Ricki could hear it throbbing with anger. "He's slumming it crewing this show. He's doing me a huge favor. He wouldn't even be here if his daughter wasn't my girlfriend. If one of us has to go, it ain't gonna be Luis."

There was a long pause. "Fine," Patrick muttered, so low Ricki had to strain to hear. He obviously resented having to cave. "But," he said, determined to have the last word, "I'm keeping my eye on him. I worked in news. I've seen his type blow before. It's in their DNA."

Ricki's jaw dropped. She stepped into the hallway ready to light into Patrick but he'd already stormed down the hall. He disappeared into the kitchen. "That nasty, racist son of a . . ." Ricki steamed. "Virgil, you have to fire him. He's a horrible human being."

"I'm working on it. Hard as I can." Virgil pinched the bridge of his nose. "It's a bad time of year to be shooting a show. No one in town has the skill set I need and no one in L.A. or New York is available. Hopefully, someone's schedule will open up. In the meantime, it's prep work right now. Patrick's in and out anyway. I swear he's got some kinda side hustle going on. Your dad and I are working on our own to block each segment and figure out the best angles to show off each dish. Luis is even confabbing with the cinematographer and the editor on the best lighting for shots."

"Thank you for believing in my dad," Ricki said, choking up.

"Chère, of course." Virgil managed a smile. "I brought him and your mom here for you. But also, very much for me. I feel guilty for getting him into this mess."

Ricki reacted with a forceful, "*No.* I'm the one who feels

guilty. If I'd never gone to see Phyllis and let her know Mom was alive and in town, neither of my parents would be in trouble right now. I wish I could send them back to P.V. The police can't force them to stay. But nothing would make them look guiltier than fleeing 'south of the border,' as our unfriend Patrick would put it. With a sneer."

"It's better for them to wait this out," Virgil agreed. He motioned to the kitchen. "I need to get back in there. Patrick will back off. I'll make sure of it. In the meantime, I'll be on the hunt for his replacement."

He strode off and Ricki allowed herself a sidebar from worrying about her parents to relive the pleasure of hearing Virgil call her his girlfriend during the argument with Patrick.

An influx of shoppers buoyed Ricki's spirits in the afternoon, especially when a local cookbook club paid a lucrative visit. The chatter in her shop had the added advantage of muting the incessant singing from the tour guide carolers. She finished the day with an hour of online auctions that would replenish her stock, after which she placed an order for branded non-vintage items she sold featuring her shop logo, like potholders, tea towels, and measuring spoons. *It's easy to repeat aphorisms about combatting worry*, Ricki thought as she reshelved cookbooks buyers had pulled out to peruse, *but nothing works better than a busy day making bank.*

Ricki was debating whether to bid on an early twentieth-century cash register so she could enjoy the aural pleasure of a sales *ca-ching* sound when her upbeat mood took a hit thanks to an unwelcome visitor.

"Nina." The greeting came out sour. The day had been good but also tiring and Ricki didn't have the energy to fake a polite greeting.

The detective sauntered in. "Hello to you too."

"I'm closing up."

"Perfect timing on my part," Nina said, dashing Ricki's hopes of evading the conversation. The detective leaned against the desk and folded her arms against her chest. "We have a development I can share with you."

"I'm listening."

"Phyllis Gibbs had a mild arrhythmia."

"That's good news," Ricki said, hastily adding, "I mean, not for her. But her death must have been an accident. She probably overdosed on whatever she took when her condition was acting up."

"Except here's the thing. She didn't have a prescription for nitroglycerin or digitoxin or any heart medication." Nina unfolded her arms. "You know Sam and me well enough at this point to know we're the suspicious types. So when we learn something like this, our first thought is, someone knew about Gibbs' heart condition. And took advantage of it. Which leads me to why I'm here. I have a question for you."

"Oh, boy, I know I'm not going to like this," Ricki said, her own heart racing.

The detective leaned on the desk and fixed a penetrating look on Ricki. "How well did your mother know Phyllis Gibbs?"

NINE

Ricki met Nina's stare. "That's an easy question for me to answer—I have no idea." She tried to ignore her own heart, which was racing faster than a Kentucky Derby winner.

"Really? None? I know you two have talked about Gibbs since this whole thing came out. Your mother worked with the victim for a number of years. They were close enough for Gibbs to fudge the records when your mother applied to adopt you."

Ricki gaped at Nina. "How did you find out?"

"A brilliant use of NOPD investigative skills coupled with a lucky guess, although it's less of a guess and more based on the reality of where we live. As you've probably figured out, my partner Sam would rather park himself at a desk than be out in the field, so he and a forensics analyst have been deep-diving into Gibbs' finances and communications, and there's evidence she's used her position handling medical records for personal gain at more than one job. If you couple that with the fact that even in the year you were born, the odds of a single Black woman adopting a white baby would have been slim to none, it's not a reach to assume whatever went down between Gibbs and your mother had to do with your adoption."

"I'm being honest when I say I don't know anything about Mom's relationship with Phyllis. And why are you asking me instead of my mom?" The reason hit Ricki. "You're trying to weasel information out of me because you're afraid she'll lawyer up!"

The detective gave a mock-apologetic shrug. "I plead guilty to taking advantage of our friendship."

"Friendship?!" Ricki exploded. "Nina, you're trying to get me to implicate my mother in a murder! Or my father! Next you'll be trying to pin it on me!"

"I wasn't, but now that you mention it, you do have motivation," Nina said, warming to the idea. "Dang, I should have thought of that. Now, you see, that's where our friendship came in handy for you."

"AGGHHHH!!" Ricki pulled at her hair in frustration. She dropped her hands and stomped to the door. She yanked it open. "That's it. Miss Vee's Vintage Cookbook and Kitchenware Shop is closed for business. And when it comes to incriminating my loved ones, so am I."

She motioned for Nina to proceed her out the door.

The two women left Bon Vee. As they descended the front steps, Theo passed at a fast clip toward the mansion. Ricki gave a small wave and he barely acknowledged it, remaining on the move. Gumbo and Jambalaya screeched at him. "Nice birdies," he said, preoccupied.

"He didn't hit on me," Nina said, surprised. Theo made no secret of his unrequited crush on the detective. "I'm a little insulted."

"Don't be. It's not about you. He just said something nice to the peacocks, which is a first. He's up to something. Hopefully legal. Although maybe he's figured out the only way he'll ever get quality time with you is to commit a crime where you're forced to catch and jail him."

The women reached Nina's unmarked vehicle, parked on the street in front of the stately mansion. Nina reached for the door handle, then stopped. "Ricki, I know I give you a little grief sometimes."

Ricki snorted. "A little?"

"But I do consider you friend-adjacent. I'll tell you something I shouldn't. The toxicology report hasn't come back to us yet. When it does, hopefully whatever cause of death it reveals will let your parents off the hook."

Nina got in her car and took off, leaving Ricki to wonder what her next step might be and what "friend-adjacent" meant.

Ricki called Josepha from the car on her way home and warned her not to say a word if Nina "dropped by" in her oh-so-Nina way. "I won't be home," Josepha said. "Your dad and I are going to St. Roch Market for dinner, then to

Frenchman Street to hear some jazz. It's hard to come by in P.V., so we wanna take advantage of it while we're here."

"Go for it," Ricki said, happy to hear her parents had fun plans for a change.

On the way home, Ricki stopped at Langenstein's, a local grocery store with a popular hot bar. Their New Orleans Monday menu meant a delicious dinner of red beans and rice, along with bread pudding for dessert. Noting that the waistband on her black-and-white checkboard pattern pencil skirt was cutting into her waist, Ricki reluctantly subbed out the bread pudding for a side of steamed vegetables.

When she got home, Ricki changed into sweats. Thor and Princess burst through the doggy door, dirty from playing in grass made muddy by a misty rain. She fended off their joyous jumps and licks until after she gave them a good wiping-down. Ravenous because she skipped lunch, Ricki wolfed down dinner and then took her laptop to the couch, where she sandwiched herself between the two snoring pups while Red Beans watched from top of her cat tree. She'd been too busy to check her work email file at the shop, so Ricki fired up the laptop and opened the file.

She let out a yell that woke up the dogs and set off a cacophony of alarmed barks.

"You two are the best friends *ever*," Ricki said to Cookie and Zellah.

The three were sitting on the antique rug covering the hardwood floor of Miss Vee's two hours before its ten a.m. opening. Each had a stack of paper about four inches thick in front of them.

"There's no way you could vet all these recipes by yourself." Zellah began turning her big stack into smaller ones.

"I underestimated how enthusiastic people would be about our community cookbook." Not for the first time, Ricki felt a tinge of regret for coming up with the idea.

"It's a good thing," Zellah said. Despite the early call prompted by Ricki's panicked Mayday, she'd taken the time to paint each cheek with possible takes on the cookbook's cover.

Ricki loved them both. Picking one over the other would be tough.

"Let's separate by category," Ricki said. "Appetizers, entrées, soups, salads, side dishes, desserts, beverages. Sound good?"

Cookie gave her a thumbs-up and Zellah nodded. The friends fell quiet as they sorted. "This entire group is gumbo recipes." Cookie pointed to an inch-thick stack.

"So's this." Ricki pointed to her own pile, as did Zellah. "We could do an entire cookbook with only gumbo recipes."

"Except no matter how special everyone thinks their recipe is, it's not much different from all the others." Zellah made a wry face. "I'll go through and pick a seafood, a chicken and sausage, and a veggie. If I can find one. Our New Orleans peeps are not a veggie-eating crowd."

"True dat," Cookie said.

"We should do the same for jambalaya," Ricki said while Zellah grouped the gumbo recipes by flavors.

"And a third for beignets." Cookie pointed to another thick pile. "Everybody has a beignet recipe too."

"They must deliver cooking oil to this city by the tanker," Ricki said, making separate piles for the jambalaya and beignet recipes that cookbook wannabes had submitted.

The sorting continued. "Ricks, what's going on with the death of that Phyllis woman?" Cookie asked. "She died of a heart attack, she didn't die of a heart attack, someone killed her. I'm hearing all sorts of rumors and I don't know if any of them are true."

Ricki realized she hadn't shared the latest developments with her friends. "It's not confirmed but the police seem sure her death wasn't natural or an accident. They're just waiting for confirmation of what killed Phyllis. And both of my parents are potential suspects."

Zellah and Cookie stopped what they were doing and stared at her. Cookie spoke first. "*What?* Why?"

Ricki hesitated, debating whether to share her mother's secret with them. She decided that if the police knew, there wasn't much point in hiding it anymore. "Phyllis worked in Medical Records. Mom didn't think she had a prayer of adopting me as a single Black woman, so she listed her status as Widowed and Phyllis helped her hide the truth from the social worker on the case. Then held it over her head for years."

Her friends responded with outrage, using colorful and profane language to speak ill of the dead. "The woman was a witch." Zellah transferred her anger into fiercely stapling together a two-page recipe that had come apart. "To take advantage of how much Josepha loved you and wanted to be your mama. I can't even."

"I know." Ricki sucked in a breath to control her emotions. "I have the best parents ever. Why couldn't I be happy with that? Why did I have to keep on with the stupid search for my bio 'rents?"

Zellah held up a hand. "Stop! Never, *ever* apologize for that."

Cookie nodded vigorous agreement. "Exactly. Ricki, you have every single right in the world to search for them. Josepha and Luis know this. That's why they've supported you."

"They have. With every single step I've taken." Tears dripped down Ricki's cheeks, threatening to mar the stack of beignet recipes in front of her. She pushed it aside and stood up, then went to the shop desk and extracted a tissue from a box housed in a 1950s pink Bakelite tissue dispenser she kept on hand for customers to use. "But my past is so not important right now. All I want to do is clear my parents' name."

"The way to do that is to find out who killed Phyllis," Cookie said. "Anyone come to mind?"

"I wish. There was no sign of forced entry or NOPD would have immediately classified her death as a homicide. It had to be someone she knew, but also someone who knew about her heart condition. If Phyllis manipulated and blackmailed a NICU nurse like my mom, it's not a reach to assume she was doing the same to other people. Charity was a public hospital. Most people who went there were poor. New Orleans is so class-conscious that if a patient was on the socio-economic bottom rung of the ladder and moved up in society or business, I could see them paying off someone like Phyllis to hide their past." Ricki's phone pinged a text. "It's Mordant," she said, checking it. "He has news. I'll tell him to come by." She thumbed a reply to him.

"Zellah, you'll have to leave," Cookie teased. "He won't be able to concentrate with you here."

"Oh, please," Zellah said with an eye roll. "You're making a big deal outta nothing."

Ricki and Cookie exchanged a knowing look. Anyone who saw Zellah and her besotted suitor together would be hard-pressed to classify the relationship as "nothing."

Mordant showed up ten minutes later, wearing a black stove-pipe and nineteenth-century mourning suit, the outfit of his day job as a haunted history guide. He beamed when he saw Zellah. "I didn't know you were here. I would've brought flowers."

"You don't have to do that every time you see me, chère."

"I like to. And you deserve them."

"All that's missing is hearts and tweeting lovebirds circling his head, like in a cartoon," Cookie whispered to Ricki, who suppressed a giggle.

"You have news for Ricki?" Zellah prompted.

"Ah. Yes." Mordant reluctantly tore himself away from gazing at his beloved and took a seat in one of the comfy club chairs by the shop's bay window. "I dug up some details of Phyllis Gibbs' life after Charity Hospital." The women stopped sorting recipes to listen. "Like pretty much everyone in the city, she was displaced by Hurricane Katrina. She relocated to Atlanta and spent five years there working as the office manager at a doctor's office."

"Any chance she made an enemy there who tracked her down to New Orleans and came here to off her?" Ricki asked, ever hopeful.

Mordant shook his head. "I didn't find any evidence of that. Her only grift in Georgia was milking her displaced hurricane victim status for free rent, a different place every year. Once a landlord got wise to her, she moved on. Katrina destroyed her home in Lakeview and she got a nice payout from her insurance company. Thanks to mooching free rent off of sympathetic Atlanta landlords, she could afford to sit on the payout. Gibbs returned to New Orleans in 2010 and got a job as an office manager for a concierge doctor."

"Huh?" Cookie sounded confused. "What kind of doctor is that? I've never heard of any part of the body being called a concierge. What exactly do they treat?"

"Not what but who," Ricki said. "Very wealthy people. VIP or concierge doctors charge their patients a retainer fee. They don't take any insurance. You pay a flat amount per year and they're there whenever you need them. They're all over Los Angeles. My old boss had his concierge doctor on speed dial."

She winced at the memory of billionaire Barnes Lachlan, whose first-edition collection she'd managed until he was arrested for the Ponzi scheme generating his fortune. Her association with the scam artist forever tanked Ricki's professional reputation in the rare book field. The career disaster came on the heels of her estranged husband's death. Chris, a struggling actor who found success as a daredevil influencer named Chris-*azy*!, died after stuffing his face with one too many marshmallows while doing an online stunt called the Marshmallow Challenge. The back-to-back traumas had motivated Ricki's search for a fresh start in the Crescent City.

"So the local rich folk have bought into this elitist trend," Zellah said, disapproving.

"If I had the money, I would," Cookie declared. "I swear, I catch more stuff waiting to be seen at urgent care than what I showed up for."

"Phyllis worked at her doctor's office here in town until about a month ago," Mordant said. "She retired, supposedly to move somewhere in South America."

"I guess she wasn't in any great rush to make the move." Ricki leaned back against the sturdy foot of the shop's desk. She tapped her lips with her index finger as she mulled over this new information. "Only wealthy people use concierge doctors. And like I said before, those are the people who have secrets they'd pay to hide. Running an office, Gibbs would see a lot of personal data. What if she threatened to use what she learned about a patient against them?"

"I believe your detective pal Nina would file that under 'Motivation,'" Zellah said with a wink.

Ricki rose. "I need to pursue this. I'm making an appointment with Crescent City Concierge. And crossing my fingers they don't charge for a consultation."

TEN

Her friends departed to grab coffee before their workdays began. Zellah and Cookie left with stacks of recipes, promising to winnow them down to the most promising submissions.

With a half-hour still to go before she opened Miss Vee's, Ricki used the time to set up a consultation at the VIP doctor's office. A mellifluous voice greeted her call. "Crescent City Concierge Care. With whom do I have the pleasure of speaking?"

Ricki gave the office props for extreme proper grammar. "Hello." She did her best to match the chi-chi tone of the receptionist. "My name is Miracle James-Diaz. I'm interested in learning more about your practice."

"I'd be happy to schedule an introductory appointment," came the smooth reply. "Are you familiar with concierge medical services?"

"I am. I'm from Los Angeles."

"Oh." The receptionist's interest perked up. "What brings you to New Orleans?"

"I run Miss Vee's Vintage Cookbook and Kitchenware Shop."

"Ah. A store."

Ricki didn't miss the hint of distaste in the woman's voice. "Yes. At Bon Vee Culinary House Museum. Eugenia Charbonnet Felice is my cousin."

"What time tomorrow works best for you?" came the instant response.

Namedropping Eugenia never fails, Ricki thought to herself. "Let me check my schedule." She counted to ten, then said, "Let's do twelve thirty. I'll have my staff cover for me. We're so busy during the holidays."

"I'm sure you are," the receptionist responded with a tinkling laugh. "You'll be meeting with Delia Robbins, our head office manager."

"You have more than one?"

"We have three. Well, two right now."

Ricki picked up a hint of stress in the response. She chalked off the practice being down an office manager to Phyllis's death.

"Can I get your cell number so we can text a confirmation?" the receptionist continued.

"I prefer to communicate via email," Ricki said. There was no point in sharing her number when she had zero intention of following up with the pricey doctor. She gave the receptionist the general email address for the shop and signed off.

Ricki sent a message to Olivia, her "staff" of one, to see if she was free to mind the store during the next day's lunch hour. Olivia shot back a Can't, sorority holiday luncheon, sorry!—so Ricki reached out to Cookie, who responded with a thumbs-up. Relieved, Ricki checked the time on her phone and saw she still had twenty minutes to spare before opening for the day— enough time to pay Cousin Eugenia a visit.

Eugenia was in her elegantly appointed office, which was painted and upholstered in a range of subtle cream shades and furnished with Charbonnet family heirloom furniture. The doyenne of Bon Vee was in the midst of clipping what looked like party invitations to the lampshade of her antique desk fixture, which was already crowded with other invitations. Ricki had come to see if Eugenia had any intel on Crescent City Concierge Care, but curiosity about the older woman's odd task prompted her to ask, "What are you doing?"

"Organizing my invitations to various krewe events taking place over the holidays."

"That's a lot of events."

"I have several friends with granddaughters the same age as Olivia, and all of them are in different krewes, hence the onslaught of invitations. I was going to use my Christmas card stand, but it's full up." Eugenia gestured to the four-foot wooden Christmas tree designed to hold cards. There wasn't an empty space on it.

Ricki got to the reason for her visit. "Do you know anything about a VIP doctor's office called Crescent City Concierge Care?"

Eugenia appeared perplexed. She tucked in a few hairs that had dared to come loose from her ash-blonde chignon, then continued clipping invitations to the lampshade. "I have absolutely no idea what you're talking about. VIP doctors? Concierge Care? Is this all some Los Angeles claptrap?" Unlike the Crescent City Concierge Care receptionist, Eugenia viewed the L.A. bona fides of the high-end medical trend as a negative, not a positive.

Ricki explained how the service operated, ending with, "Phyllis Gibbs, the woman my mother knew who died, worked there."

Eugenia stopped what she was doing. "The Peony Place Murder."

"It has a name? It's not even officially a murder."

"Olivia and I came up with the name," Eugenia said with false modesty. "Since she has a bit of a connection to it through her friend Lizette. Renate Rancourt is Lizette's grandmother and lives on the street. Olivia and I find it to be a fascinating case."

Uh-oh, I've inspired a grandmother-granddaughter amateur sleuth team. Lord help us all. "I thought you might have heard about the concierge service from a friend or something. Never mind."

"Sorry I can't be of any help. Everyone I know sees their doctor until he retires, then sees the son or daughter who takes over the practice. This concierge approach must be a new-money trend."

Ricki swallowed a laugh at the disdainful mention of "new money." The designation wasn't wrong. But often a conversation with Eugenia, a woman who could trace her lineage on her father's side back to the founding of Louisiana, felt like a verbal time tunnel. "No worries. Thanks anyway. I have to go open the shop."

Ricki started out but Eugenia stopped her. "I just had a wonderful idea. Greg and Robin are planning to throw Olivia a Christmas-themed party to celebrate her court call," she said, referencing her son and daughter-in-law, proud parents of the recently anointed krewe queen. "I'll tell them I'm going to host it, which will put me in charge of the guest list. It's New Orleans. Somebody has to have a skeleton in their closet, if not everybody." Eugenia smiled a conspiratorial smile. "I'll put it together quickly. The sooner we solve this, the better. We can search for clues together."

"Great!" Ricki said while screaming *NO!!!* silently to herself. Still, she had to admit, deputizing one of New Orleans' leading lights as an investigative assistant could come in handy.

The next day, after promising to share "all the deets" of her visit to the luxe doctor's office with Cookie, Ricki took off for Crescent City Concierge Care.

She found their facilities discreetly housed in an early twentieth-century Romanesque-style mansion on storied St. Charles Avenue. Ricki grabbed the last available spot in the practice's beautifully landscaped parking lot. Seeing her eight-year-old Prius, which was in need of a wash, at the end of a row of high-end vehicles, reminded Ricki of the Sesame Street song, "One of These Things (Is Not Like the Others.)"

A sign directed Ricki to follow the side yard path to the front of the mansion. She followed the directions, curving her way around the former home until she reached the medical practice's grand entrance. It took both hands to pull open the heavy front door adorned with beveled glass windows that glimmered with rainbows when they caught the sun.

Ricki stepped into a center hallway featuring elaborately carved walnut paneling and antique rugs. The stunning space had been turned into an ersatz reception area. A massive Christmas tree reached upward from its perch in the middle of the space, its bejeweled ornaments picking up the color scheme of a spectacular stained-glass window gazing down upon the reception area from the second-floor landing. The tone was hushed . . . or would have been if a middle-aged matron wasn't berating a beleaguered employee behind an antique reception desk.

"I don't pay what I pay here to be kept waiting almost five minutes to see a doctor," the patient barked.

"I'm so sorry, Mrs. Dabney," the woman behind the desk

responded, her head bobbing up and down in a way that indi-cated she understood, sympathized, and apologized. "It won't happen again. You have my word on that."

"It better not, or I'll take my ailments elsewhere." The patient stormed past Ricki and out the door.

"Hello and welcome to Concierge Care," the receptionist said, turning her attention to newcomer Ricki with a bright smile. "Just so you know, keeping patients waiting isn't our normal modus operandi. We lost one of our office managers a few days ago and things are a bit off."

"If I only had to wait five minutes to see a doctor, I'd celebrate," Ricki said. The receptionist laughed and Ricki recognized her from the phone call when she'd booked her appointment. Ricki noted her nametag read "Eloise Simmons." It also listed her hometown—Covington, Louisiana—as if she worked at an upscale hotel. "I'm Miracle James-Diaz. I have a twelve-thirty appointment with Delia Robbins."

"Yes. Let me check you in." Eloise's fingers flew across her slim silver keyboard. She pressed a button on an ear pod Ricki hadn't noticed. "Delia, your twelve-thirty is here," Eloise said into a tiny wireless microphone clipped to her gray silk top masquerading as scrubs.

Seconds later, a door behind Eloise opened and a woman Ricki pegged as Delia made an entrance. Her height and bone structure gave her the look of a former model, giving Ricki the impression that the Crescent City staff was cast as much as hired.

Delia came to her and extended a hand. Her grip was firm, her hand soft and supple. "I hope I didn't keep you waiting."

"Not even a millisecond. Eloise explained you lost an employee recently."

"Yes," Delia said, her tone indicating she wouldn't elaborate. "We've hired a replacement but she can't start until after the holidays. It will make things a bit tricky for the next few weeks. You know how people get around the holidays."

"Yes, very well," Ricki lied.

"Let's go to the conservatory." She ushered Ricki in the opposite direction from the receptionist desk. As they walked, she turned her head toward Eloise. "Order Mrs. Dabney an arrangement from Bonne Fleurs with a note of apology for having to wait."

"Already done."

Delia gave Eloise an approving nod, then led Ricki into a tiled, enclosed glass solarium filled with lush plants. The kind of room more associated with historic house tours than a doctor's office, it reminded Ricki of the conservatory at Bon Vee.

The women settled into the room's capacious lounge chairs and Delia launched into her spiel. "I saw from the notes on your call that you're from Los Angeles, so I know you're familiar with the concept of VIP doctors. What makes Crescent City Concierge different, especially for New Orleans, is we don't only offer primary care physician services. We're a full-service practice, offering the services of a cardiologist, endocrinologist, dermatologist, pulmonologist, and ob-gyn, plus we're connected with a satellite facility offering orthopedic care. All for an extremely reasonable rate."

She handed Ricki what looked like a wedding invitation but turned out to be a price list. The yearly cost for concierge care was in the five figures. Rather than tap out the city's limited pool of patrons willing to cough up the equivalent of private school tuition, the practice also offered an individual office rate that was mild instead of massive heart attack-inducing.

Delia droned on while Ricki wondered if any of the doctors in the practice might have had less impressive roots at Charity Hospital. "How long have your doctors been practicing?"

"At least ten years for almost all of them."

"I like doctors with a long track record," Ricki said, trying to home in on any who'd been around long enough to have worked at Charity before Katrina decimated it.

"Then you'd like our primary physician, Dr. Jeremy Mansieur. He recently attended his Tulane School of Medicine's Class of '92 reunion."

Ricki did the math in her head. "Perfect." Delia looked at her with a quizzical expression and Ricki hastily added, "A doctor with thirty-plus years of experience is what I'm looking for. Before I commit to the practice, I'd love to meet Dr. Mansieur."

"Of course." Delia extracted a cell phone from the pocket of her gray silk fake-scrubs, which appeared to be the office uniform. She opened an app and studied it. "He has a break between patients in about ten minutes, if you'd like to wait."

"Sounds good."

They left the conservatory for the reception area. Ricki took a seat and Delia returned to her office. Ricki noticed a magazine on the side table next to her chair and picked it up. The publication proved to be a sales tool for the practice, with articles touting the brilliance of each doctor. Ricki thumbed through it, eventually landing on the page for dermatologist Rachel Vernon. As with most current dermatologists, the list of services leaned toward expensive cosmetic procedures with a desultory nod toward skin cancer prevention.

Ricki, who'd enjoyed a facial now and then in Los Angeles, felt herself lured into considering the "24-Karat Rejuvenating Spa Treatment," which touted its ability to rejuvenate the skin and create a radiant, youthful glow. Ricki surreptitiously flipped her phone's camera to reflect her face. At twenty-eight she could claim youth, but stress blemishes were threatening to erupt on her chin. *And who doesn't need to glow?* Ricki thought, tempted.

An attractive woman of indeterminate age came into the medical mansion. She waved hello to Eloise. Taking a seat across from Ricki, she smiled a greeting, which Ricki returned. Sensing an opportunity, Ricki initiated a conversation. "Hi." She lowered her voice. "I've never been here before. I'm interested in signing up for their services but I'd love to talk to a patient and get their take on it."

"I get it." The new arrival leaned forward. Her wavy strawberry blonde hair fell over her shoulders. She wore a navy wrap dress that seemed designed not to deflect the attention from her gold and diamond trio of necklaces. A large diamond sparkled from her ring finger. "I can't recommend the practice highly enough. Then again, I'm married to one of the doctors."

She grinned, winked, and sat back in her chair.

A nurse appeared in the doorway that Ricki assumed led to a hallway of examination rooms. "Miracle James-Diaz?"

"That's me." Ricki stood up. "Nice talking to you," she said to the doctor's wife, whose feedback had been useless. But she'd been nice and not snooty or taken with herself, like some of the doctor's wives Ricki had met in L.A.

"Nice talking to you too. Lisa," the woman said, addressing the nurse, "can you tell him I'm here for lunch?"

"Will do, Mrs. M." The casual response indicated a long-standing relationship.

The nurse led her to Dr. Mansieur's office, where the décor was in keeping with the mansion's general style, which Ricki classified as Inherited Wealth. Mansieur was a walking ad for his practice's services: handsome, in great shape, and with a smooth complexion that belied his almost-sixty-years without looking excessively lasered. He exuded a self-confidence borne of success. After ten minutes of glad-handing, Ricki made a show of examining his framed diplomas. "Someone told me you did your residency at Charity."

Mansieur appeared puzzled. "No. Baptist before Tenet sold it to Oschner. I'll make sure Delia gives you my current bio. Now, let me tell you more about the individual care you'll get with us that you won't get anywhere else in the city . . ."

If this guy is guilty of anything, it's boring people to death, Ricki thought, pretending to listen as he bloviated about himself and his fellow practitioners. Still, while she couldn't pinpoint why, she sensed there was something hinky about Crescent City Concierge Care.

Nurse Lisa walked Ricki back to the front desk, where Delia was in the middle of what appeared to be an intense conversation with a patient. "Delia, you have to get me a jar of the Futura night cream," the woman pleaded. "Dr. Vernon said she discontinued the line, which is crazy. It's such fab skincare. I have enough of everything else to last me a while but I'm low on the night cream and I can't find it anywhere else. I searched online but it doesn't come up. It's like it never existed. There have to be a few jars left somewhere in the practice. *Please*." The woman clasped her hands together, begging.

"I'll see what I can do," the office manager responded. Ricki sensed it was an empty promise . . . and wondered why the practice's dermatologist would discontinue a product line obviously popular with her patients.

After promising to pay triple the cost of the product, the woman left. Delia turned her attention to Ricki. "I hope you've gotten everything you need from your visit." She handed Ricki a business card. "My personal line if you have any questions."

Receptionist Eloise rose from her chair. "I need to visit the ladies' room. You'll have to cover me for a few minutes."

"Right."

Delia's unhappy reaction to the mundane desk duty gave Ricki an idea. "My mother is a retired nurse who's in town for the holidays. With me working at the shop all the time, she doesn't have much to do. She'd be perfect to fill in here until your full-time hire is available, if you're interested."

"I am," Delia instantly responded as she settled into the receptionist chair. "Please have her call me on the number I gave you. As soon as possible."

Ricki sauntered out of the mansion. She checked to make sure she was out of Delia's eyeline, then hurried to her car. She hopped in and called Josepha. "Mom, put on your best church outfit. I've got a job for you."

ELEVEN

Josepha made it to the doctor's office in twenty minutes clad in her favorite navy suit. Ricki was glad to see she'd passed on wearing the bespoke hat that went with the outfit.

She'd filled her mother in on the plan over the phone and was pleased Josepha enthusiastically embraced it. "Emphasize all your experience with patients and how good you are at managing them," Ricki said. "I get the feeling a lot of the ones in this practice are Karens who throw a fit at the tiniest inconvenience to their entitled lives. The office desperately needs help or they risk losing them."

"Understood. Once I'm in and have established myself, I'll start poking around to see what I can learn about Phyllis. Like, if she ran across something she could work to her advantage. I'll get gossip going too. It's the most natural thing in the world for me to ask what happened to my predecessor."

"Proceed with caution, Mom. F. Scott Fitzgerald was right when he said the rich are different. The money they have can make them dangerous to anyone they perceive as a threat."

Josepha affected a coy expression. "Me? A threat. *Pshaw*." She adjusted her skirt and eyed the building with determination. "Like they say on the battlefield, cover me, I'm goin' in."

Ricki grinned and gave her a mock salute. "Sir, yes, sir!"

Josepha marched up the stairs and into Concierge Care. Rather than fiddle around waiting, Ricki decided to pay a visit to the shops on nearby Magazine Street and see if gift inspiration struck. She still didn't have a clue what to get Virgil for Christmas.

The street's festive holiday spirit lessened the tension Ricki felt about sending her mother undercover. White lights decorated one shop window while another was a blast of color. Green and red garlands were draped around several storefront doors. A light display declaring "Merry Christmas, Y'all" dangled over a doorway. Ricki waved to the proprietor of her favorite vintage clothing store, who had set up a speaker on the sidewalk to entertain passersby by playing Louis Armstrong's version of "'Zat You, Santa Claus?"

Ricki stepped into Nutmeg, a beloved local shop featuring exquisite items, many made by local artisans. Owner Guidry Vane was in the midst of removing a hand-painted glass replica of a paddleboat for a customer from a tree that glittered and gleamed with an array of similar ornaments depicting famed New Orleans landmarks: Jackson Square, Café du Monde, the Pontalba Buildings, even one of the city's legendary above-ground tombs. That particular ornament brought back memories of the body discovered in the tomb recreation Bon Vee had built for their Halloween haunted house.

Ricki shuddered and stepped away from the tree to admire a collection of handmade ceramic bowls painted sage green. "Those'll class up any holiday table," a voice behind her said.

Ricki turned around to see her friend Guidry, who was husband to Ky Nyugen, Virgil's business partner at Bayou Backyard, the Bon Vee gang's favorite bar-restaurant hangout. She and the shop owner exchanged greetings and a hug. "I love the bowls but I'm trying to find something for Virgil," Ricki said, "and he's not much on entertaining, especially right now with his show in production."

"I'm excited for him," Guidry said. "And for me. He's going to plug our kitschy holiday oyster plate." Guidry lifted a platter designed to hold a dozen oysters on the half-shell. Painted above each oyster space was a Santa hat and below it a Santa beard, turning every oyster to be placed on the plate into a mini-Santa Claus.

"That's awesome. I'm going to buy one for myself."

The shop owner laughed. "Isn't that how it goes when you're buying gifts. One for him, one for me. One for her, two for me."

"Speaking of 'him,' any tips on what I can get for Virgil? I'm embarrassed to ask but—"

"Don't be. The man is impossible to shop for. I wish I could point you in the right direction but it would take you out of my store to I don't know where."

"It's not just me?" Ricki flushed, mortified by how plaintive she sounded.

"No, honey," Guidry said, his expression understanding. "It's not just you."

"Thanks," Ricki said, grateful for his kindness. "You have such lovely things. I'm going to take a look around. I'm sure I'll find some gifts for my parents."

"Your mom is from here, right? I bet she'd like my line of New Orleans toile."

Guidry led Ricki to a line of items featuring his one-of-a-kind toile design. It replicated the distinctive look of toile but as with the Christmas ornaments, highlighted the landmarks of the Big Easy.

Ricki picked out a frame for her parents and sent herself a reminder to take a family photograph to place inside before her parents left town. Guidry wrapped her gifts, refusing payment for the oyster platter. "My gift to you and your man. Oysters are the food of love, amirite?"

"Ha, right," she said, playing along with the innuendo.

Despite Guidry's assurance that she wasn't alone in her Virgil shopping frustration, the lack of gift progress still bothered Ricki. As she walked back to the Concierge Care parking lot, her phone buzzed. She set down her Nutmeg tote bag, glad for the break of carrying it. The Santa oyster platter was heavy. She pulled her phone out of her brown leather crossbody bag and saw a text from Josepha. I got the job!

Yay! Ricki texted back. When do you start?

Now! See u tonight or whenever I get off. They got lots of work for me.

Ricki celebrated the success of Phase One in her plot to uncover whatever was going on at the high-end medical office and how it might connect to Phyllis. She was about to put her phone away when it rang. Her heart notched an increase in beats when she saw the caller was Nina. *I am calm, centered, and strong,* she affirmed to herself. *I am calm, centered, and strong.* Feeling none of the three, she took the call. "Hi. Are you're calling to say my parents are no longer suspects in Phyllis's possible murder, I hope, I hope?"

"Oh man, that would be a great holiday present, wouldn't it? Unfortunately, I can't wrap it and put it under a tree. At least not yet. But you don't have to describe Gibbs' murder as 'possible' anymore. It officially is one. The tox screen came back. She ingested a deadly amount of delphinium. Since it seems like an odd choice of snack, we're looking into the possibility of someone sneaking it into something Gibbs ate or drank. The Crime Scene Unit found crumbs that could have come from muffins or a sweet bread, like zucchini. Your mother a good baker?"

"To be honest, no. She likes to cook, not bake. Since I've been selling cookbooks, I've noticed that buyers divide along those lines. People who love to cook don't really enjoy baking and vice versa."

"Your mother basically said the same thing."

"You were trying to catch her in a lie, weren't you?" Ricki fumed. "Like, if I said, yes, Mom made muffins last week, she'd stay on top of your suspect leader board. Well, guess what? A lot of people who live on Peony Place have delphiniums in their gardens. That opens up your suspect list to Phyllis's neighbors."

"Or anyone who happened to walk by and help themselves to a flower. The block's silly with poisonous plants."

"The more suspects, the better. And my father doesn't bake either. And his cooking repertoire is limited, so unless Phyllis died from eating a delphinium-stuffed tamale, you're out of luck."

"I'm sorry, Ricki." To Ricki's surprise, Nina sounded genuinely apologetic. "I don't like badgering you or your parents but I have to do my job. When someone's murdered on a fancy street like Peony Place, it gets the higher-up's attention. Kind of a 'there but for the grace of God' thing."

"Look for other suspects. Because my parents are innocent."

Ricki ended the call, relieved she'd backed up her mother in the lie that she didn't like to bake. Josepha was the rare person who loved to cook *and* bake. *Mom must have picked up on what Nina was fishing for and adjusted accordingly,* Ricki thought. If so, it was a rare misstep on the detective's part. One she wasn't likely to make again.

*   *   *

Having missed lunch, Ricki paid Langenstein's another visit to pick up a pre-made sandwich which she ate while driving back to Bon Vee. Once there, she stopped at the staff offices in the carriage house to pick up a box of books she'd bought from an online estate sale. They'd belonged to an elderly society matron who lived in one of the stately homes on Exposition Boulevard, which ran along the eastern edge of Audubon Park, and were heavy on Louisiana-themed recipe collections.

As she headed back to her shop, Ricki saw her father practicing one of his tai chi routines on the side yard grass. She watched, making sure she was out of view so she didn't disrupt him. Luis's moves were slow and hypnotic. Ricki relaxed simply watching him. Even the peacocks appeared mesmerized by the large man's grace and fluid motion.

Ricki tore herself away, resuming her trek to the shop, where Cookie and Zellah sat behind the shop desk, snacking on cheese straws. "Thank you so much. How did things go?"

"Very well," Cookie said through a mouth of cheese straw. "Shoppers came by who weren't even here for tours. Word's out this is a cool gift shop with one-of-a-kind items."

"Yay for that."

"I inventoried everything I sold and printed it out for you."

Ricki deposited her box of the books on the table. She picked up Cookie's list. Under it was a note of some kind. "What's this?"

"Read it."

Ricki scanned the page. In big block letters it read, *Gloria Allen's recipe for hush puppies is from a 1984 issue of* Southern Living. "Uh-oh. Someone narc'd on poor Gloria." The woman was one of Bon Vee's most-requested docents and well-liked by the staff.

"Me and Cookie got the same note," Zellah said. "Which is anonymous, of course, because no tattletale is ever gonna name themselves."

"Is it true?" Ricki asked the café owner. "Is the recipe from *Southern Living*?"

"Sadly, yes. I located the recipe on the internet. If Gloria had modified it, it'd be one thing. But it's exactly the same. Word for word."

"Then we can't use it."

"Someone's gonna have to break it to Gloria," Cookie said. "Let's draw cheese straws. Which Zellah made from a recipe the lady across the street submitted, and are delish."

"I'll take a cheese straw, but we don't have to do a draw." Ricki helped herself to one and verified that they were indeed delish. "This cookbook thing was my idea, so I should be the one to break the bad news."

"This time," Zellah said. "But it can't always come from you. We'll divvy up delivering the news if it happens again. These wannabe contributors are out for blood. You could wind up getting death threats."

"I'm regretting my cookbook brainstorm more and more every day."

Cookie and Zellah took off. Ricki made the dreaded phone call to Gloria Allen, who responded to the news her recipe had been declined with more embarrassment than anger. "I am so sorry. The recipe's handwritten. I must have copied it from a friend's issue of the magazine."

"Nothing to apologize for, Mrs. Allen. It happens to all of us."

"How did you find out it was from *Southern Living?*"

"We're doing our best to vet all the recipes." Ricki purposely gave a vague response, not wanting to inflame the situation, especially since there was a good chance the anonymous competitor was a friend of Gloria's who knew she turned in a recipe and wanted to make sure it didn't rule out their own entry. "Let me know if you have any other recipes you'd like to submit. We'd love to include you in the cookbook."

"I will."

Ricki finished the day by selling almost all of the books from her estate sale haul. Between that and learning the toxicology report would force Nina to widen her circle of suspects, Ricki left the shop in a good mood. Rather than cut through the Bon Vee grounds, she opted for the sidewalk to enjoy the holiday decorations on the front lawns lining Persephone Street.

A deer family gamboled by a Christmas tree in one yard display; in another, giant colorful ornaments dangled from the branches of a giant oak tree. The air had a chill to it that felt almost wintry, adding to the festive atmosphere. Ricki breathed it in, enjoying the cold sensation.

She was almost at her car when Mordant pulled up next to her in his hearse. "Tell me you're free in the morning," he called to her through the driver's side window.

"I don't open until ten, so if it's before that, yes."

"That's what hoped."

"Why?" Ricki asked, curious.

Mordant pulled over to park. He got out of the hearse. "Phyllis Gibbs' house is going on the market and I made a nine a.m. appointment for my fiancé and me to view it. Which in this case would be you."

"Mordant, you're awesome," Ricki said, excited. "It's the perfect opportunity to poke around her house for clues. I know NOPD has already done this, but they're operating on such a bare-bones level they may have missed something, especially since everyone thought she died of natural causes at first. It'll also give us a chance to find out more about her neighbors." She filled Mordant in on the results of the toxicology report.

"It's a fake date, then," he said. "Wear a ring that looks like an engagement ring."

"I have a real one. That Chris gave me." Ricki felt a stab of grief. She'd taken off her engagement and wedding ring when she and Chris separated. Putting either of them back on would feel strange.

"Excellent. I'll pick you at eight thirty."

Ricki eyed the hearse. Large magnets on every car door advertised the guide's haunted history tours featuring Mordant in costume with his usual mournful expression. "I think we better take my car."

TWELVE

After tending to the pooches the next morning, Ricki texted her mother to see how her first day at work went. Josepha replied that she was already at the medical office. Ricki raised an eyebrow. It was barely eight a.m. She hoped the exclusive practice didn't work Josepha so hard she wouldn't have time to focus on the real reason she was there: to search for clues that could lead to Phyllis's killer.

Ricki rummaged through her closet and drawers to put together an outfit that would sell her as a serious potential home-buyer to the real estate agent handling Phyllis's house. She settled on black wool slacks that she paired with a dark gray button-down silk blouse. The outfit looked funereal because it was. Ricki had bought it for the funeral of Luis's grandmother.

Mordant met her at Bon Vee, where his handyman skills were being put to use restringing the white lights threaded through holiday garlands draped over the estate's black iron fence. Ricki did a double take when she saw him. Clad in navy trousers, a beige polo shirt, and brown boat shoes without socks, he resembled a frat boy turned successful businessman. "Mordant! I almost didn't recognize you."

"Leftover costume from when I was an extra on *NCIS: New Orleans*," he said as he squished his long frame into Ricki's car. "I was in a crowd scene at an insurance salesmen convention. I thought about adding fake blood and turning it into a preppy serial killer costume for Halloween but never got around to it."

"Good thing you didn't. It's perfect for what we need to do."

"I hate it. I'm not comfortable being a normal guy."

"You still have your deathly pallor, so you don't look completely normal."

"You're just saying that to make me feel better." Mordant cast a glance at Ricki. He took in her outfit. "Who died?"

"Dad's abuela. It was the best I could do."

Ricki followed the short route to Peony Place. She parked behind a gleaming new model BMW hybrid stationed in front of Phyllis's house, where a large wooden lawn sign announced it was for sale. Ricki assumed the car belonged to the real-estate agent, a slim, perfectly dressed brunette in her mid-thirties who was on the landing outside the home's front door, eyes glued to her cell phone.

Ricki made a point of slamming her car door shut. The noise did the trick of separating the agent from her phone. She flashed a smile that revealed veneers bright enough for Ricki to see from where she stood on the sidewalk. Ricki waited for Mordant to extricate himself from her car, then the two proceeded up the sidewalk.

"Hi, Madison Carter from Reve Realty." The agent extended her hand to each of them. "Awww, cute ring," she added, noticing Ricki's engagement ring.

"It's an antique," Ricki said. Annoyed by the agent's patronizing attitude, she felt compelled to defend the cubic zirconium ring her late husband once admitted he'd dug out of his mother's costume jewelry drawer.

Madison got down to business. "Just so you know, this is the first time anyone from my agency has been able to get inside the house."

"The police had it locked down until the crime scene unit was done going over it on account of the owner's murder," Mordant said.

"Riiight." Madison, obviously not thrilled by the mention of the murder, made a face like Mordant had passed gas. She instantly replaced the expression with her go-to smile. "But I can guarantee you any house on Peony Place has great bones. Apparently the lawyer handling Ms. Gibbs estate is owed his fee, so he's interested in a quick sale. Whoever buys this stunning home will be getting a fabulous deal." The agent pressed a code into the lockbox, then removed the key. She opened the door and the three stepped inside.

They walked through the center hallway to the living room. Madison let out a little "Eep!" and Ricki's eyes widened at the sight in front of them. The home's outside was neat and spare. The inside was anything but, the "great bones" advertised by the agent hidden under a morass of stuff. The space was packed, the floor barely visible. Furniture duked it out with a horde of boxes, many sealed.

Madison made an expansive gesture with her arms. "Will you look at all this. It's proof how large the room is. You can fit so much into it."

"Yes. We see." Ricki had to admire Madison's brave spin on what was close to a hoarding situation.

The agent held a hand over her nose. "It's a teensy bit musty in here. I'll open some windows. Use your imagination to picture all of this gone and y'all having a cozy nightcap in front of the fireplace."

Mordant glanced around the room. "Where is the fireplace?"

"Somewhere." Madison's face crumpled for a split second. "I don't think I can create a path to any of the windows in here. I'll meet you in the dining room."

She left on her fruitless mission to freshen the home's dank air. The minute she was gone, Ricki pulled out her phone. "You hunt for anything that might be a clue. I'll take as many pictures as I can before Madison comes back." She snapped shots of the labels on several boxes. "Some of these are incoming, but a lot are marked for a hotel in Nicaragua. Our Phyllis was planning a move."

"To the only Central American country that doesn't have an extradition agreement with the U.S. Ah, here's the fireplace."

Ricki navigated her way through the boxes and furniture. Glass sculptures crowded together on a side table. She picked one up and a mark on the bottom identified it as Lalique, a pricey collectible brand. Ricki snapped photos of the collection, then moved on. She stopped to check out a folding table loaded up with a variety of skincare products. She picked up a bottle and examined the label. Sleek lettering spelled out "Futura Next Gen Cleanser." The tagline underneath read "Tomorrow's skincare today." Ricki digested this. "Hmm. I heard a woman begging for Futura night cream at the VIP doctor's office yesterday. They told her it was discontinued and she said she'd pay triple what it cost to get her hands on some. Phyllis is sitting on a skincare goldmine here. I wonder how she scored all this."

"Grifters gonna grift."

Ricki joined Mordant at the fireplace. The mantle was crowded with framed photos—all of the same cat. A vase in the center of the display held dead roses. "Looks like Lizette's grandmother was right when she blamed Phyllis for stealing her roses." Ricki moved in closer to read a small card resting against the vase. "Oh, this is so sad. It's a mass card for the cat. Her name was Sparkle." Ricki found herself unexpectedly moved by the first glimmer of Phyllis's humanity.

"Uh-huh." Mordant had forged a path to one of the room's side windows. "I see the wall you told me about. The one between Phyllis and this neighbor. It's pretty new. And high."

Madison appeared in the doorway. "I got a couple of windows open. I'd love to show you the rest of the house."

"What's the deal with this wall?" Mordant was still staring out the window. "There's not one on the other side of the house. Is there a problem with these neighbors?"

"No, not at all. Peony Place is a close-knit community. It's more of an architectural choice. Wait until you see the dining room. It's huge. We'll just have to move a few boxes out of the way."

Ricki and Mordant exchanged a look as they followed the agent out of the living room. "Architectural choice my keister," Mordant whispered. Ricki nodded in agreement.

The two kept up their act of being a house-hunting couple throughout the rest of the tour, the only bump occurring when Mordant fixated on trying to get a look at the neighbor's side of the tall wall from the windows facing in their direction. Sensing the realtor growing suspicious, Ricki pulled him away from the window. "Honey, relax. I'm sure they're very nice people who wanted a little more privacy than they'd get from a hedge." Ricki whispered to Madison, "We have problems with our current neighbors, so it's an issue with him." Judging from the change in the agent's expression, she bought it.

They finished the tour and thanked the agent. After doing one last sales pitch while she led them outside and exacting promises to let her know if they were interested in moving forward with the house, Madison took off.

"That was . . . a lot." Mordant scratched behind the collar of his polo shirt. "Ugh, this thing itches. I think I'm allergic to polo shirts. Anyway, we learned a couple of interesting things. One, Phyllis planned a move to a country without an extradition agreement."

Ricki held up two fingers. "And two, she has a big stash of a much-desired skincare line."

"Madison danced around the wall issue, so we didn't learn anything new there."

"I think the only way to find out about neighbors is to ask other neighbors. I bet Lizette's grandmama is a wealth of gossip on that score. I still have time before I open the store. Let's pay her a visit."

"Do you know which house is hers?"

"No." Ricki perused the block. "My money's on that one."

She pointed to the oldest and largest house on the block, an antebellum number with heavy columns and a gallery that wrapped around the second floor. An American flag, a Louisiana flag, and a flag Ricki didn't recognize wafted back and forth due to a light breeze. The front yard was a veritable rose garden, filled with blooms of every shade. A few other plants were mixed in, including sturdy and colorful stalks of the block's omnipresent delphinium.

"Logical choice," Mordant said, eyeing the front yard in question. "Let's give it a shot."

They headed down the block to the mansion in question. Ricki inhaled the unmistakable scent of roses as they trod the path to the front door. "I can see why Phyllis would want to pilfer these. They're gorgeous and smell fantastic, even at this time of year. I hope someday I get to own a house where I can plant roses."

"You sound wistful."

"Sorry. I'll get back on track."

Ricki rang the doorbell. She and Mordant heard motion inside the house, then a voice. "Hello?" The word came with the hint of a Caribbean accent. "Can we help you?"

"My name is Miracle James-Diaz. My cousin Olivia Felice is friends with Mrs. Rancourt's granddaughter. I run the gift shop at Bon Vee Culinary House Museum. I'd love to have a short chat with Mrs. Rancourt."

"Hold on a minute, please."

A muted conversation on the other side of the door ensued. Ricki and Mordant waited a minute. Then Ricki called to the door, "Please tell Mrs. Rancourt that Eugenia Felice, Olivia's grandmother and another cousin of mine, says hello."

"Name-dropper," Mordant muttered.

"Watch."

The door flew open. Ricki shot Mordant a triumphant grin. A maid dressed in full maid mufti ushered them into the home's grand foyer. And grand it was, with a sweeping staircase that went up to a second floor and beyond, and a parquet floor polished within an inch of its life. A giant vase filled with roses graced an eighteenth-century entry-hall table, filling the room with more of the heady rose scent. Ricki was so taken with the magnificent surroundings she almost missed the geriatric woman judging her from a wheelchair.

"Mrs. Rancourt will see you in the front parlor," the maid said in her lilting Islands accent.

Their elderly hostess pressed a button on her wheelchair and expertly maneuvered out of the foyer. Ricki and Mordant followed her into a massive room awash with antiques and good taste. They meekly took a seat across from Mrs. Rancourt on a plump sofa upholstered in a soft peach damask. "Tanice, bring us coffee," the elderly woman said to the maid.

"Yes, ma'am."

Tanice headed off to fulfill the request. Mrs. Rancourt continued to eye them with such disapproval Ricki wondered why she'd admitted them in the first place. "You wanted to have a short chat. May I ask why?"

The question was phrased more like an order. Now that they

were in the belly of the high society beast, Ricki debated what approach to take. Continue the lie they were a newly engaged couple looking to buy on Peony Place? Or tell Mrs. Rancourt the truth? She was old-school New Orleans, fully made up and in a navy wool crepe dress, even though her day probably consisted of meals with her maid and watching her "stories." She might be in her eighties, but the steely glint in her eyes telegraphed she was as sharp as a thorn on one of her roses. Ricki decided to go with the truth.

"We wanted to talk to you about your late neighbor Phyllis. Innocent people are suspects in her murder. We want to clear their names."

"Are you from one of those awful true crime podcasts?"

The tone in the woman's voice made Ricki fear she was about to throw them out. "No. The innocent people are my parents. Phyllis worked with my mother at Charity Hospital years ago. They had . . . issues."

Mrs. Rancourt's face cleared. "Ah." She looked puzzled. "But I assumed Phyllis was the victim of a robbery. We heard the suspects were colored."

Mordant made a strangling sound. "Those were my parents. And there was no robbery," Ricki said, giving herself credit for delivering this calmly and not screaming, *you racist!* "I'm adopted. My mother is African American and my father is Hispanic."

"I see." Her tone telegraphed her disapproval loud and clear.

Tanice returned with a tray of coffee cups and a plate of cookies. She placed the tray on the table and distributed the coffee, then left. Mrs. Rancourt took a delicate sip. "Your parents weren't alone in having problems with the late Miss Gibbs. That awful woman was helping herself to my roses. If she hadn't died, I'd be pressing charges for trespassing and stealing."

"Did other neighbors have conflicts with her?" Mordant asked. "We noticed a wall on one side of her house but not the other."

"You mean the Sachs. They're the most recent addition to the block." Lizette's grandmother assumed a crafty expression.

"They crossed swords with Miss Gibbs over an issue with the trees dividing the property between the two homes. I've never spoken to them, so I'm not aware of the exact issue. Personally, I believe that wall was more of a safety measure on Miss Gibbs part, if you know what I mean."

"I don't." Ricki knew exactly what the bigoted woman meant but couldn't resist forcing her to articulate it.

Mrs. Rancourt took another sip of coffee. "Let's just say, they're neighbors of a different stripe. First on the block. If you don't count the house sitter in the house across the street from Miss Gibbs, who's been there so long he's practically moved in. I have my suspicions about him, believe you me."

"I'm sure they have nothing to do with his 'stripe.'" Ricki affected a bland expression and took a sip of her coffee. Mordant choked on his. She put her coffee cup back on the tray and Mordant did likewise. "Thank you so much for seeing us."

"You're welcome. If you discover anything about who ended Miss Gibbs' life, please let me know. For future reference, I prefer visits around the cocktail hour."

Mrs. Rancourt extended her hand. For a brief moment, Ricki wasn't sure whether to shake it or kiss it. She opted for the former and Mordant did likewise. They rose to their feet. Mrs. Rancourt rang a tiny bell Ricki hadn't noticed sitting on the coffee table and Tanice appeared to escort them from the house.

"Wow," Ricki said as they hurried to her car. "Just . . . wow."

"That was by far the creepiest twenty minutes I've ever spent. And in this city, that's saying something."

"Aside from the blatant and unapologetic racism, did you hear how she kept calling Phyllis 'Miss' Gibbs? No Ms. for Mrs. Rancourt. She rang a bell to summon the help! I've only seen that in movies. *Old* movies."

"And I'm guessing the coffee in her cup was one part coffee to three parts bourbon."

They got into the car. "We did learn something," Ricki said. "Phyllis and the Sachs didn't get along. If she pushed them too far, it wouldn't be the first neighborhood squabble that turned deadly. We need to find out what the problem between them was."

"I have some thoughts about that."

Ricki started the car engine and pulled out of the parking spot, eager to drive away from the toxic block. She glanced at Phyllis's house as they went by it. "I think realtor Madison should add a warning label to the For Sale sign: Living on Peony Place could be hazardous to your health."

THIRTEEN

Since she was running late, Ricki texted Olivia, who'd finished her finals at long last, to open Miss Vee's. On the drive to Bon Vee, Mordant and Ricki made a plan to return to Peony Place later that evening under the guise of being potential homebuyers checking to see what the neighborhood was like at night. "I'll also remind Nina to look into the dispute between Phyllis and the Sachs," Ricki sad.

Mordant had tours scheduled for the rest of the day, so Ricki dropped him off at his hearse. She stopped in the Bon Vee staff lounge to get a cup of coffee and a protein bar for breakfast. Once at the shop, she was glad to see Olivia replacing a string of burned-out lights with help from Lizette. "Hey," Olivia greeted Ricki. "Did you get the e-vite from Grandmama for my party?"

"E-vite?" Ricki asked, confused. "From Eugenia?"

"I know, right?" Olivia grinned. "Gran's going hi-tech. She says she has to because the party's happening so soon. She's throwing it together in about a week. I don't know what the rush is."

Ricki did, but rather than get into a conversation about it, responded with a vague, "I'm sure it's because she's excited and can't wait to celebrate you." She took out her phone and scrolled through a barrage of emails, mostly recipe submissions. "Ah, there it is." She opened the e-vite and clicked "I will attend," then settled in behind the shop desk. "So, Lizette, I just had an interesting chat with your grandmother."

Lizette chortled. "'Interesting.' Nice word choice. Super polite. Did you see Gram's fake queen flag?"

"I saw a flag I didn't recognize."

Olivia tested the new light strand to confirm it worked. "What do you mean, fake?"

"Rex queens are the only ones who get their own flags to

fly during carnival season. This really ticked off Gram, so she had a flag made up to show she'd been queen of Gaia like, a hundred years ago."

"I'm surprised your gram didn't die of a broken heart when I became queen instead of you this year," Olivia teased.

Lizette sighed. "I wish."

The girls helped Ricki manage a bus full of tourists from Paris, rattling off gift recommendations in French, a language Ricki didn't speak. Due to the state's Gallic roots, Ricki had found a few cookbooks written in French at local estate sales and her customers left happy, but not happier than Ricki, who recorded the best sales of the month.

Grateful to the girls, Ricki sent them off to have lunch on her. Alone for the first time that day, she texted Nina to call her, then used the lull in customers to go through recipes for the Bon Vee community cookbook. She rejected a half-dozen that had vague or indecipherable directions, or completely out-of-date ingredients. *I don't think there's a big market for finnan haddie recipes these days*, she thought to herself after looking up the mysterious ingredient on the internet and learning it was cold smoked haddock.

Her phone pinged a text, but not from Nina. In the dining room, Cookie wrote to Ricki and Zellah. Now!

Ricki left the shop, locking the door behind her, and walked up the hallway, making a left into the dining room. Zellah was already there. She and Cookie were staring at a messy, melted slice of ice-cream cake. "Is that the awesome take on Mile High Pie someone submitted?" Ricki asked, shocked by the sight. All three women had loved the coffee and chocolate version of the Pontchartrain Hotel's legendary tower of an ice-cream pie topped with a tall layer of baked meringue. "What happened? Where's the meringue?"

"Looks like someone scraped it off," Zellah said.

Cookie, who'd been appointed Bon Vee cookbook photographer, gestured at the slice with her camera. "I set it up for my shoot, but didn't like the plate it was on, so I ran to the kitchen to get another one and when I came back, the meringue was gone."

"Great." Ricki's good mood deflated. "The carolers are leading the tours today. When they come by, I'll find out if they saw anything." She let out a frustrated *argh!* "The cookbook was supposed to be a positive for Bon Vee, not a negative. If people are going to undercut each other and rat each other out and even resort to sabotage, we may have to cancel the whole thing. Cookie, what are you doing?"

"Anger eating," Cookie said, spoon and plate of pie in hand. "And this delicious blend of coffee, chocolate, and hazelnut ice cream is making me feel much better."

Zellah picked up a spoon from the table. "Share, please."

Ricki left her friends taking turns treating themselves to remnants of the failed photo shoot. She emailed a white lie to the woman who'd dropped off the recipe and pie that the dessert was such a hit it had been devoured before its photo could be taken, and would she mind making another? The contributor was a housekeeper from a nearby Garden District mansion and Ricki wanted to make sure she got the recognition she deserved in the cookbook. To Ricki's relief the housekeeper wrote back that she was flattered and would deliver another pie tomorrow.

Caroling from the hallway indicated the approach of a tour group. Ricki grimaced as caroling soprano Ruth hit a high note. She plastered on a smile for shoppers. "Hi, happy holidays," she greeted the group. "I'm Ricki and this is Miss Vee's Vintage Cookbook and Kitchenware Shop. Take a look around. If you have any questions, I'm here to answer them."

The dozen or so guests browsed the displays, picking up items to show each other. "Does this toaster still work?" a man who looked to be in his early sixties asked, holding up a circa-1920s silver two-sided toaster with embossed cut-outs.

"Yes. It's been rewired too, which is better for today's electrical currents. The toasting arms swing out so you can turn the bread and toast both sides." Ricki demonstrated.

"My grandparents had one like this but without the swinging arms. Honey, what do you think?" He held it up to his wife.

"It's lovely," his wife replied. "Our kitchen is retro, so it will fit in beautifully."

"A yes from the missus means we'll take it," her husband said.

"Great. I'll write it up."

The man wandered away to continue browsing. His wife replaced him at the desk. "Do you happen to have any wet wipes?"

She asked this in a whisper, which Ricki found curious. "Sure."

She pulled a container of wipes out and handed it to the woman, who took one and wiped her hands. "My fingers are a little sticky. Must be the humidity."

Coming from Los Angeles, Ricki still had a lot to learn about humidity. But she'd never heard anyone mention it caused sticky fingers. She noticed a tiny white blob on the corner of the woman's mouth. "You know, I have a cookbook I think you'd love."

Ricki went to the shelf housing more recent "pre-owned" cookbooks. The one she pulled out had been released in 2012. She handed it to her customer. The title simply read, "Meringue."

The woman turned beet red. "I love meringue. I can't resist it."

"I understand." Ricki gave her a conspiratorial wink.

The woman paged through the cookbook. "This is gorgeous. I'll take it too."

Ricki rang up the total. She bagged the toaster and cookbook. After the room emptied of customers, she texted Zellah and Cookie: I found our Mile High culprit. Tour guest so not a problem. All good.

Her cell rang. Finally, a return call from Nina. Ricki moved away from her customers to take the call. She spoke in a low voice. "Thanks for getting back to me. I know you're busy, so I'll keep this quick. Mordant and I found out there was a dispute between Phyllis Gibbs and her neighbors, the Sachs. The ones who built the wall. We don't know the details but I'm sure you guys can drill down on that."

"Right, thanks."

Ricki heard the exhaustion in Nina's voice. She couldn't

remember ever hearing the detective sound so tired. "Are you OK? You don't sound it."

"Tired. We have a new criminal in town. Some cities have burglars who dress up as Santa around this time of year. But that's too normal for New Orleans. Nope, we have a yutz who's dressing up as the city's very own holiday character, Mr. Bongle."

"You mean Mr. Bingle," Ricki said. She had a vague recollection of the iconic character, a snowman with a red bow tie and an ice-cream cone hat created as a mascot for the Maison Blanche department store in the 1940s.

"Nope, not Mr. Bingle. I said it right. Around twenty years ago, someone thought they'd cash in with a knockoff of the original Mr. Bingle and call it Mr. Bongle."

"Ah. We'd moved to L.A. by then. That's why I never heard of him."

"The brain trust trying to rip off Mr. Bingle created a design and had it manufactured somewhere in Asia. But when it got to the states, it was so cheaply made, it was laughable. The snowman was gray instead of white, the smile was crooked, his tie wouldn't stay tied, and his red fedora tipped to the side. Basically, he looked like a drunk who fell into a dirty snow bank. But New Orleans being its sweet, quirky self, Mr. Bongle became as beloved in town as Mr. Bingle."

"That really is so NOLA," Ricki said, feeling a surge of warmth for the city of her heart.

"What's also very Big Easy is that there's now a guy dressed as a low-rent snowman breaking into homes and businesses. The news is calling him the Bongle Bandit. They worked real hard for that one."

Ricki gazed at the images of Mr. Bongle plushies she'd called up on her screen. "The toy is kind of creepy looking."

"Imagine him life-size. He's more Halloween than Christmas. City officials are putting the pressure on us to bust the Bongle Bandit because a holiday icon turned criminal is bad for the city's reputation. Anyhoo, I'll share what you learned about the Sachs with Sam. Hopefully he'll take a break from counting down to retirement to look into it. Meanwhile, I'm off to defend the honor of America's weirdest Christmas character."

Nina ended the call. Ricki closed the screen. She didn't need Mr. Bongle taunting her with the fact his criminal doppelganger had dropped Phyllis Gibbs' murder down the list of NOPD priorities.

But clearing her parents' names was Ricki's top priority and would stay that way until she proved them innocent . . . with or without Nina, Sam, and NOPD's help.

FOURTEEN

Twilight transitioned into night as Ricki and Mordant parked on Peony Place that evening. Clad in their costumes of young homebuyer togs, they got out of the car and sauntered down the street hand in hand. "We're spending a lot of time together," Mordant said. "I hope Zellah doesn't start to think something's really going on between us."

"I wouldn't worry about it," Ricki said, knowing her artist friend would burst out laughing at the thought of Ricki putting the moves on her boyfriend. The women were devout believers in the friend code of honor that prohibited such deceitful behavior. "But I'm beginning to think this wasn't a great plan. No one's out now and we can't ring a doorbell to ask questions like we want to know if the block is safe at night. People would call the police on *us*."

They continued strolling down Peony Place. Suddenly, Mordant grabbed Ricki's arm. "Stop."

"What is it?"

"There's a light on in Phyllis's house. If I remember the layout right, it's her living room."

"We can peek in through the side window. The wall between her and the Sachs will help block us." They glanced around to make sure no one was watching, then darted to the side of the house. "I'm too short to see into the window but you can."

"I need to make sure whoever's in there doesn't see me."

"It might be no one. A real estate agent showing the house might have accidentally left the light on."

"True." Mordant took out his tiny pair of binoculars. He raised his head only to his eyeline and peered into the house.

"Do you see anyone?"

"Nope."

Ricki heard a voice coming from the sidewalk. "People! Duck."

The two dropped to the ground on Phyllis's side yard and lay flat. Through a corner of her eye, Ricki saw a matronly looking woman walking a puffball of a Pomeranian pooch. Ricki combat-crawled through the grass to see where the woman was going. She and the dog turned onto the front path of the house on the other side of Phyllis's—the one sans wall. The woman unlocked the front door and she and the dog went inside the house.

Ricki stood up and snuck back to Mordant, who'd resumed peeking into Phyllis's living room. "Now I know how to connect with the Peony Place residents, at least the ones who have dogs. As a dog mom, I know we all generally do our walks around the same time of day and night. I'll come back with Thor. A cute chihuahua is less intimidating than a German shepherd, although Thor is an alpha terror and Princess is a shy sweetie."

"Good idea." Mordant adjusted his binoculars. "From what I can see in the living room, a bunch of Phyllis's boxes got moved to under the window."

Ricki hopped up and down, trying to reach the window. "Argh, I can't see. Curse you, short genes, whoever I got them from."

"Duck!" Mordant dropped to the ground, pulling Ricki down with him. "There *is* someone inside. I saw their shadow."

"Could you tell if it's a man or woman?" Mordant shook his head no. "We'll have to wait and see when they leave."

Mordant had barely finished saying this when the front door opened. A young man exited Phyllis's house carrying a plastic tote bag. He glanced up and down Peony Place, then took quick strides down the front path to the house across the street, a three-story redbrick Georgian.

"That must be the house sitter Mrs. Rancourt mentioned," Ricki whispered. "The one she was suspicious of."

"Judging by his behavior, much as I hate to admit it, her instincts might be right in this case."

"I know." Ricki pulled off a piece of damp grass stuck to her cheek. "Why does he have a key to Phyllis's house? And what's in the bag? The way he looked up and down the street and then hurried across seemed sketchy to me."

"He's coming back outside from his place. With the bag."

The assumed house sitter popped the trunk of a nondescript compact sedan. He put the bag in the trunk, then got into the car.

"We need to follow him."

"I don't know if we'll make it to your car in time."

"If he's like ninety percent of America, he'll spend at least five minutes checking his phone before he starts driving." Ricki rose. "Ugh, I'm never going to get the grass stains out of this top."

She plastered herself against the wall of Phyllis's house. Mordant did likewise. They inched toward the front yard and sneaked to the sidewalk, where they resumed their roles as a house-hunting couple. They casually strolled to Ricki's car and got in. They waited while, as predicted, the house sitter scrolled through whatever he was checking out on his phone. He finally put the phone down, started the car, and drove off . . . unaware Ricki had pulled out right behind him.

Ricki made sure there was at least a car-length between her and the house sitter as they drove down Napoleon Avenue. Many of the streetlights were blocked by branches of the city's massive oak trees, providing a cover of darkness.

The house sitter made a right on Tchoupitoulas, then a left into the parking lot of Rouses Market. Ricki pulled into a spot with a vantage point of the sedan. The sitter got out and headed into Rouses.

"I think this stop might be a nonstarter," Mordant said. "The guy's probably making a grocery run."

"True. But his next stop might be important. Or the one after that. I better call my parents and ask them to walk the dogs tonight."

Fifteen minutes later, the sitter reappeared pushing a grocery cart. He loaded grocery bags into his car before driving off, Ricki and Mordant on his tail. He made a left onto Tchoupitoulas, following it for a mile before pulling into the Winn-Dixie parking lot.

"I'm getting hungry from these grocery store stops," Mordant said.

"I guess he couldn't find everything he needed at Rouses."

The pattern repeated, with the sitter leaving Winn-Dixie about fifteen minutes after arriving, again pushing a cart with grocery bags he loaded into his car.

"I'd say he's going to go to Robert's next but they close at eight," Mordant said as they followed him down Arabella Street.

The sitter made a right onto Annunciation in front of a shotgun house. He got out of the car and retrieved several bags of the groceries from Winn-Dixie, which he left on the home's front doorstep. He stopped to type something on his phone, then got back in his car. He repeated the task for another hour, never knowing Ricki and Mordant were following him. His car finally empty of grocery bags, he drove back to Peony Place. The sleuths watched the house sitter park and re-enter the redbrick house.

"I think it's safe to assume," Mordant said, "that our suspect is a delivery gig worker."

"Agreed." Stiff from the hours spent in the car, Ricki pulled her shoulders back to stretch them. "But that doesn't explain the key to Phyllis's house and why he was so furtive when he left it. And the tote bag he left her house with must still be in his trunk. We need to find out more about him."

"I will. Tomorrow. Right now, I need to hit Popeye's before it closes."

"Me too. My stomach is making sounds like when Thor growls at a dog on the TV."

The two treated themselves to combo dinners from Popeye's, chicken for Mordant, shrimp for Ricki. She then dropped Mordant off at his home, a shotgun cottage painted all black in the Marigny, a funky and artsy section of town on the east side of the Quarter.

She returned home to find Josepha there, having heeded Ricki's request to feed her animal brood and walk the dogs. "I brought you a chicken sandwich and fries from Popeye's as a thank-you for helping out," Ricki told her mother.

Josepha patted her thick stomach. "I shouldn't but I will." She took the bag. "Your kitten's a terror." With her free hand,

Josepha gestured to Red Beans, who was lolling on her cat tree, tail wafting to and fro. "She parked her little self in front of Princess's food dish and no amount of barking could get her to move. I had to pick her up and cart her off."

"She tortures poor Princess. I'll have to find a way to get her to stop. You want a glass of wine?"

"I never say no to a nice glass of Sauvignon Blanc. Or even a not-so-nice one."

Ricki went to the kitchen. She retrieved a bottle of wine and poured two glasses, then returned to the living room. She handed her mother a glass and sat down on the couch next to her. "Where's Dad? I thought you could walk the dogs together."

Josepha glowered. "Back home, fast asleep after a double round of his tai chi routines. He needed it. That director is abusing your dad. He's making him do things that violate union rules, like run errands. Luis is a respected camera operator, not someone you send out to pick up a mango smoothie. He leaves a lot on interviews for other jobs and expects Luis to cover for him. I get that the man needs another job after this shoot is over, but it shouldn't conflict with the job he's doing right now. Of course, your dad won't say a word against him. He says it's his Código de honor. Well, I sure hope this code of honor of his don't work him into an early grave."

Josepha punctuated this with a large bite of her sandwich, followed by a few fries. "Cajun fries go a long way to making a person less grumpy. Now, what about you? How'd your snooping go?"

"I prefer to think of it as investigating rather than snooping, which makes us sound like cartoon or sitcom characters." Ricki filled her mother in on how she and Mordant tailed the house sitter. "We don't know why, but he has a key to Phyllis's house. When he left, his behavior was suspicious. He was carrying a bag and looked up and down the street like this." Ricki acted out the young guy's furtive glances before hurrying to his car and putting the bag in the trunk. "After that, he made grocery runs for people. All of them appeared to be legit. We didn't learn anything else, so Mordant is going to see what he can find out about him." Ricki sipped her wine. "What about you?

Have you heard any gossip about Phyllis at Crescent City Concierge?"

Josepha frowned and shook her head. "I think her co-workers would love to dish about her but not at the office or around the doctors. I'm gonna see about putting together an after-work happy hour to try and loosen them up."

"What's your take on the doctors?"

"Mansieur, the primary, is pompous and arrogant but not sketchy. I can say pretty much the same for all the other doctors." Josepha paused. "Except for the dermatologist, Dr. Vernon."

This got Ricki's attention. She knew her mother had excellent instincts about people. "What about her?"

"I don't exactly know but I get a bad feeling. With all the procedures she's tried on herself, her face is just short of one of those faces in L.A. I can't bear. You know, those faces which are basically masks because the women have had too much work. Dr. Vernon's patients adore her, so she's good at her job. But . . . You know how Red Beans goes like this when Princess tries to come back at her?" Josepha mimed arching her back. "I brought up Phyllis to Dr. Vernon. First, I asked what she wanted me to do differently and she said, 'Everything,' in this angry tone. When I pushed for specifics, I got her version of Red Beans' attitude." The nurse arched her back again and made a hissing sound. "She didn't actually hiss. But she might as well have."

Ricki pondered this. She recalled the skincare products in Phyllis Gibbs' house—products from a line Dr. Vernon refused to sell anymore. Ricki's entire career, first as an editor of a rare book collection and now as a shopkeeper specializing in vintage items, was based on her ability to identify treasure among people's trash. Her gut sent the message the skincare stash was treasure—and the story behind how it ended up with Phyllis might be the clue to her murder.

She ran a hand over her cheeks. "I haven't seen a dermatologist since I got to New Orleans, and the switch from dry air to crazy humidity is doing a number on my skin. I think it's time for me to make an appointment with Dr. Vernon."

"She's booked for months ahead." Josepha said this with a cunning grin. "But luckily, you have an in with someone who can make an adjustment to her schedule."

FIFTEEN

Leaving the next investigative steps in the hands of Josepha and Mordant allowed Ricki to spend the rest of the week replenishing her depleted stock. She bid online for a batch of vintage cookware, picked up cookbooks being set aside for her by library sale volunteers, and finished her shopping spree with a run to thrift stores on both sides of the Mississippi.

Ricki saved her favorite resale shop for last. Good Neighbor Thrift Store was a low-key spot on a nondescript stretch of Tulane Avenue. She'd developed a friendship with store manager Lady Smith-Foucault, who reminded Ricki of a much younger version of her mother Josepha.

Lady greeted Ricki with a shopping cart and a cheery "Hello, baby. How ya doin'?"

"Good." Ricki took the cart and pushed it up the aisle to the kitchenware section with Lady in tow. "My parents are in town. Of course, it's turned out to be complicated." She filled Lady in on the drama of Phyllis's death as she perused the aisle. "The murder's dropped down the list of NOPD priorities thanks to this stupid Mr. Bongle bandit."

Lady responded with a sympathetic nod. "You'd think some richy-rich lady killed on a richy-rich block would be the top story on the news, but someone dressed up as one of New Orleans' own Christmas mascots is gonna get way more airtime. The crook can't be anyone from the city. A New Orleans native would never take a character so beloved here and turn it into a wanted criminal. Shameful."

"I haven't kept up with the story. Do they have any clues about who it might be?"

"One of the reporters last night said they're thinking it might be a woman now, going by height. They can't tell anything by weight because of the snowman belly. I don't know how they can figure height either, with that fedora."

"Don't tell the rest of New Orleans, but Mr. Bongle gives me the creeps," Ricki whispered.

Lady guffawed. "Baby, can I tell you how many nightmares Mr. Bongle gave my son? He was all, 'I want a Mr. Bongle for Christmas!' when he was seven. So I got him one, a big one that was about a foot high, and he was so happy. That night, he wakes up screaming. I run in and he's all, 'Mr. Bongle won't stop staring at me, Mommy! I'm scared!' So, Mr. Bongle went bye-bye."

The women shared a laugh. Ricki stopped the cart in front of an ancient microwave. "This is a find. It must date back to the 1970s. Does it work?"

"Yes, but the better question is, do you want it to work?" Lady looked askance at the old kitchen appliance. "Aside from the questionable electricity, I gotta wonder what kinda rays something this old is giving off."

"True," Ricki had to acknowledge. An idea came to her and her face lit up. She scurried over to the book section and returned with a handful. She placed them inside the microwave and closed it. She then pressed the power button. The microwave dinged and the door popped open. "Ta-da! The world's weirdest bookcase."

Lady applauded. "Brava to the lady who knows her clientele. There's enough kooksters in this city to buy ten of these. If more old microwaves come in, I'll save 'em for you."

Ricki didn't find anything else of interest at the thrift store, so she bought the microwave and made the drive to Bon Vee. Once there, she put the microwave on the dolly she kept in her car and wheeled it through the mansion to her shop.

Olivia, who'd opened for her, sat behind a desk covered with plates, pans, and baking dishes, all laden with a variety of food and baked goods. "Hey. Look at what people have dropped off with their recipes." She held up a cookie bar. "These rum pecan bars are lit. If I eat any more of them I won't fit into my queen gown. What's that gross old thing?"

"A fifty-year-old microwave I'm turning into a bookcase."

"Oh. Cool."

Ricki parked the microwave in a far corner of the shop.

Olivia waved her over. "We're still trying to figure my gown design. Lizette's an artist. She's thinking about going into fashion design and she drew some sketches for me. What do you think?"

Olivia handed Ricki her phone. And Ricki began swiping through designs. They all showed talent—and were wildly inappropriate. "It's hard to pick one," Ricki obfuscated.

"I *love* the black one. Wearing that would make a statement like, I'm here but I'm showing you through my dress that I am *not* here for your dated positions on important issues. Climate change is real!"

"I'm not up on all the krewe politics but I think it's pretty safe to assume they wouldn't be thrilled with you using them to make a political statement. Did you show these to your parents, since they're the ones paying for your ball gown?"

"Just my mom."

"What did she say."

"She just went, '*Agh!*'" Olivia mimed a panic attack. "I was running out the door, so we didn't get to have a conversation about it. But she texted this." Olivia called up a message on her cell: a giant **NO**, followed by a screenful of exclamation marks. "I'm gonna ask Lizette to come up with a couple of alternatives."

"Maybe have Lizette design a dress for your sorority formal and let your mom handle this one. She's more keyed into the boundaries for Krewe of Gaia-ware."

"Yeah. I guess you're right." Olivia pocketed her phone.

Ricki studied her young cousin. "Liv, I love you but I have to be honest—I'm getting mixed signals from you about the whole queen thing."

"I am excited." There was a hesitancy to Olivia's tone that belied this. "But it's . . . It's a lot. Like, I met with my maids for breakfast this morning. I can tell a couple of them are super disappointed they weren't chosen to be queen. Penelope Vogelspack hardly said anything. She spent the whole time on her phone. I know she only went because she had to."

"New Orleans society confounds me," Ricki admitted. "We don't have anything like it in Los Angeles. Maybe when they chose the queen for the Rose Parade for the Rose Bowl? Anyway, if we do have debs and society events, nobody cares about it except the people involved. My guess is that once the carnival season parties start up for all the different krewes, your friends and even your frenemies will be having too much fun to care about who's what anymore. Plus, for every girl who's a maid, there's someone who isn't."

"That's true." Olivia scrunched up her face. "That's sad. I'm sorry for them."

"Then make sure any party you're invited to is inclusive and diverse. In every way. That's a political stand you're entitled to. Start with your grandmother's party."

Olivia brightened. "That's a good idea. Gran'll totally be open to it. I already made her promise the party would celebrate the whole krewe and not just me, so that'll take some of the pressure off too. Thank you so, so much." Olivia threw her arms around Ricki in a tight hug. She let her go and motioned to a platter. "Want a crab-filled deviled egg?"

Ricki eyed them warily. "How fresh are they?"

"Dropped off right before you got here."

Ricki's expression cleared. "Oh. Then yes." She helped herself to two of the eggs. And after polishing them off, went back for a third and made a note that the recipe was a keeper for the Bon Vee community cookbook.

At the end of the day, Ricki decided to stop by the kitchen, ostensibly to say hi to Virgil. But her real mission was to see if he'd made any progress finding a replacement for director Patrick. First, she read a text Lady had sent from the thrift store: Christmas hoarder kicked the bucket. Only been through 3 boxes and already have 10 ornaments for u. Ricki texted back a thumbs up emoji, along with a promise to stop by the next day.

She followed the delicious aroma of chicken, tomatoes, and onions to the kitchen, where Virgil had just pulled a large baking dish filled with simmering deliciousness from the oven. A production assistant put a finger to his lips indicating Ricki be quiet.

Virgil inhaled the scent of his creation and tilted it toward the camera with his signature smoldering smile and a gaze that bordered on seductive. *He makes cooking so sexy*, Ricki thought, entranced. *It's enough to get me into the kitchen. Almost.* The irony of Ricki selling cookbooks when she rarely turned on a burner or oven herself wasn't lost on her. As she often explained—a touch defensively—to amused friends and family, she loved the vintage tomes for their history and imagery, with every cookbook representative of the decade in which it was published, offering a window into the world's culinary past.

"For me, a great Réveillon dinner is a mix of unique recipes and traditional dishes," Virgil intoned. "And you don't get much more traditional in New Orleans than when you serve chicken creole over a bed of white rice. For an elegant main course, this is deceptively simple—an easy recipe from the Big Easy."

"And . . . cut." Patrick, whose eyes had been glued to a small monitor, removed his headphones after issuing the order.

"They were recording?" Ricki whispered to the assistant.

He shook his head. "Camera blocking. You're good to go in now."

Ricki stepped into the kitchen in time to hear Patrick tell her father, "Lock down that camera position. Nice work."

Luis, who'd taken a bite of a large praline, nodded thanks. He saw Ricki and waved the praline to say hi. She approached him. "Hey, sweetheart. You want a praline? Patrick brought a box from a place near him."

"Near my family home in Jefferson, not where I live now," Patrick said. "My family's been getting our pralines from T'Marie's for generations."

"I'd love one, but I'm full," Ricki said, disappointed to learn Patrick was a NOLA native. She'd remembered Lady's declaration that no local would ever besmirch the memory of Mr. Bongle and for a brief, admittedly out-there moment, fantasized exposing Patrick as the Bongle Bandit. *No such luck*, she thought, heeding his recommendation to take a praline anyway for the road. She comforted herself by noting the director appeared to be much less edgy and had even paid her father a compliment. Unable to resist, she nibbled on the praline, which was indeed homemade and wonderful.

Virgil finished confabbing with a few crew members. He held a fork up to Ricki. "Can I lure you my way with an invitation to taste-test?"

Packed as she was from the praline, along with the recipe samples delivered to Miss Vee's, Ricki couldn't resist tasting Virgil's take on chicken creole. He speared a moist forkful of chicken, doused it in sauce, and fed it to Ricki, who swooned. "They need to invent a new word to describe your cooking. Delicious doesn't do it justice. And I hate the word scrumptious. It's so twee. Hmm . . . another bite might help me come up with it." Amused, Virgil fed her another piece of tender, flavorful chicken. "How about . . . amaze-alicious?"

Virgil chuckled. "I'm flattered, chère. But I'll take a pass on amaze-alicious."

One of the myriad of crew members with some form of producer title approached Virgil. "We need to go over tomorrow's shopping list," she said, holding up a tablet.

"Sure. Give me a minute to say goodbye to my girlfriend."

Again, the pleasure she got from being described as such superseded Ricki's insecurities about her relationship with Virgil. "Go ahead," she told him. "I'll see you tomorrow."

"You sure?"

She nodded.

Virgil gave her a gentle kiss on the lips and went off with the producer. Ricki floated out of the kitchen. She would have forgotten about her next task had she not set an alarm. It went off, reminding her that the time Phyllis's neighbor walked her dog was fast approaching.

Which meant so was the time for Ricki to walk Thor on Peony Place.

SIXTEEN

Ricki went home to retrieve Thor. Feeling guilty for leaving Princess on her own with the mischievous Red Beans, she gave the German shepherd comfort food in the guise of a juicy beef bone. On her way out the door, she got a text from her mother confirming she'd scored Ricki an eight thirty a.m. consultation with dermatologist Rachel Vernon.

Ricki parked around the corner from Peony Place to make it look like she'd come from a neighboring block. She put on the reflective vest she wore when walking Thor and Princess at home, as well as the headlamp whose beam proved useful for scouting potholes or sidewalks cracked open by the tree roots of the city's old oaks.

She hesitated before getting out of the car, suddenly nervous. *Am I making a mistake? Maybe I should leave this to the police.* Then she replayed her conversation with Nina. The detective sounded weary, which earned her sympathy from Ricki. Nina had a tough job, made more difficult by chronic budget and staff shortages. But Nina's response to questions about Phyllis's case had been pro forma. The possibility of the murder being relegated to a cold case file loomed, which would doom Josepha and Luis to living with a cloud of suspicion hanging over them.

Her resolve strengthened, Ricki got out of the car. She and little Thor started down Peony Place, for all appearances just a local woman taking her dog for its evening constitutional.

They circled the block a couple of times without any sighting of the woman and doggy living wall-free on one side of Phyllis's house. Ricki was about to start another loop when a white SUV rolled down the street and pulled into the driveway of Phyllis's other neighbor. Ricki debated her next move. This offered an unexpected opportunity to strike up a conversation with the neighbors whose conflicts with Phyllis escalated to wall-building level. *But hopefully not a murder-y level*, Ricki thought, which could put herself and Thor in danger.

A woman dressed in yoga leggings and a hoodie in the same shade of blush pink, her black hair short and natural, got out of the driver's side. Ricki made her decision. "Excuse me," she called from the sidewalk. The woman turned, a wary expression on her face. She clutched her car key in a way that she could use it if she needed to protect herself, a gesture Ricki recognized because she'd taught herself the same thing via an online video.

Ricki attempted to disarm her with a friendly smile and wave. Thor helped by barking and wagging his tail. "I'm so sorry to bother you. My fiancé and I live a couple of blocks away. We're in an apartment and are looking to buy our first house. We toured your neighbor's and liked it but I wanted to find out a little more about the block."

"Ah. Got it." The woman relaxed. "Sure. I'm Melissa. Melissa Sachs. I'd be happy to answer any questions, if I can."

Ricki took this as a sign to walk Thor partway up the drive. A security light came to life, illuminating Melissa. She was a stunning woman in her early thirties, with sculpted cheekbones, full lips, and an aquiline nose. She reminded Ricki of an Ethiopian model from a fashion magazine one of her customers had left behind at Miss Vee's. Her lithe figure sent the message her yoga leggings were put to use in an exercise studio and not just as athleisure wear. Melissa's stomach bulged with a small bump indicating the early months of pregnancy.

Ricki introduced herself. "Thank you so much for taking the time to talk. I'm Ricki. I promise I'll keep it quick."

"Not a problem." Melissa crouched down to pet Thor, who did his best impression of a docile pet, dropping to the ground and rolling over to expose his tummy for a rub. "My husband Dave and I will be thrilled to have any neighbor besides Phyllis. A drug lord would be a trade up."

Ricki didn't have to fake being taken aback by Melissa's vitriol. "She sounds like a horrible person."

"The worst. You see that?" Melissa gestured to the infamous wall. "Phyllis claimed the tree roots between us were on our side of the property and created piping problems that led to mold in her house. She said she had Lyme disease, which weakened her body and made her susceptible to symptoms from mold toxicity, and sued us. We had to take down a bunch of beautiful old trees, put up the wall, and pay for Phyllis's medical treatments. And of course she had to go to some incredibly expensive doctor. My husband David and I are sure the whole thing was a hoax to squeeze money out of us."

Crescent City Concierge Care, Ricki thought to herself, making a mental note to have Josepha check Phyllis's medical records. "I'm so sorry. I heard she died, which is why the house is for sale."

"Murdered," Melissa said with more than a hint of satisfaction. "And power to whoever did it. David and I can finally stop living in fear that she'd find a new way to bleed us dry."

"How come there's no wall between her and the neighbors on the other side of the house?"

"Good question. One we never got an answer to and believe me, we tried. Phyllis didn't seem to have any problem with those neighbors, the Broussards. They got to keep their trees." Melissa sounded resentful. "I'll be honest. The fact they were the only people on the block she got along with made me suspicious. I always wondered what was going on there."

"That's a bit disturbing. Any other neighbors to be worried about?"

Melissa shook her head. "None except that racist old witch Mrs. Rancourt. If she had her way, she'd bring back one of those covenants that forbid people of color from buying homes on the street. Of course, that wouldn't be a problem for you." Melissa walked around the car to the passenger's side. "I can give you my number if you have more questions but I better get the groceries inside." She extracted a tote bag brimming with foodstuffs.

"Do you need help?"

"I'm good, but pretty soon I'll be hiring Tomas to make groceries for me," Melissa said, using what Ricki had learned was New Orleans' specific phrase for grocery shopping. "He house-sits for the people who own the house across the street. They live in Dallas and only come for holidays."

"Did Phyllis use him?"

Too late, Ricki realized the question sounded like something Nina would ask during a police interview. Fortunately, Melissa wasn't about to pass up another chance to badmouth her late neighbor. "Oh yes. 'Used' him is the exact right description. She used him until they had a falling-out. I don't know over what, but after that, I never saw Tomas pull out of the driveway without flipping off Phyllis's house as he headed down the street." Melissa balanced herself with a grocery bag in each hand. "Nice talking to you. I hope you get the house."

"Me too," Ricki said, feeling a smidge guilty about her eager homebuyer act. "When are you due?"

"June. What about you?"

Ricki's cheeks flushed. "Um . . . I'm not pregnant." She made light of the moment. "Food baby."

Melissa released a mortified gasp. "Oh no. I am so, so sorry."

"I've been heavy on snacks and low on exercise lately," Ricki joked while making a mental note to ignore any recipe sample that came through Miss Vee's doorway. "It's OK. Really. But before you go, I'd love your number."

"Right. Of course."

Melissa shared it and Ricki typed it into her phone. After apologizing again, Melissa went into her house.

"We're going to do another lap to see if the Broussards come out," Ricki, now armed with the neighbors' name, said to Thor. "Then tomorrow, you and me and Princess are going to step up our game from walks to jogs. Mama needs to lose her food baby."

As she and Thor walked, Ricki thought about her exchange with Melissa. She'd exhibited a lot of bitterness toward her late neighbor. Ricki had to imagine her husband David either matched or exceeded it. Phyllis's lawsuit cost them. With her gone, they no longer had to "live in fear," as Melissa herself put it. Which in Ricki's mind ranked as motivation for murder.

She finished circling the block and was about to write off the night when the Broussards' front door opened. The matronly woman and Pomeranian Ricki had seen the night before stepped outside. "You're such a good boy, Meringue," the woman cooed at the dog. "Bad Mommy for falling asleep. Blame that silly old *Real Housewives of Baton Rouge*."

The woman, who Ricki assumed was Mrs. Broussard, breezed down her front path humming. She had a shoulder-length cloud of well-tended blonde hair and soft features, and wore perfectly pressed khaki slacks, penny loafers, and a blue pinstriped button-down shirt under a navy cardigan. Ricki guessed her age at early sixties. Mrs. Broussard reminded the shopkeeper of the sorority alum who occasionally booked lunch at Bon Vee and a house tour as a chapter get-together.

Thor barked at Meringue, doing Ricki the favor of initiating contact. "Hi! Is your dog friendly? Mine would love to say hello."

The woman beamed. "Meringue loves other doggies."

Pet parents and pooches met on the sidewalk, where the dogs engaged in the ritual of sniffing each other's tushies. They began to play, forcing Ricki and Mrs. Broussard to twirl in different directions as they untangled their leashes. Ricki used one twirl to introduce herself. "I'm Ricki."

"Brenda. Brenda Broussard. Oops! Meringue, no humping."

"My Thor's a boy too." Ricki gave the pup's leash a gentle pull to spare him Meringue's advances.

"I haven't seen you on the block before," Brenda commented. "Are you new to the neighborhood?"

"I live in one of the duplexes on Penniston," Ricki said, taking a chance that the housing on the cross street included the two-story abodes. "My fiancé and I are interested in buying this house, so I thought I'd walk Thor on the block at night to see what it's like." Ricki gestured to Phyllis's house with an eye on Brenda to gauge her reaction.

"The Gibbs house," Brenda said with a sage nod. "Smart move. You won't get a better deal on this block. They did tell you why, didn't they?"

Good, she wants to gossip! "I heard the owner was murdered," Ricki said sotto voce.

Brenda eagerly bobbed her head up and down. "It's true."

Ricki continued to speak in a low "just between us" voice. "Do you think it was one of the neighbors? I heard she didn't get along with the people on the other side of her and that's why there's a wall between them."

"The Sachs. Phyllis had health issues and their trees exacerbated them. Personally, I think the Sachs overreacted. It didn't have to go as far as it did."

The Broussards' front door opened and a man exited the house, pulling the door shut behind him. He was dressed in the male version of Brenda's outfit to the point where the couple looked like they were twinning. "Sorry for the delay, sweetie. The client was on Pacific time."

"Arthur's a retired financial advisor, but some of his clients just won't let him retire," Brenda said, obviously proud of her husband.

Arthur made his way toward them. Up close, Ricki noticed he either had a good ten years on his wife or appeared like he did. His gaunt face had the vestiges of once being handsome, and his frail build made Ricki wonder if he was suffering from an illness.

"Art, this is Ricki. She and her fiancé are thinking about buying Phyllis's house. I was telling her about the conflict between Phyllis and the Sachs."

"Completely unnecessary," Art said, shaking his head. "We lived next door to Phyllis for, what? About fifteen years? Never had a problem."

"We spoke to Mrs. Rancourt up the street and she mentioned there was animosity on the block."

Brenda made a face. "Ugh. If there was ever a person who could be called an old biddy, it's her. The stories that woman spreads. I won't insult her poor victims by repeating them. After seeing her and Phyllis going after each other about Rancourt's roses, I would've put money on Mrs. Rancourt as the prime suspect in Phyllis's murder."

"She would have had to run Ms. Gibbs over with her wheelchair," Ricki said, framing the reality as a joke.

"The wheelchair is new," Brenda said. "She had a hip replacement recently."

"Believe me, up until that operation, Renate Rancourt was one tough broad," Arthur said. "She could've taken *me* out."

Noting Arthur Broussard's fragile build, Ricki didn't dispute this.

Tired with being used as a decoy, Thor gave an impatient bark and tugged on his lead. "I better get going. It was nice talking to you."

"Same here," Brenda said. Her husband nodded agreement.

Thor pulled Ricki in the direction of where she'd parked. On the way back to the car, she glanced across the street at Renate Rancourt's house, where elaborate outdoor lighting showcased her garden. Ricki tried imagining the old woman manipulating her way into Phyllis's home and somehow slipping her a toxic amount of delphinium. The scenario was far-fetched.

But having been exposed to Renate Rancourt and her general vitriol, Ricki didn't write it off as impossible.

SEVENTEEN

Ricki put in a call to Josepha on the way home to report what she'd learned from Phyllis Gibbs' next-door neighbors. She finished by saying, "See if you can find out anything about whether Phyllis really had Lyme or mold disease."

"I'll bring it up tomorrow night. I talked the ladies I work with into going out for happy hour, so it'll be the perfect time to do a little digging into what they know about her."

When Ricki got home she found Princess in the closet again while Red Beans watched, amused. Every time Princess made a move to leave Red Beans lazily batted a paw at her and the shepherd retreated. "Devil kitten, that's enough," Ricki reprimanded. She scooped the kitten into her arms. "You're growing, and super-fast. I swear you didn't weigh this much two days ago."

Ricki deposited Red Beans on top of the cat tree with a grunt. Thor, exhausted by the evening's machinations, passed out on the couch, so Ricki leashed up Princess for a solo walk, which turned into a run on the return when black clouds delivered on their threat to storm.

In the morning, Ricki decided her pooches needed a break from the mischievous kitten. She reached out to another Kitty Kat for help.

"You sure you don't mind keeping her at your place today?" Ricki asked her landlady, who held the miscreant pet in her arms.

"I'm off today and don't have any rehearsals," Kitty said, stroking the red-gold fur of the Abyssinian cat. Ricki noted with amusement the fur was pretty much the same color as the landlady's died red curls. "I'd love the company."

After Katrina closed down Charity Hospital, Josepha's best friend had transitioned into a position as a traveling hospice nurse. She balanced the emotional demands of her job with membership in the ABBA Dabba Do's, one of New Orleans many quirky parade dance troops.

"Princess and I owe you."

"Really, it's a pleasure. And I think what you're doing to support your parents is beyond words. I wish I could be more help to y'all."

"You're being a huge help, Kitty. You're letting Mom and Dad stay in one of your places for free."

Kitty frowned. "I feel bad I didn't know Phyllis still walked among us. I read her 'obituary' and never thought it was anything but right." Her face darkened with anger. "If I'd known she was still around and what she put your mama through, I might've taken her out myself."

"Well, that wouldn't have helped at all."

The anger disappeared, replaced by a helpless expression. "I feel so useless."

"Don't even think that," Ricki said, determined to relieve the kind woman's distress. "We're gonna find a way to put you to work, Kitty, I promise."

Ricki gave Red Beans a pet, then departed for Crescent City Concierge and her dermatology appointment. The minute she entered the practice, the head office manager pulled her aside. "Your mother is a godsend," she raved. "I can't thank you enough for gifting us with her."

"I'm so glad it worked out." *If you only knew why she's really here.*

Delia dropped her voice. "We're trying to talk her into sticking around longer. Maybe never going back to Puerto Vallarta."

Delia winked and walked away, leaving Ricki conflicted and nervous. Could her plan be working out *too* well? If Josepha's co-workers discovered she was sneaking around behind their backs looking for clues to who murdered Phyllis, their anger might be exacerbated by a sense of betrayal.

Dr. Mansieur came into the waiting area from the procedure room hallway, a patient in tow. The man was tall and stocky, with a florid complexion. "Make an appointment for Mr.

Vogelspack with the new knee guy at the ortho practice," Dr. Mansieur told Eloise. "Make sure he knows Owen is my patient, so he gets priority on all appointments." Dr. Mansieur clapped Vogelspack on the shoulder. "We're gonna get you back on the pickleball court ASAP, buddy."

The men shook hands while Ricki weighed why the name "Vogelspack" sounded familiar. After a minute, it came to her. "Vogelspack" was the last name of Penelope, the malcontent maid in Olivia's court. *I wonder if he's her father,* Ricki thought. She texted the question to Olivia, who sent back confirmation a few seconds later, along with a string of emojis, including a couple of dollar signs and eyerolls, followed by the green-faced sick emoji. Olivia obviously wasn't a fan of her court maid's father.

Curious, Ricki leaned forward, hoping to pick up some of the man's conversation with Eloise. "I don't have time to figure out what day works best for me," he declared to her. "I'll have my girl call you."

Ricki bristled at the contemptuous use of "my girl." *If he is Penelope's father, I feel for her,* Ricki thought with newfound sympathy for Olivia's peer.

The businessman strode out of the facility. A nurse appeared in the hallway and called Ricki's name. Ricki followed the nurse to a procedure room designed to the nth degree. If not for the medical equipment, the space could have subbed for a luxe she-shed. Guidry Vane's New Orleans toile provided the room's wallpaper. A small club chair upholstered in leather oxblood echoed the wallpaper's color.

The nurse took Ricki's vitals, then directed her to sit in the dermatology examination chair. "Dr. Vernon will be with you shortly," she said as she exited.

"Shortly" wasn't hyperbole at the practice. No sooner had the nurse closed the door than the dermatologist opened it. "Hello, I'm Dr. Vernon."

She announced this with a smile that bordered on desultory. *Or maybe she's just being professional,* Ricki thought.

"Thank you for filling out the paperwork online," the doctor said. "It's a big help."

While Dr. Vernon perused Ricki's forms, Ricki studied the doctor. She was an attractive woman in her mid-forties with a medium-brown bob that hung below her shoulders. She was slim to the point of being boney. Between that and the worry lines her own procedures couldn't make disappear, Ricki sensed the doctor was under a lot of stress. Was it from her demanding job or did other factors play into it, Ricki wondered. Like whatever went on between her and Phyllis.

"So, I see here your main concern is how the change in climate from Los Angeles to New Orleans is affecting your skin."

"Yes. But I'm also interested in anti-aging procedures. I know I'm on the young side—"

"There's no such thing as too young for preventive skincare," the doctor said in a tone that defied anyone arguing with her. "Let's take a look."

Vernon placed the tablet on the counter and turned on a light bright enough for an interrogation room. She aimed it at Ricki, who squinted under its harsh gaze. The doctor took a tool from her physician's jacket pocket that appeared to be a combination light and magnifying glass. She slowly moved it over Ricki's face.

"My mother has been helping out while your office staff is down an employee," Ricki said by way of introducing Phyllis into the conversation. "I hope that doesn't conflict with me being a patient."

"Not at all." The dermatologist moved her apparatus from one of Ricki's cheeks to the other. "From what I hear, your mother is doing a wonderful job."

"She's gotten an earful about the woman she replaced. Was she a problem?"

"I'm sorry, I can't talk about my patients."

"She was a patient?" Ricki asked, genuinely flummoxed. "Wasn't she on staff?"

"Employees at Crescent City have the option of also being patients. Has the area around your chin always been prone to breakouts?"

"Not since middle school when I hit puberty."

"Then it's the one-eighty of moving from a very dry to a very wet climate."

The doctor continued to assess Ricki's skin. "About the anti-aging thing," Ricki said, taking another tack on the subject of Phyllis. "The day I toured Crescent City Concierge, there was a patient begging for one of your creams. Futura something?"

"We no longer carry that line."

"The office manager told her so." Ricki thought of the products at Phyllis's home and forged ahead. "The patient said she'd get the cream from Phyllis."

The doctor's hand tensed and her small magnifying light slipped. "I have no idea what you heard or thought you heard. We stopped carrying the line months ago." Dr. Vernon straightened up. "You have excellent skin. I'm going to have my nurse apply a mask that will draw out the impurities causing your current blemishes. After that, I only have to see you on an as-needed basis."

Ricki was sure the doctor stopped herself before "or never" slipped out. "Thank you," she responded as blandly as possible.

The doctor and her chilly attitude left, to be replaced by the nurse seconds later. She lowered the chair and instructed Ricki to lie back and close her eyes. Ricki did. She started as the nurse began applying a goopy mask all over her face. "That's cold," Ricki said, shivering. "And it stings."

"Which means it's working. You're a lucky patient. This is one of Dr. Vernon's proprietary masks and she told me not to charge you for it. Hmm, that's interesting."

Not liking the sound of this, Ricki cracked an eye open. "What is?"

"Her instructions say to leave it on for an extra five minutes. Let me double-check this." The nurse tapped a message on her tablet. After a brief wait, she read the reply. "It's to counteract your skin's reaction to our humid weather. That's a new one. The doctor must be adjusting her approach to the problem. Anyway, rest and relax. I'll be back in fifteen minutes to remove the mask."

True to her word, the nurse returned fifteen minutes later

to find a mortified Ricki had dozed off. The nurse removed the mask and applied moisturizer. "Here." She held a mirror up to Ricki, who had to admit her skin looked better than it did after the one visit she paid to a "to the stars" celebrity dermatologist in Beverly Hills.

"Those are some fast results," Ricki said, admiring herself.

"If you think it looks good now, wait a couple of days. There will be a little peeling, which is natural. But after that, you'll have the skin you were born with."

Maybe Dr. Vernon's problem isn't something sketchy, Ricki thought to herself. *She just doesn't have a great bedside manner.*

But even as she admired her reflection, Ricki couldn't help feeling this was wishful thinking.

EIGHTEEN

Ricki and her glowing complexion made a pit stop at Good Neighbor to pick up the ornaments Lady had on hold for her. She strolled up to the door—or what used to be the door—and came to a dead stop.

The door was gone, replaced by now-all-too-familiar yellow crime scene tape. She saw Lady conferring with a handful of patrol officers standing by their police cars. Ricki hurried to her friend. "What happened?"

"The Bongle Bandit," Lady said, making a sour expression.

"What?!" Ricki reacted, appalled. "Who robs a thrift store?"

"Apparently, New Orleans' very own Christmas mascot." Lady folded her arms across her chest and glared at the empty space where the door had been. "We're an old-fashioned cash business. A lot of our customers are poor and don't have good credit. Luckily, Bongle didn't get our safe. But he did get money left in the register by a trainee more interested in making social media videos than doing her dang job." Lady directed this at a young woman wearing a Good Neighbor apron, who finished shooting a photo of the battered door frame and shrugged a halfhearted apology.

"This is outrageous," Ricki fumed, furious on her friend's behalf, as well as the customers who relied on Good Neighbor for everything from clothing to household goods. "What can I do to help?"

"Grab the ornaments I put aside for you before Mr. Bongle comes back."

Lady gestured for Ricki to follow her. They gingerly stepped over the door's broken glass into the store. Except for the open cash register, it appeared untouched. Lady led Ricki into the back room, which served as a de facto employee lounge and storage facility, its walls lined with shelves holding merchandise destined for the sales floor. An ancient iron safe remained bolted to the floor in a corner of the room. "This Bongle clown must've taken one look at it and thought, *This ain't happenin'*, so he hit the register," Lady said.

"Is Good Neighbor going to be OK?" Ricki asked, concerned. "I can head up a fundraiser to make up the cash you lost."

Lady shook her head. "There was barely a hundred dollars in the register. Replacing the door would cost more but the landlord's gonna do it for free in the spirit of the holiday season. Also, because it's his mama's favorite store."

"I'm glad. But if you need *anything* . . ."

Lady gave Ricki a warm smile. "I know who to call. Thank you, friend. Now, let's get those ornaments."

She pulled a banker's box off a shelf and handed it to Ricki, followed by a second box. Ricki plopped down on the floor and carefully removed the paper towel wrapped around an ornament by its previous owner. She held up a hand-painted German glass eggplant. "I love this! Some of the paint's worn off, which shows it's vintage."

"Half that box is veggie or fruit ornaments. They're breakable, so I packed the heavier ornaments separate from 'em."

Ricki lifted the second box. "I can see. This is heavier." She rose to her feet and placed the boxes on the dolly Lady pushed her way. "I have cash." She reached into the wallet housed in her fanny pack and handed Lady two hundred-dollar bills.

Lady held up her hands. "No, no. Way too much."

Ricki pushed the money into Lady's hand. "Take it. I'm sure I'll make it back. And I don't care if I don't. Think of it as a being 'in the spirit' of the holiday season."

"Can't say no to that," Lady responded, her voice husky. "Thank you. By the way, your skin looks more pretty than ever."

"Thanks. I have a new dermatologist." *Who I hope turns out to be a keeper.*

They wheeled the dolly out of the back room. On their way out, they passed the section of the store displaying beauty products, prompting a question from Ricki. "Has anyone ever donated products from a skincare line called Futura?"

"Doesn't ring a bell. We only take healthcare and beauty

products from companies or stores, never individuals. Too risky. Even when companies donate, I think twice about it. We once got a box of makeup from China. The stuff looked nice, but you never know what another country is putting into their products, so I passed on it. But after that, I found out that a lot of makeup sold in America is made in China and other countries, so I kinda regret passing."

Ricki placed the boxes in her car. She made Lady promise to call if Ricki could help her or Good Neighbor in any way, then she drove to Bon Vee, arriving minutes before her regular opening time of ten a.m. She carried the boxes of ornaments into Miss Vee's and spent the next hour entertaining herself by adding her new purchases to the shop Christmas tree.

Cookie stopped by around lunchtime to show Ricki the cookbook layout she'd come up with, but not before showering Ricki with compliments on her complexion. "I had a procedure with the dermatologist at Crescent City Concierge," Ricki explained. "I was there to see if I could find out anything about the doctor's relationship with Phyllis."

"How much does this dermatologist of yours charge?"

"She's not 'my' dermatologist, she's a suspect, and a lot."

Ricki named a figure that made Cookie swallow the gum she'd been cracking. "That's a car payment. Of a Beamer. It'll have to go on my list of wishes if I ever meet a genie. Moving on to the layout." She opened the file on the shop computer. "Do you like how I put a little cookbook icon over the paragraph explaining where each recipe came from?"

Ricki studied it over her friend's shoulder. "Yes. It looks wonderful. And I love how you used a signature font for the name of the person donating the recipe. I'm almost afraid to say this but I'm starting to get excited about the cookbook."

"Wait until you see Zellah's illustrations." Bon Vee's resident artist had utilized her talents to create themed artwork introducing each section of the cookbook.

"Did I hear my name?" Zellah grinned at them from the shop doorway. She held a cup of coffee in each hand. "A supplier dropped off samples of a new syrup flavor. Hazelnut rum. I need taste testers."

She came in and distributed the cups. Ricki and Cookie took sips. They shook their heads. "That's a hella no from me," Cookie said. Ricki nodded agreement.

"Yeah, I had the same reaction," Zellah said. "Thanks for confirming it." She squinted at Ricki. "You've got something on your chin."

"I do?" Ricki pulled a circa 1940s butter knife from a display of flatware on the desk and checked her reflection. She noticed a white flake on the edge of her chin. "Huh. I guess all of the mask didn't come off." She rubbed the spot and the flake disappeared.

A tour group passed by the shop. Ricki saw the guide was a museum volunteer who usually assisted Eugenia with administrative duties. "I thought it was quiet this morning. Why is Jerry leading tours? Where are the carolers?"

"I guess y'all didn't hear this morning's drama," Zellah said. She leaned across the desk and dropped her voice. "Someone dropped off a casserole dish of grits and grillades along with their recipe. That's too heavy a breakfast for me, so I left it in the staff lounge with a note it was up for grabs. The carolers helped themselves to it. But between the time I left it and they had at it, someone doctored the dish. They must've added laxative herbs because all four carolers became 'indisposed.'"

"*Nooo.*" Ricki groaned. "More sabotage? Great. I take back being excited about the cookbook."

"I think your morning just got worse."

Cookie cocked her head toward the shop entrance. Ricki's stomach churned like she'd ingested doctored grits and grillades when she saw Detectives Nina and Sam standing outside the shop doorway.

"Hey there." Ricki's voice cracked as she tried feigning nonchalance at the sight. She gave up. "Please tell me you're here to do a little holiday shopping. I just got in some adorable vintage Christmas ornaments."

"Afraid not," Sam said. The detectives stepped into the shop. "Although that eggplant ornament is cute. My teens would get a kick out of it. According to them, the eggplant emoji has a sexual connotation." He chuckled.

"Save it for the precinct break room, Sam," Nina said to her partner. She addressed Ricki. "We're not here to talk to you or your parents."

Ricki relaxed. "That's good news."

"We're here to talk to Virgil Morel."

Ricki registered Nina's deadline serious tone. *And that's not.* Her stomach resumed churning.

NINETEEN

Ricki and her friends waited until the detectives were gone to hash out what they wanted with Virgil. "It can't have anything to do with Phyllis's murder," Ricki said. "He'd never heard of her until I brought her up."

Cookie gasped. "Do you think he's Mr. Bongle?"

Zellah and Ricki gaped at her. "*No*," Ricki said, affronted. "My boyfriend is not the city's most notorious current criminal. He doesn't need the money. And he doesn't have the time."

"Who knows?" Zellah said. "Maybe Virgil is hiding the truth and he's secretly broke from gambling or something and is knocking off stores when he's not cooking."

"Zellah, how dare you—" Ricki began, furious. Then she saw the grin on her friend's face. "Oh. You're joking."

"Uh, *yeah*. It's the dumbest idea I ever heard."

"You have to admit, it'd make a great story," Cookie said. "The city's famous chef secretly masquerading as the city's most famous robber." Zellah shot the petite blonde a look. "Well, it would," Cookie said without a hint of apology.

"I'm texting Virgil to tell me as soon as he's free," Ricki said, thumbing the message as she spoke. "It's probably nothing. Right?" Her friends didn't respond. Ricki sighed. "Yeah, I don't believe that either."

She endured a tortuous hour-plus waiting for Virgil to get back to her. Unable to concentrate, she forgot to charge one customer for the ornament they added to their cookbook purchase, and almost overcharged another.

"I know this is a rare cookbook," the visitor said, holding up a 1955 collection of Pillsbury Bake-off contest winner recipes. "But a thousand dollars is a little steep."

"I'm so sorry." Mortified, Ricki corrected her mistake. "It's ten dollars. I accidentally added two zeroes." She added a potholder with the shop logo to the visitor's shopping bag, "An apology gift from me."

Finally, blessedly, Virgil returned her text: **U free tonight?**

Ricki texted back **YES**, followed by a row of exclamation marks.

Meet at 6. BB.

Ricki texted back a thumbs up. She hesitated, then added a heart. She checked the time on her phone. The wait to meet up with Virgil at the Bayou Backyard would make her antsy, but at least she'd know why the detectives were on a mission to meet with him.

At the end of the day, she locked up the shop and said goodbye to tour guide Jerry who'd filled in for the carolers. "Thanks for all the upselling with your groups. Sales were great today."

"You have great merch," the senior said. "I barely had to do anything. Hope you didn't miss the carols. My family says I sound like a dying moose when I sing."

"Jerry, the silence today was truly golden."

Ricki made the short drive to the Bayou Backyard. Before exiting the car, she checked her reflection in the rearview mirror. A small flake of skin floated off when she touched her cheek, which she attributed to the residual effects of the mask.

She walked past a group of fraternity brothers playing cornhole at one of the bar's outdoor game sites. A cute blond with hipster stubble flashed a flirtatious smile. "Hey," he said, beckoning to her. "Wanna play with us?" The innuendo in his voice wasn't subtle.

"Thanks but I'm meeting someone." Ricki, flattered, returned his smile. The BB was religious about checking IDs, as opposed to a lot of bars in the Big Easy, so the frat boy was only six or seven years her junior. *No cougar to your cub today, young friend*, Ricki thought as she continued to the indoor portion of the bar. *But if things go south with Virgil, it's nice to know I have options.*

She walked past the picnic tables providing seating indoors and outside for the hangout, and saw her boyfriend chef nursing a club soda at the long tiki-style bar that ran the length of the

BB's back wall. Ky Nyugen, Virgil's business partner, waved to her from the opposite end of the bar and she went to give him a hug. "Guidry told me you stopped by Nutmeg," he said. "On the hunt for a Christmas gift for the Impossible One." He indicated Virgil with his thumb. "If you crack that code, let us know so we can copy you."

"I will," Ricki said, amused. "But at this point I think I'd have better luck finding Amelia Earhart's plane."

She followed the length of the bar to Virgil, who was so lost in thought he didn't notice her. She was touched to see he'd gone ahead and ordered her usual, a glass of Chardonnay.

Ricki laid a gentle hand on his shoulder and he started. He looked up and his haggard face brightened. "Hey, you."

"Hey." Ricki took the seat next to him. "Thanks for ordering my drink."

"I'd be some bad boyfriend if I didn't. I also ordered us each a crawfish boudin."

"Yum." Remembering Melissa Sachs' food belly faux pas, she added, "I'll skip the bun on mine." She eyed Virgil with concern. "You look wiped out."

"I am. Luckily, we're off tomorrow. The caterers for Eugenia's Olivia party need the kitchen. I get to sleep in. If I can."

"What's going on?" Ricki asked. His morose tone scared her.

Virgil took a swallow of bourbon. "Guess who's been added to an NOPD suspect list?"

She stared at him. "You? For Phyllis's murder?" He nodded. "What?! Why? You had never heard of her until I brought her up."

"They found her will in a pile of mail at her house. The estate attorney sent it back because she never paid his final fee. But it was signed and witnessed, so it'll hold up in court."

"How does any of this relate to you?"

"After paying off her estate's debts, whatever's left goes to her favorite charity: New Pawlins Kritter Krewe."

"Your mom's nonprofit was her favorite?" Ricki repeated the odd development, bewildered. "I don't understand."

"Neither did I. When I wasn't working on the show today,

I spent my time trying to solve the mystery of why us. I had Amanda, our executive director, go through our records looking for any connection to Phyllis. She finally found one. About fifteen years ago, Phyllis Gibbs adopted a cat from New Pawlins. Helene tracked down Ruben, the volunteer who helped her on the adoption form. Ruben was our favorite kind of volunteer—the kind who follows up with adopters over the years to make sure our pets are doing well and are in a safe, healthy environment. Sometimes people fall on hard times. They're not thinking to let us know so we can help out financially or even by rehoming if it's called for."

"Was that the case with Phyllis?"

Virgil shook his head. "She told Ruben, the volunteer, that her cat passed away. He was very sympathetic and they were on the phone a while, which is why the conversation stuck in his memory. He recommended giving another kitty a home but she was so broken up about the loss she couldn't even think about adopting again."

"Sparkle." Ricki got a lump in her throat remembering the shrine to the cat on Phyllis's living-room mantle. "I guess the cat was the one positive in her life. I feel terrible for her now."

"Don't worry, you won't after I finish my story. So, due to me being board president of New Pawlins and my mom having founded it, being in the will put us in NOPD's eyeline. But here's the catch. A big chunk of the money we'd supposedly get comes from one of those websites where people set up pages to raise money to pay for medical bills or other emergencies. Phyllis had one set up to help offset the cost of treatment for a rare form of Lyme disease she claimed she had. Notice my use of the word 'claimed,' because according to your friend Nina—"

"I'm not sure I'd call Nina a friend. I mean, sometimes, yes, it feels like we are, but other times, like now, it doesn't at all—" Virgil gave Ricki a look. "Sorry. Go on."

"Phyllis's autopsy results show no evidence of her ever having any form of the disease. It was a grift."

"Why am I not surprised? But I have to give her credit for

going with Lyme disease. There's not a person alive who doesn't hate ticks."

"Bottom line, since the money was raised under false pretenses, it all goes back to the donors. Still, there will be other money in her estate, like from the sale of her house. Which means I'm still a suspect in the eyes of NOPD."

Ricki sipped her wine. She drummed her fingers on the bar's tin tabletop. "But you know who else could be? Anyone who donated to Phyllis's fake illness. Especially a big donor. They'd be furious they were scammed. Hopefully NOPD is thinking the same thing, but in case they're not I need to let Mordant know so he can look into it."

Ricki typed a message to Mordant. Ky delivered the couple's boudin. Ricki set aside the roll and regretfully pushed Ky's homemade hardboiled egg and potato salad to the far side of her plate, vowing not to succumb to its deliciousness. She cut her crawfish-and-rice stuffed sausage into bite-size pieces. As she ate, she noticed Virgil hadn't touched his meal. "I'm sure NOPD is just going through the motions, like with my parents," she said, doing her best to allay his fears. "They haven't landed on any real suspects but they have to make it look like they're doing *something*. As soon as the Bongle Bandit hits another store, you can bet NOPD will shelve Phyllis's case again. And when they come back to it, they'll see how way off they were to suspect you."

Virgil toyed with his potato salad. "Maybe. But if it doesn't go away . . . If word gets out I'm under suspicion in a murder case . . . even if the evidence is non-existent, it will tank my show."

TWENTY

Ricki didn't speak for a minute, gutted by the thought of her boyfriend's passion project being derailed by what she could only describe as a drive-by association with a crime. "That can't happen."

"Unfortunately, it could. I'm lucky no one involved with the production has gossiped about your poor dad being in NOPD's crosshairs. I told the crew that if they're looking to be out of a job, have at it. If they want to keep working on the show, lips zipped. Production companies are jittery about anything that could spark bad press, even if it's just rumors."

"Who knows about the New Pawlins connection to Phyllis?"

"NOPD and me—and now you—know about the financial angle. Helene and Ruben only know that a woman who adopted one of our cats was murdered. I told them this was all under the cone of silence. They love my mom and the organization, so I trust them."

"I'm glad. But too many people know too much. I've learned the hard way that's what leads to leakage." Ricki clapped her hands to her face. "Argh, this is crazy-making. Nina and Sam are smart and great at their jobs but I feel like they're all over the place on this case. Probably because they're distracted by the Bongle Bandit and who knows how many other crimes happening in the city."

"I don't know what they expect to find going down the New Pawlins path," Virgil said. "I guess they have to check every box but this one feels like a nonstarter."

"And time-waster." Ricki's phone pinged a text. "It's from my mom. She's doing a happy hour with her co-workers at Crescent Concierge and wants to stop by my place on her way home. Maybe she picked up a clue that'll steer this murder investigation in a more useful direction."

Virgil took one of Ricki's hands and caressed it. "You're a blessing, Miracle James-Diaz. A true blessing."

He lifted her hand to his lips and kissed it. Ricki felt a rush of desire she reluctantly tamped down. "I better go meet Mom."

Virgil squeezed her hand, then released it. "Go."

Ricki drained her wine glass and hopped off the barstool. She kissed Virgil on the cheek. "Love you."

She cursed herself for the slip of the tongue. *What was I thinking? Did I sound too casual? Too serious? Will he feel like he has to say it because I said it? Ricki, stop blurting! Think before you speak, girl!*

She came out of her self-flagellating spiral to see Virgil grinning at her. "Love you too."

Ricki got home to find Thor and Princess curled up together on the couch. She hadn't seen them so relaxed since Red Beans joined the family and vowed to work on socializing the three critters as soon as her beloved humans were crossed off the NOPD suspect list.

She changed into sweats and kicked the temperature up a couple of degrees. While the winter temperature in New Orleans rarely dropped below the forties, the city's perennial dampness made the cold cutting, especially in a historic home like Ricki's where insulation was an afterthought.

Her doorbell rang. "It's your mama," Josepha said from outside in a sing-songy voice.

Ricki opened the door. "You sound like you had a good time," she said with amusement as her mother sauntered in.

"I did. It was me, Delia, Eloise, and a couple of others who man the office. No nurses. There's a hierarchy at Concierge Care, more than other places I worked. We office folk are the bottom rung, then nurses, then the doctors." Josepha made room for herself on the couch between the dogs, each of whom rested a head in her lap. She petted both of them. "I got 'em talking by being all, 'I want to do a good job while I'm here, what do I need to know about everyone to make sure it happens?'"

"Excellent way to get the gossip going," Ricki said, making herself comfortable in the club chair across from her mother.

"Oh, you betcha. Girl, the things I learned! Dr. Banes, the cardiologist, belongs to an S&M club in the Quarter. The pulmonologist and endocrinologist are having an affair. One of the nurses has started transitioning but hasn't announced it even though it's obvious to everyone. Dr. Mansieur is on his third or fourth wife, I can't remember which."

"I met her," Ricki said, recalling the attractive strawberry blonde of undefinable age she'd chatted with in the waiting room.

"According to Delia, who's been there forever, there are rumors about Mrs. Mansieur's background but no one's gotten the story."

"Maybe Phyllis did," Ricki mused. "And used it against her. Or used any of this against one of the doctors. Or all of them. Did your new friends talk about Phyllis?"

Josepha shrugged. "There wasn't much to say. She was reserved, professional, and kept to herself. No one had any idea whether or not she had Lyme disease. She never brought it up. She had cordial relationships with all the doctors except one: the dermatologist, Dr. Vernon."

Ricki raised an eyebrow. Once again, a potential link between Phyllis and the doctor behind the coveted but illusive Futura skincare line surfaced. "Really. How so?"

"Delia said Phyllis went out of her way to avoid Dr. Vernon and when they did have to have contact, the doctor always seemed hostile. Come to think of it, my happy-hour friends didn't say much about Dr. Vernon in general. They seemed . . . almost afraid of her."

Ricki considered this. "I wonder if Phyllis was holding something over the doctor's head in exchange for free expensive skincare products like I saw at her house. Although that doesn't explain why Dr. Vernon doesn't sell her line anymore. The Futura products are beloved by her patients, so discontinuing them makes no sense. Oooh." Ricki sat up straight, excited. "I read a mystery where a hand cream included a product the creator of it doesn't want anyone to know about. Maybe Phyllis uncovered something sketchy about what's in Dr. Vernon's line."

"Sounds a little far-fetched. Like something you'd only find in a book."

"Yeah, you're probably right," Ricki said, deflated. "I need to get into Phyllis's house again. I'm sure there's a clue there I'm missing. I'm texting Mordant to get in touch with the real estate agent." She typed on her phone. Mordant responded with a thumbs up. "Oops. I forgot something." She texted, But not tomorrow. It's Eugenia's party 4 Olivia! Mordant sent back another thumbs up, followed by a disco dancing emoji.

Josepha yawned. "We shared two pitchers of sangria. I'm feeling it now. Good thing I've got tomorrow off to get ready for Eugenia's fancy event." At first, Josepha and Luis had begged off attending the party, not sure if they'd fit in with the crème de la crème of New Orleans society, who'd snatched up invitations the instance Eugenia issued them. But Ricki convinced her parents they should attend the party to see if Josepha could spot anyone from the past who might connect to Phyllis and her murder.

"Let's get you home," Ricki said. "I'm assuming you didn't drive to your happy-hour get-together."

"Took a cab. I can walk home. It's only two blocks."

"I'm driving you. It's late, it's dark, and I'm a little nervous about how murder-y it's been around us lately."

Ricki retrieved her car keys. Josepha rose from the couch and met her at the door. Ricki opened it and Josepha blinked from the bright security light. She squinted at her daughter. "You're shedding."

"Skin flakes? It's from the mask at your office. By tomorrow I'll have the complexion of a newborn."

Ricki patted her cheeks and her mother chuckled.

Ricki overslept the next morning, necessitating a race to get ready for work. Her face wash landed another batch of flakes in Ricki's sink. "I better get baby's-butt-smooth-skin soon," she muttered, impatiently cleaning the sink. Due to the time crunch, she skipped putting on makeup. She threw on jeans and a T-shirt Luis had received as swag from a film shoot, then headed out the door.

Bon Vee was a hive of activity when Ricki arrived, with a pool of workers hustling to set up for Eugenia's much-anticipated soirée. She waved to Hailey, head of the Fairy Fresh Cleaning Company, whose team was busy making the whole estate sparkle from inside to outside. A party tent took over the entire side yard. Fleur du Monde, Eugenia's favorite florist, was loading in stunning holiday-themed floral arrangements of holly, red roses, plumosa ferns, Queen Anne's lace, and white lilies, whose pungent perfume wafted Ricki's way. The scent and sight put her in a festive mood and she found herself looking forward to the party and the break from what felt like a 24/7 of either obsessing about or investigating Phyllis's death.

On her way to the shop, she stepped over lighting cords and dodged rental suppliers delivering everything from chairs to crates of wine glasses. Once inside Miss Vee's, Ricki used a heavy marker to write a sign informing customers the shop would close at four, which would give her a couple of hours to run home, tend to the dogs, and get dressed for the party.

She was in the process of taping the sign to the door when her first customer showed up, an elderly woman Ricki recognized as a neighbor she'd seen walking an equally ancient Yorkshire terrier. "I'm Babette Undine," the woman said in a soft New Orleans accent, her voice quavery with age. "I live over on Prytania. I've wanted to visit your shop for ages."

"I'm thrilled you made it, Mrs. Undine." Ricki helped the woman over the raised threshold. "If you have any questions or need help, just let me know."

"Thank you."

Ricki checked the shop email while the woman browsed. Out of the corner of her eye, she saw Mrs. Undine pull a piece of paper from her purse and let it flutter to the floor. "Oh my goodness, it's my recipe for date nut pudding. However did it get into my purse?"

"Let me get that for you." Having decided to humor the sweet woman, Ricki bent down to pick up the recipe. She glanced at it. "This looks delicious. You know . . . we don't have anything like it submitted for the community cookbook. Is there any chance you'd let us include this?"

Mrs. Undine beamed. "I would be honored. My late husband's mother came up with the recipe. He'd be tickled to see it in a cookbook. He passed away in early November."

"I'm so sorry." A lusty rendition of "The Holly and the Ivy" came from the hallway, announcing the return of the carolers and drowning out Ricki's response. She gritted her teeth and tried again, this time louder. "I'm so sorry!"

The older woman recoiled slightly. "Thank you so much. And I'm happy to say that I've still got my hearing. Although the caroling does provide a challenge."

Mrs. Undine made a cursory purchase of a tea towel. She showered Ricki with more gratitude on her way out the door, passing a customer Ricki hadn't seen enter the shop. "Hi, sorry, I didn't see you come in," Ricki said to the newcomer.

"Not a problem," the woman responded. She was stylishly dressed in beige wool slacks and a delicately patterned sweater under a navy jacket. Ricki picked up the hint of a New York accent. "I saw what you did with the woman's recipe. You were very kind to her."

Ricki shrugged, suddenly feeling awkward. "She's a Bon Vee neighbor. We want to stay on her good side. Can I help you find anything?"

"I'm visiting my mother. She's in the mid stages of dementia and is in a facility on Carrollton. I thought a copy of a cookbook she used to have might trigger a few memories."

"What a great idea. My boyfriend's mother is in a memory care facility. I'm going to recommend he do the same thing. Maybe with one of his own cookbooks. He's a chef."

"Cool. What's his name?"

"Virgil Morel."

The woman smiled, revealing dimples. Her hazel eyes lit up. "I have his first cookbook, *My Creole Table*. I've made Mom dishes from that. My copy is in New York. Do you happen to have one here?"

"Do I ever." Ricki led the customer to a shelf she'd dedicated to copies of Virgil's five cookbooks. She pulled out a copy of *My Creole Table*. "It's even signed." She opened the book to show off Virgil's signature.

"Fantastic. I'll take it."

Ricki walked the customer back to her sales desk. They made small talk while Ricki rang up the purchase, to which the woman added several Christmas ornaments. Ricki placed the book and ornaments into a shop tote bag and handed it to the woman. She responded with a strange expression. "Um, I know booksellers give out bookmarks, but this is a little unusual."

Ricki, baffled, peeked into the bag. She gasped in horror. A large flake of skin lay on top of Virgil's cookbook. "Oh my *God*. A mirror. I need to find a mirror." She twirled around, frantic.

"I've got one."

The customer pulled a compact out of her purse and passed it over. Ricki took one look at herself and released an anguished cry. "*No!* The mask!"

Her complexion didn't resemble a baby's smooth skin. Instead, red and peeling, it looked like the skin of a reptile.

TWENTY-ONE

"Oh no, oh no, oh no, oh no." Ricki, panicked, just kept repeating this. "I have an event tonight! I can't look like a zombie. That's what I look like. Something that crawled out of a New Orleans tomb!"

"It's not that bad." The customer did her best to sound like she meant this.

"I need to talk to my friends." Ricki returned the compact, hand shaking. She picked up her cell from the desktop, took a selfie, and sent it to Zellah and Cookie.

"Can I do anything to help?"

"Thank you. I don't know. I don't know." Ricki wrung her hands.

"I'm not going anywhere until your friends get here. I'm Beth. Beth Norris."

"Hi, Beth. I wish we were meeting under better circumstances."

"Please, don't worry about." Beth gave her a warm smile. "I'm glad I got to meet you and visit your beautiful shop under any circumstances."

The women heard the sound of running coming, the thump of feet muffled by the hallway's antique rug. Cookie and Zellah burst into Miss Vee's. They stopped short at the sight of Ricki.

Cookie stared at her friend, open-mouthed. "What the actual f—"

"It's the mask." Ricki scowled, which shed more skin flakes. "Now that I think about it, Dr. Vernon's nurse was surprised the doctor wanted to leave the mask on an extra five minutes. I bet the doctor did it on purpose to punish me for asking too many questions." Ricki remembered her customer and added for Beth's benefit, "It's a long story."

Zellah drew close to Ricki. With her artist's eye, she carefully examined every inch of Ricki's face. "It looks like they gave you a face peel, the kind where you shed the top layer of your skin and then it's bright red until your skin calms down. Hopefully leaving it on too long won't damage your skin, but it'll probably be red for a while longer."

"How can I go to Olivia's party looking like this?" Tears bubbled over Ricki's lower lids and dripped down her cheeks. "Ow! My skin is burning from the salt in my tears."

"That sounds like a lyric from a country song," Cookie commented.

"*Not helping!*"

Customer Beth weighed in with an idea. "Could you get away with wearing a fascinator? One with netting to cover your face?"

The other women contemplated this. "I like it," Zellah said.

"Won't I stand out too much?" Ricki worried. "I don't want it to backfire and call more attention to me."

"You're in the one city where you can get away with a quirky look," Cookie said. She clapped her hands together, excited. "Ooh, why don't all three of us wear them? I have fake jewels and other stuff I'm going to use for a kids' holiday project. I can get headbands and netting and we can make three fascinators. We'll say we're dressing up for Mardi Gras early. It totally ties in with Olivia's krewe court."

"Well, look at you, makin' a great suggestion," Zellah teased. Cookie stuck her tongue out at her.

"Thank you so much," Ricki said to Beth, immensely grateful to the customer for coming up with a plan that could save the night. "The cookbook is yours. A gift from me." Beth started to protest but Ricki stopped her. "You came here to shop, not do crisis management."

"You've got a lot going on, so I won't waste your time arguing," Ricki's new friend said. "Instead I'll come back when things settle down and do more shopping. In the meantime, here's my card so you have my contact info if you need it." Beth reached into her black leather Coach purse and pulled out a matching wallet. She removed a business card and handed it to Ricki. "I'm working remotely while I care for my mother, so it's got my local address. I wish I were a doctor and could do something to make you heal faster, but unfortunately, I'm an ad exec. The only help I can offer at this point is a free ad campaign."

"I may take you up on that sometime," Ricki said. "Right now, I've got three fascinators to make."

Beth left and the others jumped into action. Ricki cleared a display table and Zellah covered it with the brown deli wrap paper she used for her café po'boys. Cookie placed an order for headbands and tulle netting with one of her craft suppliers, then retrieved glue guns and decorations from her office. The headbands and tulle arrived a half-hour later and the friends got to work creating fascinators festooned with sparkling sequins and faux gems in the Mardi Gras colors of purple, green, and gold.

An unforeseen benefit of the crafting was that it proved a draw for curious museum visitors, who wandered in to watch and stayed to shop. Ricki did her best to hide her face but it wasn't easy. When she saw a shocked reaction on a customer's face, she responded with "Allergic reaction" and a helpless shrug. This unintentionally generated a few pity sales.

Within a couple of hours, three fascinators were completed and claimed by each wearer. Zellah went off to relieve Mordant, who had stepped in to man the café for her, and Cookie returned to work creating a schedule of child-oriented activities for Bon Vee, albeit reluctantly. "It's way more fun to make crafts than to organize them," she said on her slow walk out the store door.

The emergency had thrown a wrench into Ricki's own schedule for the day, cutting out the time she'd planned to return home and get ready for the party. She called Josepha and Luis with an urgent request to stop by her house and tend to Thor and Princess. "Also," she told her mother, "thanks to Dr. Vernon, I have to wear a different dress than the one I picked out for tonight." She filled Josepha in on her skin debacle.

"I don't like this," Josepha responded, distressed. "Dr. Vernon should have gone over all the details of the mask, including possible side effects."

"She didn't and I'm convinced it was intentional. I'm sure she's hiding something and I'd tell you to poke around her more than the other doctors . . ." Ricki caught a glimpse of her reflection in one of the bay window's panes and grimaced. "But my face tells me it's too dangerous. Anyway, pull out any purple, green, or gold dressy dresses in my closet and bring them to Bon Vee. I'll figure out which one doesn't look ridiculous with the fascinator I made. Oh, and my black satin sandals. I need to balance whatever outfit I pull together with generic footwear."

"Of course. Love you, baby girl. And . . . be careful."

Ricki thought about her mother's admonition as she cleaned up the ersatz craft station and returned cookbooks, kitchenware, and gift items to their proper places. This wasn't the first time threats to people she cared about propelled Ricki into risking her own life by sticking her nose into a criminal investigation. She'd learned the hard way that being on the receiving end of a killer's ire was no fun and potentially lethal. Ricki had no desire to repeat the terrifying experiences.

But the entire motivation behind Eugenia's party was to bring a bunch of potential suspects together in one place. The lure of ferreting out a murderer among them was impossible to resist. *If anyone comes for me, I can always rip off my fascinator and scare them away with my face*, she thought, as a large skin flake fell from her forehead and drifted to the floor.

TWENTY-TWO

Josepha and Luis showed up with armfuls of clothing for Ricki to sort through. "Nightgown. Nightgown. Bathrobe." Ricki tossed the rejects onto one of the club chairs in Miss Vee's reading nook.

"These are so pretty," Josepha said, fingering the lace on one of the nightgowns.

"I'm embarrassed to say they're from my wedding shower. I don't know why I've held on to them." She held up a long, sheer lavender number. "This one still has the price tags on it. Considering I only wear T-shirts to bed, I really should rehome them. When I have time, I'll donate to Good Neighbor." She continued going through the pile. "Here we go." She put on the fascinator and held up a dark purple, full-length, slinky dress in front of her.

"It works," Josepha said. Luis nodded agreement. Her expression darkened. "Although I still want to kill Dr. Vernon for doing this to your beautiful face."

"We better avoid the concept of killing anyone, even if it's hyperbole," Ricki said, taking off the fascinator and placing it back on the table. "Hopefully my face will come through this without any permanent damage."

"Text me the exact name of the mask," Josepha said. "I'll check it out when I'm back at the practice tomorrow."

Ricki did so, then draped the dress over her arm. "I'm going to change in the hall bathroom. I'll meet you in the tent. Did you confirm with Kitty Kat?" She'd kept her promise to find a way her landlady could make herself useful by inviting Kitty Kat to the party as Ricki's plus-one. This way, there would be another set of eyes from Charity Hospital on the crowd.

"Yup, she's all set. And boy, was she excited about coming to such a fancy do. I had to talk her out of bringing a plastic bag in her purse so she could pirate leftovers."

"If there are leftovers, they'll probably end up in the staff fridge," Ricki said. "I'll see if I can bring something home to her."

"Before you go, how do your mother and I look? We presentable?"

Luis pirouetted like a model, then put his arm around his wife's waist. He wore a gray suit perfectly tailored to his sturdy build. The gray of the suit complemented his salt and pepper hair, which was stylishly slicked back. Josepha was clad in a black velvet midi dress embellished with black and silver beads at the neckline. Her short dark hair miraculously retained its natural color and she only wore a touch of makeup—enough to add a rosy glow to her cheeks and lips and bring out the rich brown of her eyes.

"You look fantastic," Ricki said, filled with love and pride for her parents.

A string quartet began playing, signaling the start of the cocktail hour, and Josepha and Luis headed off to the party. Ricki scurried to the restroom discreetly lodged off the mansion's capacious front hall. "No point in putting on makeup," she muttered to the mirror reflecting her red, peeling face back to her. She returned to Miss Vee's and put on the fascinator, making sure to position the net veil completely over her face. She closed her eyes to center herself and focus on affirmations that would give her confidence. *I have faith in my journey. I am strong and brave and can overcome every obstacle.* She opened her eyes and saw the fascinator netting had rubbed a patch of skin on her chin lose. *It's going to be a loooong night.*

The tent was packed with revelers when Ricki arrived. Eugenia's party planners had done a wonderful job of creating a magical setting. Fairy lights bounced off the prisms of petite chandeliers strung throughout the tent adding crystal rainbows to the décor. Six-foot-high pine trees adorned with white bows and red ornaments emitted a Christmasy scent. The partygoers were elegantly dressed in an array of satins and velvets for the women and crisp, high-end suits for the men.

Ricki spotted guest of honor Olivia, who wore a simple,

stunning gown of crushed navy velvet cut on the bias. Her thick blonde hair was styled in a low ponytail, which showed off small sapphire drop earrings that matched her sapphire and pave diamond necklace. She'd told Ricki she was nervous about wearing the set, a family heirloom, but she looked completely at ease—downright queenly, in Ricki's eyes—as she mingled with guests, proud parents Greg and Robin at her side. Ricki caught her young cousin's eye and waved. Olivia waved back, then pointed to the fascinator with a quizzical expression. Ricki mouthed "Long story," to which Olivia mouthed back an eager "Tell me later!"

Olivia moved on but Ricki stayed stuck in place, self-conscious about her appearance. She wished Virgil was there, but he had begged off due to both a need for sleep and maintaining a low profile given his current circumstances. *You can't stay glued here forever*, she chided herself. She saw Zellah and Cookie at the bar wearing their headpieces. This gave her the courage to start working her way through the crowd.

The first guest Ricki recognized was Dr. Mansieur from Crescent City Concierge, pontificating among a cluster of people. The attractive woman she'd chatted with in the waiting room was by his side, holding a glass of champagne and laughing. Having met with the doctor and found him consumed with self-importance, Ricki doubted his wife was reacting to anything he'd said. She recognized Penelope Vogelspack's father Owen standing on the sidelines of the group, swigging a glass of what looked like Scotch. Figuring this meant Penelope was there, she scanned the room. She saw Lizette huddling with a few other girls, all wearing tight, shiny dresses and sky-high heels. One girl with a gloomy expression stood apart from the others, playing with her phone. Noting the square-jawed, large-boned resemblance to Owen Vogelspack pegged her as his daughter Penelope.

Ricki continued cutting a path through the guests but came to a dead stop when she spotted dermatologist Rachel Vernon. Clad in a teal sheath instead of a white physician's coat, her brown hair loose and hanging below her shoulders, Ricki almost missed the doctor. Ricki was debating whether to confront her about the ill-fated mask when someone grabbed her arm. She whirled around and came face-to-face with Eugenia.

The party hostess wore a plum peau de soie beaded jacket over a matching, full-length gown. Ricki noticed she was wearing black loafers that didn't go with the refined evening dress. "I've been discreetly inserting Phyllis's name into conversation with my crowd," Eugenia whispered. "So far, no one has even heard of her and I haven't detected anyone lying."

"Uh-huh." Ricki kept her response and tone neutral, doing her best not to encourage Eugenia's snooping.

"Guests are still arriving, so I'll keep going. I've got on my most comfortable shoes so I don't wear myself out." She poked a sturdily clad toe out from under her dress.

"*Oh-kay*," Ricki repeated, a little less neutral this time.

"You'll be proud of the wide net I managed to cast regarding the invitation list. It's heavy on Krewe of Gaia members, which includes at least several doctors from Concierge Care. But I also invited a few residents of Peony Place. Renate Rancourt, of course, since she's Lizette's grandmother and a former Gaia queen herself. But them too."

Ricki looked to where Eugenia pointed and saw Melissa Sachs standing next to a handsome man she assumed was husband David. Each held a plate of hor d'oeuvres. Eugenia moved her finger toward the center of the tent and it landed on Art and Brenda Broussard, who were in conversation with another couple. "Both of Phyllis's neighbors," Ricki said, impressed. "Nicely done."

"Merci. I found out a bit about them. Art was Phyllis's financial advisor until he recently retired. David Sachs is a contractor and does very well."

"The Sachs are the only people of color here besides my parents. I hope they don't feel uncomfortable."

"I'll bring these over and turn on the charm," Eugenia said, lifting two glasses of champagne off a passing tray. "And remind me to widen my circle of friends and acquaintances to make it more inclusive."

"Highly recommend that."

"Oh, I almost forgot to tell you, the fascinator is a wonderful idea. It will make it much easier for you to eavesdrop."

Eugenia's comment turned out to be an astute observation. As the cocktail hour extended into two hours, the fascinator proved a handy disguise, offering Ricki opportunities to create the illusion of mingling while spying on conversations. Mrs. Rancourt was giving off noblesse oblige vibes as she held court in her wheelchair, which she obviously considered the equivalent of a throne. Ricki saw Owen Vogelspack kowtowing to her and maneuvered herself near enough to hear him say sotto voce to the old lady, "I'll have my business manager get on it tomorrow." He glanced around to ensure no one heard him, ignoring the woman in the weird headdress, and hurried off. Ricki banked the comment and continued eavesdropping.

She circled the tent a few more times. Nothing seemed out of the ordinary. She walked past her parents who pretended not to see her, but Luis mouthed like a ventriloquist, "We got eyes on everyone." Ricki spotted a tray of crab puffs and reached for one at the same time as Kitty Kat, who was dressed so understated she appeared more like a mourner than a partygoer. With her free hand, Kitty Kat tapped a finger to the side of her nose, indicating they were in cahoots, then sauntered off. Ricki rolled her eyes.

"What the A-F are you wearing?"

Ricki realized the comment was directed at her. She turned and her jaw dropped. "Nina?! What are you doing here?"

The detective *tsked-tsked*. "That's a rude way to greet a guest. I have half a mind to tell your hostess that you failed New Orleans High Society Manners 101. Eugenia invited me. She explained this party is an excuse to corral suspects, like in a golden age mystery. Apparently Bon Vee is now a breeding ground for 'amateur sleuths.'" Nina mimed air quotes.

"Tell me about it," Ricki said, thinking of her parents and Kitty Kat, in addition to Eugenia. "What does Scooby Doyenne want you to do?"

"Her plan is to introduce me as a detective and gauge people's reactions. You know, see if anyone cuts and runs when they hear I'm a proud daughter of the NOPD."

"Oh boy."

Nina chortled. "I know, right? Anyway, it's not too often I get invited to a baller shindig like this, as in never. I'm looking forward to a night of fine food and wine. How do I look?" She held out her hands to show off her black velvet pants and jacket she wore over a white silk button-down blouse.

"Like a detective wearing velvet instead of jeans. But the look works on you. Theo would fall at your feet if he wasn't so busy sucking up to potential donors." A thought occurred to Ricki. "Actually, there is someone you can scare with your law enforcement status. You asked about this stupid fascinator." Ricki shared a quick version of her run-in with Dr. Vernon's face mask. "I'd love to see her reaction when I introduce you as a detective. She's here somewhere." Ricki scoured the tent. "She's a couple of inches shorter than you, has mid-length dark brown hair, and is wearing a long teal slip dress. I don't see her."

"Neither do I. But that fits the description of a woman I saw when I came into the tent. We made eye contact when I was adjusting my gun holster under my dress jacket. I'm not used to wearing them together."

"And now she's gone. Why do I feel like that's not a coincidence?"

"I'll make a note to take a look-see into the good doctor's background." Nina deftly lifted a glass of champagne from one of the many passing trays. "I'm not on NOPD time, so I'm going to knock back a few of these to wash down . . ." She lifted an appetizer off another tray. "This delicious steak tartare appetizer."

Nina followed the tray. Tired of looking at the world through netting, Ricki lifted the tulle on her fascinator. She happened to do it at the exact moment Melissa and David were glancing in her direction. Melissa appeared puzzled, then her face cleared. She said something to David and they approached Ricki. "Hi!" Melissa greeted her. "You're Thor's mom. We wondered how we wound up on the guest list tonight, and now we know."

"Guilty as charged," Ricki lied, not wanting to reveal

Eugenia was the brains behind the Peony Place invitations. "Eugenia is my cousin. I own the gift shop at Bon Vee, Miss Vee's Vintage Cookbook and Kitchenware."

"I'll have to stop by and thank you with some sales," Melissa said. "This is my husband David."

"Hey," David said. He extended a hand and clasped Ricki's in a firm, calloused grip. "We appreciate the invitation. A party like this, I could make some good connections. I already eyeballed dry rot on a couple of the house eaves on this place."

Melissa playfully swatted her husband's arm. "David, no talking about business. Oooh, they're putting out the buffet." She patted her stomach. "Let's use David Sachs Junior as an excuse to cut in line."

She pulled David toward the buffet. He almost collided with their block neighbors the Broussards, who were paying homage to Mrs. Rancourt. Ricki couldn't hear what the two couples said to each other, but judging by their frosty expressions, the exchange was forced. The Sachs headed to the buffet, oblivious to whispers behind their backs on the part of their neighbors.

Ricki decided to target the Broussards next. She pulled her veil over face and followed them to the buffet line. "'Scuse me," she said to Mrs. Rancourt as she zipped past the old lady, who was having trouble directing her wheelchair toward the food. Ricki lucked out and landed a place in line right behind the Broussards, who were bickering with each other. "I don't care how well-placed in the city that wizened gorgon is, I can't wait for the day I don't have to genuflect to her anymore," Arthur said to his wife. "I'm retired. I don't have to be nice to people I can't stand." Ricki silently applauded his stance.

"It's important to me," Brenda responded. "I could never show my face at my book club again if they found out I was cut from her annual tea party guest list."

Art grumbled something Ricki couldn't hear. He read the menu posted on a stand next to the buffet and cheered up. "Here's some good news. For dessert, there's three different kinds of bread pudding and an assortment of macarons."

His wife glared at him. "Don't even think about bread

pudding. A toe isn't enough? The way you eat sugar, you're going to lose a whole foot to the diabetes."

Arthur, who was piling crawfish mac and cheese onto his plate, retorted, "I'm gonna go sometime and it might as well be doing what I love: eating good food."

The Broussards' conversation devolved into the small talk of a long-married couple. Bored and hungry, Ricki took a break from scouting suspects to fill her own plate with a sampling of every dish.

She was hunting for a place to sit, full plate in hand, when Kitty Kat scurried over to her. "Ricki, it happened!" Excited, she waved her hands up and down. Noticing other guests glancing at her, she clasped her hands together and spoke in a low voice. "I recognized a guest from my Charity days."

"You did?" Ricki set her plate down, anxious to hear Kitty Kat's news. "Who?"

"One of the doctor's wives." Kitty Kat's voice dropped to a whisper. "And I can tell you for sure she ain't the high-falutin' upper cruster she's pretending to be."

TWENTY-THREE

Ricki quickly put her plate down at an empty spot, earning an annoyed "Hey!" from a man about to sit there. "Sorry, emergency," she apologized. She took Kitty Kat's arm and led her away from the table. "This party is loaded with doctor's wives. Which one did you make? I think I used that term right. I'll have to ask Nina. She's around here somewhere."

"First, let me tell you what happened and why I'm sure the woman is who I think she is." Kitty Kat's round body practically quivered with the thrill of sharing a story that might link to a murder investigation. "Back in the Charity days, there was a very pretty young woman who we all knew was the paid escort for Damian Arvois, one of the hospital's top administrators. One night, they were having . . . relations . . . in an operating room. His . . . lady friend . . . had lit a candle for mood lighting. But security tracked them down and she burned her hand rushing to put the candle out. I treated the burn, which was bad enough to leave a scar. Right here." Kitty Kat held the side of her hand up to Ricki. "I saw the scar tonight on a woman holding a glass of champagne."

"Who?" Ricki asked, dying to know.

The nurse examined the crowd and pointed. "Her."

Ricki glanced at the table of guests in question. She almost gasped out loud when she saw who was on the receiving end of Kitty Kat's identification: Helene Mansieur, wife to Dr. Mansieur of Crescent City Concierge Care. "*Her?*"

Kitty gave an emphatic nod. "Yup. I'd recognize her without the scar. It's been twenty years since my Charity days but she's still pretty as ever. We chatted while I fixed her up. She said she was adding the bill for the treatment to Victor's sex tab. It must've ended the relationship because I never saw the young woman again."

"Would Mom recognize her?"

Kitty Kat shook her head. "She'd have only heard the story. It made for great gossip. But your mama never worked a shift when Venus showed up, so she wouldn't recognize her by sight. That was the gal's real name. Venus Love. No joke. She got a kick out of telling me and showing it on her license." Kitty Kat gazed at Helene, who appeared to be listening to a long story from her husband with rapt attention. "It looks like she's done well for herself."

Ricki studied the woman formerly known as Venus Love. "Is there a chance Phyllis recognized her?"

"Possibly. Phyllis had a nine-to-five position but from what Venus told me when I was dressing her burn, Mr. Arvois had a busy schedule and daytime rendezvouses did happen. Plus, Phyllis had a finger in a lot of hospital pots. She'd be all over something this salacious."

A tinkly laugh from Helene/Venus rang out and sailed over the table to Ricki and Kitty Kat. "If Phyllis did figure out who Helene was," Ricki mused, "it's a perfect setup for blackmail."

"You mean Venus could be the killer?" Kitty Kat's attitude morphed from excitement to anxiety. "What should we do?"

"You don't have to do anything, at least not right now. Nina Rodriguez, the NOPD detective, is here. I'll tell her what you told me and we'll take it from there."

"Sounds good. If you need me, I'll be sitting down to eat. I wanna get a big helping of the crawfish mac and cheese before it's all gone."

Ricki stopped for a quick bite from her own plate of food before tracking Nina down. Even stone cold, everything was delicious. She reluctantly stopped eating and looked around the tent for the detective. She spotted Nina at a table near the entrance and beelined toward her.

"And you'll never guess where we found the vic's torso," Nina was saying to her tablemates, who were staring at her with a combination of fear and fascination.

Ricki bent down and murmured, "We need to talk."

"Can it wait? I'm in the middle of telling my new friends about the most gruesome case I ever solved."

"It's all right," a guest who looked queasy jumped in. "You can finish the story later."

"Or never," an equally queasy guest added.

Nina rose. "Fine. But trust me, you wanna hear where we found the head."

Ricki led Nina out of the tent to an isolated part of the side yard. "I have to go to more of these fancy parties," the detective said as they walked. "They're an absolute sea of white-collar criminals. I jotted down a few names to pass on to my compadres at NOPD."

"I'm sure they'll thank you for it. NOPD, not the potential criminals. But right now, I have a possible new suspect in Phyllis's murder." Ricki repeated what Kitty Kat had told her about Venus/Helene, the assumed call girl turned doctor's wife.

"Interesting," Nina said. "Tomorrow I'll check the database and see if we have a record of arrests for a Venus Love."

"Great. Although my money is still on Dr. Vernon."

Nina crossed her arms in front of her chest and leaned back on her heels. "Miracle, my friend, you're giving me a lot of theories and names but that's about it. We've had this talk before." She wagged a finger at Ricki. "What's the most important thing I need for a case?"

"Concrete evidence," Ricki said with a sigh.

"Correct. First thing tomorrow, I'll check out Love/Mansieur and Vernon. If there's cause for questioning, I'll bring them in. But there's always the chance they'll alibi out."

"I get it. It's just . . . the case *has* to be solved. My mom, my dad, Virgil. The most important people in my life are living with the threat of being arrested. I don't know if I should buy them Christmas presents or start a legal defense fund." Ricki lifted the tulle netting off her face. "Ugh, I'm so tired of wearing this thing."

"You dropped something."

Ricki looked down. "That's a big skin flake."

"I thought so but didn't want to say it out loud and embarrass you." Nina's cell pinged a text. She read it and her teasing demeanor disappeared. "Great. The Bongle Bandit burgled a bodega. I defy you to say that three times fast."

"This is going to take priority over the Phyllis case, isn't it?"

Nina gave a rueful nod. "It shouldn't. Technically I should be doing my job as a homicide detective. But stopping a beloved local character from giving kids nightmares instead of sweet holiday dreams, as well as cutting into tourism and business profits, means they need me to weigh in on the investigation."

Ricki sighed. "Fine. I'll keep poking around on my own."

"I know you don't want your folks or Virgil to find handcuffs in their Christmas stockings, but please don't take any unnecessary chances," Nina said, serious for a change. "I've looked the other way a lot with you. But it doesn't mean I don't feel guilty about it when you get into trouble. Which has happened a few times."

"I'll watch out for myself. Promise."

Nina started toward the tent. Ricki kept pace with her. "I hate to split before dessert," the detective said. "You think Eugenia will sign off on a to-go sampler of the bread puddings?"

"Yes, but she may want your list of friends who are potential white-collar criminals in exchange."

"Not if someone doesn't tell her about it," Nina said with a wink.

She strode into the tent and straight to the table where the bread puddings and assorted desserts were on display, leaving a frustrated Ricki to wonder if her time would be put to better use unmasking the Bongle Bandit than trying to get her loved ones off the hook.

TWENTY-FOUR

Having done her due diligence in reporting to Nina, Ricki checked in with her parents, who were sitting at a table with Kitty Kat. The three seniors had each built themselves a dessert sampler plate. "I was going to see how you two were doing but those plates speak for themselves."

"Highly, highly recommend the bananas foster bread pudding," Luis spoke with a mouthful of the dessert.

"Kitty Kat told me all about Venus Love being Dr. Mansieur's wife," Josepha said, her voice low. "I remember the stories, but I never met her in person. I'm gonna see if I can dig up anything on Mrs. Mansieur from my new pals at Crescent City."

"That would be awesome," Ricki said.

She left her parents to their dessert smorgasbords and spent the rest of the party hanging out with her friends. Toward the end of the night, she caught up with guest of honor Olivia, who was ensconced at a table with the maids from her court who'd stuck around for the whole affair.

Ricki gave her young cousin a hug. "Did you have fun tonight?"

Olivia lifted her hand and tilted it back and forth to indicate half-and-half. The Gaia krewe queen had shed her high heels and parked her bare feet on an empty chair. "People were nice to me but it was weird being the center of so much attention. A couple of ladies *bowed* to me. I was like, 'Nooooo. Do *not* do that!'"

Lizette gave her a gentle jab in the ribs. "Bull. You loved it."

"Did not," Olivia shot back, defending herself. "Oh, and Lizzie, can we talk about the looks your grandma kept shooting at me? You know the old-timey expression, if looks could kill? I'm pretty sure she wished hers could have."

"My parents are waiting for the day they're free from her

but my dad says she's gonna outlive us all and I bet he's right," Lizette said with a chuckle.

Olivia picked up a small jewel box. "Penelope left her favor. I had pearl drop earrings made for all my maids." She added the explanation for Ricki's benefit.

A maid on the other side of Lizette spoke up. "Pen hasn't been here for hours. She left right after the cocktail party."

"Oh. Then I'll drop them off at her house tomorrow."

Ricki saw Lizette and the other maid exchange a surreptitious look. "I'll do it," Lizette said.

"I want to do it. I want Penny and me to be friends. The whole court thing will be awful if we're not."

Ricki recognized Olivia's stubborn tone. "I'm sure Penny will get past this, Liv. But she may need more time. It would probably help to give her space and let her come to you when she's ready."

Olivia appeared like she was going to argue with Ricki. Then she backed off. "Fine. Lizette, you can drop off the earrings. And thanks."

She managed a smile, but Ricki knew Olivia was upset by the awkward situation with Penelope. When Ricki was growing up, her mother used to repeat the saying, "You're only as happy as your unhappiest child." Since Ricki was an only child, it was more of an in-joke between them. But as Ricki gave her cousin another supportive hug, she thought to herself the expression could be paraphrased as "You're only as happy as your unhappiest court maid."

Ricki went to find her parents, who were no longer at their table. She located them at the dessert station, where they were transferring bread pudding into to-go containers, along with Kitty Kat.

Luis gleefully held up a container so full the lid barely fit. "Mirar—breakfast, lunch, dinner."

Josepha gestured to her husband's stomach with her equally packed container. "Maybe pick one meal, mi amor. Ricki, you want me to make you a to-go box?"

"My pants are already threatening to go up another size, so I'll pass. I came to say goodnight."

Ricki kissed each parent on the cheek and did the same with Kitty. She cast a longing glance at the array of desserts, then summoned up her last ounce of willpower and left for home.

In an attempt to wrangle her shedding skin, she slept with a towel over her pillow, which she tossed into the laundry in the morning. She woke up tired and achy, residual effects from the party the evening before. After showering, she steeled herself for the day's first glance at the mirror. She stared at her image in disbelief.

Her complexion had never looked better.

Nascent worry lines seemed to have disappeared. Her cheeks, forehead, and chin were smooth. Her skin had initially looked lovely post-mask, then came the awful reptilian shedding. But now it literally glowed. "It's a miracle," Ricki murmured to the lovely creature reflecting back at her from the mirror. She felt a mixture of shock, delight . . . and guilt. Had she judged Dr. Vernon too harshly? She thought about this as she fed and walked the dogs. On the drive to Bon Vee, she was still wrestling with the question.

She parked and went to the café to grab a cup of coffee before opening Miss Vee's. Cookie and Zellah were already there. "Morning," she greeted her friends.

"Morn—" They stopped mid-word and gaped at Ricki.

"Your skin." Cookie put down the chocolate chip muffin she'd begun eating and leaned into Ricki to study her face more closely. "It's flawless."

"I know. Dr. Vernon's mask worked."

"That's an understatement," Zellah said. "It's a dang magic potion. She took ten years off you."

"I don't think you mean I look eighteen, so that's sort of a backhanded compliment." Ricki took a seat next to Cookie at the café's limestone counter. "Cookie, stop staring. You're making me uncomfortable."

"I can't help it. It's like a movie where a character sheds their epidermis and turns into someone completely different."

"That's a big dose of exaggeration. And again, kind of insulting. Also, that's usually what happens in horror movies and it never ends well."

Zellah placed a mug of coffee in front of Ricki. "Considering your face was such a disaster yesterday that you couldn't show yourself to people, I'm surprised you're not delirious with joy at the result."

"I am. And I'm not." Ricki stirred milk into her coffee as she debated how to explain why she felt so conflicted. "I mean, I'm thrilled with how my skin turned out. I didn't expect this at all. Which makes me think I was wrong about Dr. Vernon and she's an excellent dermatologist who's awkward with patients."

"There's a 'but' coming," Cookie said.

"Oh, most definitely," Zellah agreed.

Ricki ignored her friends' gentle teasing. "*But* . . . I keep going back to the products Phyllis had in her house from a skincare line that Dr. Vernon is adamant she's not selling anymore. And how the doctor didn't stick around the party last night after realizing Nina was with NOPD." Ricki frowned. "I have to get back inside Phyllis's house. Mordant is supposed to be setting it up but he hasn't heard back from the realtor yet."

"So you still think she could be the killer," Zellah said. Ricki nodded.

"Well, do me a favor and don't bust the doctor until after she's given me whatever treatment she gave you," Cookie said.

Ricki glanced toward the street and saw a mini tour bus slowing to a stop. "The first tour group of the day just pulled up. I have to go open the shop. New and improved me will see you later."

Ricki decamped for Miss Vee's. Despite her coffee she still felt lethargic, so she turned on her holiday playlist hoping the spirit of the season would energize her. The first song wasn't halfway through when caroling alto Jennifer stuck her head into the shop. "Hi, sweetie. You mind turning off the music? It conflicts with our singing."

"Sure," Ricki said, managing to hide the fact the carolers were working her last nerve.

"Thanks so much. You're the *best*." Jennifer sang the last word. Tired and grumpy, Ricki responded by closing the door the instant Jennifer cleared it.

She spent the morning helping customers, several of whom complimented her "lovely complexion." This only exacerbated Ricki's conflicted feelings about Dr. Vernon. She shoved them aside to concentrate on imbuing the shop and shoppers with the holiday sales spirit—sans shop music, thanks to the caroling divas.

At the end of the day, Ricki tallied receipts to the tune of "Hark! The Herald Angels Sing" wafting in from the hall, when she heard a lyric turn into a screech and then a scream.

"Glory to the newborn king*aaahh ahhh*!!!"

The sound of scuffling and an argument followed. Ricki locked up the day's income and hurried into the hall, where she was stunned to see baritone Larry had bass Edgar in a headlock while Ruth and Jennifer ineffectually tugged at the men to separate them.

"You stole the recipe from my grandmother's headstone!" Larry roared as Edgar tried to free himself.

"No I didn't, you lunatic! It's my own recipe for shrimp étouffée!"

Edgar managed to free himself but in doing so, a folded piece of paper fell out of his pocket. Larry grabbed the paper, opened it, and waved it in dour triumph. "Proof! It's a photo of my grandmother's headstone." He scowled at Edgar and spoke through clenched teeth. "You son of a—"

He lunged for his fellow caroler and the two toppled to the ground. Ricki joined the women in trying to stop the fight, which devolved further when Ruth and Jennifer began screaming insults at each other. It turned out Ruth was Team Edgar and Jennifer, Team Larry.

Suddenly, a stentorian voice commanded, "*Stop*."

Everyone froze. As one group, they glanced at the end of the hallway to see Eugenia standing there, appearing much displeased. "Thank you for your time with Bon Vee," she said, her tone so cold Ricki shuddered. "Your services will no longer be needed. Whatever payment you are owed will be deposited in your bank accounts."

The men struggled to their feet. "Is my recipe still eligible for the cookbook?" Edgar asked.

"It's not your recipe!" Larry pulled back a fist. "You're not even from New Orleans. You don't belong in the cookbook!"

"Go!" Eugenia ordered. "*Now*!"

Larry dropped his fist and the carolers quickly cut out of Bon Vee, muttering threats at each other under their breath. Ricki picked up the piece of paper that triggered the brawl. It was indeed an enlarged image of a recipe on a cemetery headstone. She pocketed it and went to Eugenia.

"Hiring them was not my best idea," Eugenia said.

"It was a great idea. Just the wrong group to implement it."

Eugenia sighed. "I'll put out an ad for a replacement immediately. I hate to impose on my docents to do extra free work to cover the carolers' tour groups but I have no other choice. I'll have to call on the staff to fill in as well."

"It's an emergency. You know we'll all be there for you and Bon Vee. My only recommendation is maybe skip hiring other carolers to replace these."

"Noted."

Eugenia strode off. Ricki texted Zellah and Cookie to meet at the café. She finished her tally and went to meet her friends.

They were waiting for her at a table. Zellah held up her phone as Ricki approached. "We all got a text saying we're going to be put on temporary tour duty due to 'unforeseen circumstances.' You know anything about this?"

"Oh yes." Ricki joined them at the table and told them about the carolers' kerfuffle.

"So, what I'm hearing is no more caroling," Cookie said. "If this means I have to pick up a couple of tours until Eugenia finds a replacement for them, I'm good with it."

"Me too," Zellah said. "Those four were not bringing joy to *my* world."

"Agreed, although I'm fascinated by a recipe on a headstone. I've never heard of such a thing." Ricki passed the paper with the recipe photo to Zellah.

"It's uncommon but they're all around the world," Zellah said. "More than a few of them here in New Orleans because we have such a connection to food. It's a wonderful way of honoring someone who had one special recipe they were beloved for."

Zellah passed the page to Cookie, who scanned it. "If this was my headstone, the title of the recipe would be 'Nuking Frozen Food' and the instructions would be 'Open microwave, set timer, eat meal.'"

"Mine would be the same," Ricki confessed with a grin.

Zellah shook her head, bemused. "I will never get over the fact you are obsessed with old cookbooks but don't cook."

"I know. It's weird. I love the artwork of them, and the way they're so emblematic of the era when they were published. It's really an anthropological thing with me." Cookie passed Edgar's stolen headstone recipe to Ricki. She held it up. "And now I'm obsessed with headstone recipes."

All three of their cell phones pinged an alert. "Good news for a change. Docent Jerry Feldstein wants to change from volunteer to employee, so he's going to take over the carolers' slots."

"He's a super nice guy," Ricki said, adding with a grin, "and won't be singing carols, that's for sure."

Zellah held up a glass of iced tea. "Mazel tov, Jerry!"

Cookie held up her glass of water and Ricki mimed holding a glass. "Mazel tov!"

The three toasted and laughed. Then Ricki grew quiet. Something from the caroler's altercation niggled at her. She replayed the argument in her mind and was about to land on what it was when Cookie's phone alerted her to another text. Cookie read it and her smile faded. "Oh boy."

Zellah leaned over to read the text. "What? Did Jerry have second thoughts about taking on the tours?"

"No. This isn't from Eugenia. I get notifications from OhNo!La," Cookie said, referencing the city's popular social app. "This one just popped up."

Zellah read over Cookie's shoulder. "Uh-oh. This ain't good."

"What is it?" Ricki craned her neck to read the headline. Her brow wrinkled with concern at what she saw.

"Breaking News!" the headline blared. "Drama Hits Krewe of Gaia. Queen Might be Removed from Court."

TWENTY-FIVE

"This is terrible," Ricki said, upset. "Poor Olivia."

"Does the post say why?" Zellah asked.

Ricki handed Cookie her cell and opened the app on her own phone. She scanned the post and read out loud, "An unsolved murder with links to Bon Vee Culinary House Museum, site of other recent murders, has created an optics problem for the Krewe of Gaia, whose queen is Olivia Ramona Charbonnet Felice, granddaughter of the museum's executive director Eugenia Charbonnet Felice, whose aunt was Bon Vee homeowner and legendary New Orleans restaurateur, Genevieve Charbonnet. A rumor that someone close to the Felice family is now a person of interest in the murder of Peony Place resident Phyllis Gibbs has prompted a faction of the Gaia court to encourage Queen Olivia to resign as queen or be forced out." Near tears, Ricki put her phone down. "I can't read anymore."

Cookie placed a comforting hand on Ricki's back. "I'm sure the 'person of interest' isn't one of your parents. Everyone loves them but I don't think they'd be classified as close to the Felice family."

"It's not them," Zellah, scrolling on her own phone, said. "I'm reading the comments. Someone wrote they heard there was a connection between the victim and Virgil Morel."

Ricki released an anguished cry. "No. That's Virgil's worst fear. If the production company or streamer hears about this, it could tank his show."

"Don't freak out, Ricks," Cookie said. "These stories have such a short shelf life." Her phone pinged. "I just got another notification about a five-car pile-up on I-10. You see? The Gaia story will blow over."

"Or blow up," Ricki said, distraught.

"Let's hope it's door number one," Zellah said, her voice laced with sympathy and kindness.

Unfortunately, it soon proved to be door number two. Instead of blowing over, the story blew up.

Ricki left her friends to check on Virgil, who was wrapping up the day's filming. She immediately noticed director Patrick appeared grim. "Hi," she said, aiming for friendly and low-key. "How'd the shoot go?"

"Fine until the news broke our chef might be a wanted man." Patrick delivered this in a caustic tone. He gestured to Ricki's dad. "Diaz, I need you. I want to go over your shot list for tomorrow."

"You got it." Luis spoke from the corner of the family room where he was packing up his equipment. Ricki caught his eye and he tilted his head to indicate she should separate herself from Patrick's presence, which Ricki was happy to do.

She went to Virgil, who was on the room's couch finishing a phone call. "Like we said, it's gossip," he said into his cell. "Nothing more. Rich people here got bored with talking about how much they hate the mayor and found a new topic. By the time my show airs, whoever killed Ms. Gibbs'll be remanded to one of our famous horrific prisons." He saw Ricki and mouthed "Please God." She crossed herself, then clasped her hands as if praying. Virgil returned to his call. "I'll keep you updated." He ended the call and rolled his eyes. "Thanks, OhNo!La."

Ricki sat down next to him. "Production company? Streamer?"

"Both. Emergency conference call. A lot of 'We believe in you, it's not a big deal, blah blah blah.' Then came the 'But.' As in, 'But if the case is still open and people'—meaning me—'are still under suspicion, we can always bump to next year.' Translation: no show."

"That can't happen," Ricki said, adamant.

"It can't. But it could." Virgil's cell rang. "It's my seafood supplier. I gotta get this."

"If you need me, call me."

Virgil nodded. He blew her a kiss and took the call.

Ricki barely slept that night. She staggered into the shop the next morning, sleep deprived. Seconds later, Olivia showed up. Her face was red and swollen, her cheeks wet. "I can't stop crying," she said, proving it by bursting into tears.

Ricki wrapped her cousin in her arms. "I'm so sorry, Liv."

"The krewe is split into two sides," Olivia sobbed into Ricki's shoulder. "The ones who want me out, and my dad's side who want me to stay. My parents are furious. They're threatening to sue if I'm kicked out. The whole krewe may fall apart and it's all my fault."

"No," Ricki declared, holding Liv tighter. "It is *not* your fault. It's the worst of circumstances. You've done absolutely nothing wrong. I hate the word victim because it implies being passive, but in this case you *are* a victim, Liv. You can't beat yourself up for something you have zero control over."

"I could have said no when they asked me to be queen," Olivia said. "I would've been fine being a maid. Or not even being in the court."

"You were given the honor for a reason and you need to respect yourself for earning it."

Olivia made a face. "I only got it because my family goes back to prehistoric times in New Orleans."

"Plenty of girls in this city could say the same thing. But you're the one they chose."

"Ugh." Olivia dragged herself to a club chair and collapsed into it. "I'm sure this happened because Penny Vogelspack was so bent out of shape about not being picked. Dad said her father pitched a fit about it. I'm going to tell her she can have the stupid crown. It's not worth all this."

Ricki wasn't sure where she stood on the whole krewe scene in general, but she hated to see her cousin cave. "Please don't be intimidated by bullies into quitting, Liv."

Olivia ignored her. She removed her cell phone from the pocket of her leggings and sent a voice-text. "Penny, it's me. I give up. You can be queen. I can't take all the drama." She stopped talking into her phone. "There. Done. It's over." Her phone rang. "Or not. She's FaceTiming me. Help! What do I do?"

"Talk to her," Ricki advised.

"Can you be with me?" Olivia pleaded. "I don't know what to say."

Ricki glanced into the hallway. Seeing no evidence of potential customers, she joined Olivia, parking herself on the arm of the club chair. Penny Vogelspack's face popped up on Olivia's phone screen. To Ricki's surprise, the girl appeared as upset as Olivia. "Olivia, this whole stupid court thing has gotten insane. I swear, I never said anything to anyone about wanting to be queen. And I was never going to be."

"What do you mean?" Olivia asked, exchanging a confused look with Ricki. "You've been giving off so much attitude ever since we got court calls. I thought it was because you were mad about me being chosen."

Penny shook her head vehemently. "No. I've been in a bad mood because I'm hating on my parents right now. They've been on my case because I switched my major to International Business and I have to learn a second language, so I signed up for Chinese and it's *hard*. I'm really bad at it. My dad isn't supposed to tell me anything about Krewe of Gaia but he was mad at me because my grades sucked last semester. He told me to forget about being queen. He had to bust his butt just to get me on the court as a maid."

"Wait." Olivia tried to process this. "If it's not you, who will be queen when I quit? Do you know?"

"Yes." Penny gave a grave nod. "Lizette Rancourt."

Olivia and Ricki gasped simultaneously. Ricki clapped her hand over her mouth to cover her reaction. *It's not what Olivia needs right now*, she reprimanded herself.

"I can't believe it," Olivia said, stunned. "Lizette's my best friend. Or was."

A doorbell rang on Penny's end. "I have to go," she said. "My tutor for Chinese is here. I'm really sorry about everything."

Penny ended the call. Olivia stared at the blank screen of her phone. "How could Lizette do this to me?"

"You don't know if she had anything to do with this. Penny said the krewe members aren't supposed to reveal what goes on in their meetings. Lizette may not know she's next in line after you. I bet she doesn't."

"It's all so weird because Dad said Penny's dad was the one who most wants to get rid of me as queen. But why is he making such a big deal about it when his own daughter can't replace me?"

Ricki gave a helpless shrug. "I have no idea. This whole krewe thing is beyond me. The drama and subterfuge makes me feel like I'm in a Machiavellian medieval court. I know it's an awful time for you right now, sweetie, but don't jump to conclusions about Lizette. Talk to her first."

Olivia's lower lip quivered. "Everything is *such* a mess."

"I know. But I'm sure everything—and *everyone*—will calm down once the police arrest Phyllis's killer. OhNo!La will have a whole new story to salivate over."

"When will that be?" Olivia, exasperated, phrased this as a rhetorical question.

"Soon," Ricki said.

Olivia gave a skeptical grunt. "I wish."

So do I. Ricki kept her doubt to herself, aware it would only make Olivia feel worse. Between Olivia's friend drama and Virgil's show teetering on the edge of cancellation, the urgency to solve the murder of Phyllis Gibbs had been amped up to the nth degree.

And time was running out.

TWENTY-SIX

Knowing Olivia had a lot to deal with, Ricki sent her home for the day. Then she texted her friends a Mayday to meet at the Bayou Backyard at six p.m. It was time to call up her investigative support team.

"Ricki? Are you free?"

Ricki looked up to see Eugenia standing in the doorway. A loose chunk of hair dangled from her chignon, telegraphing how distressed the matron was.

"Of course." Ricki went to Eugenia and ushered her into the shop. She shut the door and discreetly flipped the OPEN sign to CLOSED.

"This is all my fault." Eugenia wrung her hands. "I never should have invited the detective to the party. I thought she would scare the killer into exposing themselves. Instead she just fueled the fire of gossip."

"It's not your fault, Eugenia," Ricki said. "Gossip is impossible to control, and that's especially true in this case."

Eugenia stopped wringing her hands. "You have a point. Murder. Krewe court shenanigans. It's a one-two punch of salaciousness."

"And enough to get people going, with or without Nina sashaying around the party."

This made Eugenia smile. "She did seem to be enjoying herself. Perhaps I'll get a free pass the next time I'm clocked at doing twenty-one in one of those godforsaken twenty-mile-an-hour school speed zones." She breathed a sigh of relief. "Thank you. I feel better. In the future, though, I'm limiting my amateur sleuthing to what's in my wheelhouse." Her eyes narrowed. "Like uncovering who's responsible for the drive to unseat my granddaughter from the Krewe of Gaia."

Eugenia threw open the shop door and exited, intent on her new mission.

The day dragged on for Ricki. Impatience made her antsy. She was dying to meet with her friends and run a murder theory or two past them and considered closing the shop early. But knowing sales would slow down post-holiday season, she powered through, using down time to scribble her thoughts.

The last tour group of the day dawdled in her shop and when she got to the Bayou Backyard, Cookie, Zellah, and Mordant were already there. To her surprise, Theo also showed up. Absorbed in whatever mysterious thing he was pursuing, he'd been MIA at recent group events.

Zellah gestured to the group's picnic table, which was loaded with plates of popcorn shrimp, crawfish handheld pies, mini corn dogs, and mini po'boys in addition to pitchers of beer. "We got here on the tail end of happy hour, so we put in a bunch of orders before it was over."

"Perfect." Ricki took a seat next to Cookie on one of the table's two picnic benches. Mordant poured her a glass of beer and reached across the table to hand it over. Ricki thanked him, then said, "Y'all know about Olivia and how she might be forced out of the Gaia court?"

"It's an insult to the whole Felice family," Theo said, glowering.

"The Bongle Bandit is taking up a big chunk of NOPD's time, so we can't count on them to move along the investigation into Phyllis's murder," Ricki said. "But if we can deliver solid clues to her killer I think it will speed things up." She took out her cell phone. "I made a list of possible suspects. Nina and Sam may find out some of them have alibis but since we don't have information, I think it's worth considering all of them."

"Because as we know from TV shows, alibis can be faked," Cookie said. "Oooh, listen to me, I sound like a TV show myself."

Ricki opened her Notes app. "When I was writing names, they broke into two groups. People who were linked to Phyllis in the past and people who had links in the present. I'll start with the past. At the party last night, Mom and her friend Kitty Kat identified Helene Mansieur as a professional escort who had a relationship with a Charity Hospital administrator named Damian Arvois. Her real name is Venus Love and yes, that is her birth name. Anyway, Helene/Venus is married to the primary care physician at Crescent City Concierge, Jeremy Mansieur. Since Mom and Kitty recognized her, it's not a reach to assume Phyllis did too."

"And Phyllis could have used this to blackmail the doctor's wife," Theo said.

"That's what I'm thinking."

"She's got motive, but so does her husband if he thought Phyllis might leak his wife's past," Mordant posited. "Or if he knew she was blackmailing his missus and wanted to put an end to it."

"He's on my list too," Ricki said.

"What about the Charity guy having the affair with her?" Zellah asked. "I'm guessing he's not the type who'd want the world to know about his extracurricular activities."

"Agreed, but he passed away ten years ago," Ricki said. "I found his obit this afternoon. He died a pillar of the New Orleans community."

"I bet," Zellah said dryly.

"There may be other people from Phyllis's Charity past, but they haven't popped up on NOPD's radar. So, moving on to the present. Sticking with Crescent City Concierge, there's dermatologist Dr. Vernon."

"Your skin still looks incredible," Cookie said.

"I know and thank you. I'd say I was paranoid in thinking she used the mask to warn me off by making the nurse leave it on longer than it was supposed to be but as Cookie points out, my glowing complexion contradicts this. Still, there's something hinky about how Phyllis had so many items from the doctor's discontinued skincare line. The doctor shut me down when I brought up the line in my appointment with her. She wasn't subtle about it either."

"Definitely suspicious," Mordant said.

"Or, and hear me out," Cookie said, "she's a fantastic doctor who has crummy social skills."

"You really want that mask, don't you?"

"A thousand percent," Cookie said without an inch of apology.

"Sorry, the doctor is still on the list. Which reminds me, Mom was going to find the correct directions to applying the mask. That way we'll know if Vernon followed them." Ricki texted her mother, then paged down on her phone. "On to the residents of Peony Place. We have the Sachs, who were forced by Phyllis to pay for an expensive wall between their properties. They were convinced Phyllis scammed them into paying medical bills for a nonexistent condition—"

"Meaning she pocketed the money," Mordant added.

"And they were right. Nina told me Phyllis's autopsy showed no evidence of Lyme disease. But the Sachs don't know that. Melissa Sachs told me they were terrified the threats and lawsuits wouldn't stop. Well, they did when Phyllis was murdered. Husband David is ambitious. And he's a contractor. The contentious relationship with Phyllis could have created a lot of problems for him."

"And again, with her gone, their problems are gone."

Mordant gestured with his hands to illustrate this, then helped himself to a crawfish pie while Zellah gazed at him with admiration. "Can I just say I find your whole P.I. persona hot?"

Mordant flashed a grin that was as cocky as his basset hound face would allow. "You can, but may you?"

Everyone groaned at the ancient joke. Ricki held up a hand. "Hello. Back to me. Next up, the Broussards, who are the neighbors on the other side of Phyllis. She had a very cordial relationship with them. Which, given who Phyllis was, I don't trust for a minute."

"What do you think was going on between them?" Cookie asked through a mouth stuffed with a mini oyster po'boy.

"I don't know but it's something we should take a deeper dive into. We also have Tomas, the house sitter across the street who's a gig worker. Mordant and I followed him thinking he might be up to something but he was only making grocery runs."

"Why is he a suspect?" Zellah asked.

"He worked with Phyllis but they had a falling-out. Mordant and I caught him inside Phyllis's house. I say 'caught' because when he came out, he looked both ways . . ." Ricki imitated Tomas's clandestine exit from the house. "Like he didn't want anyone to see him. Which means he was up to something. And last of the Peony Place folks, we have Mrs. Rancourt."

"The old lady who was in the wheelchair at the party night?" Cookie sounded perplexed. "She looked like every bone would break if you blew on her. How could she be a murder suspect?"

"As a puppet master," Mordant said. "She's one of those Uptowners whose genealogy bleeds purple, green, and gold. All she has to do is go like this . . ." He crooked an index finger. "And people will do her bidding."

"But we're talking about murder," Cookie said.

"I know." Mordant delivered this in the deep, sepulchral voice he used on his haunted history tours.

Ricki's phone pinged. She read the text. "It's from my mother. Aha, I was right. The mask instructions cautioned in big letters not to exceed the limit. Doing so could create lasting skin damage. Dr. Vernon knew exactly what she was doing. I'm lucky all I had to deal with was a ton of flaking."

"Which was . . . worth it?" Cookie sounded hopeful. Ricki raised an eyebrow at her and she backed off. "Guess not."

Ricki drummed her fingers on the table, then wiped them with a napkin before helping herself to a popcorn shrimp. "We *have* to get back inside Phyllis's house. Mordant, any word from the real estate agent?"

"Um . . . yes," Mordant said, obviously uncomfortable. "I led a tour past what turned out to be one of her listings in the Garden District."

Ricki grimaced, knowing what was coming. "Which means she saw you in your undertaker costume."

Abashed, the tour guide/P.I. nodded. "She figured out I wasn't the kind of guy who'd be in the market for a house in the seven figures and shut down any thoughts of getting back inside with her."

Ricki held up her index finger to indicate she had an idea. "'With her' is the operative term here. We don't need Madison, we only need another agent who will let us. Does anyone know someone they think would help us out?"

Theo raised his hand. "I do. Me."

The others turned their attention to him, expressions perplexed. "What do you mean, 'you'?" Zellah asked, speaking for all of them.

Theo stopped slouching and sat up straight. When he spoke, it was with a mix of pride and diffidence, rare for someone whose default was usually arrogance. "I got my real estate license."

The others reacted to the unexpected news. Ricki was the first to speak. "Theo, that's awesome. Congratulations."

"Is that what you've been so secretive about?" Cookie asked.

"Yup," Theo responded. "I wanted to do something more substantial than be the Bon Vee 'Director of Community Relations.' I mean, I made up the title myself, and have basically made up the job. I figure real estate is a good side hustle. I can also use it to generate more donations for Bon Vee, so I'm genuinely putting my fake title to use."

Zellah leaned back and eyed him with approval. "Well, well, well. I never thought I'd say these words but Theo Charbonnet, I am impressed."

Theo tilted his head to acknowledge this and there was a flash of the old hubris. "Thank ya verrah much," he drawled, imitating an extreme Uptown accent.

"Back to the problem at hand," Ricki said. "Can you use your agent status to get in touch with Madison and tell her you have clients who are interested in viewing Phyllis's house?"

"I can."

"Fantastic," Ricki enthused. "How soon can you get us in?"

Theo tapped a message on his cell and sent it. Seconds later, the sound of a slide whistle indicated an incoming message. He read it, then said to Ricki, "How's tonight?"

TWENTY-SEVEN

"We shouldn't stay too long," Theo whispered.

True to his word, he'd arranged a showing of Phyllis's Peony Place home for his "clients." They'd only just walked inside the door and Ricki could tell the brand-new real estate agent was already regretting it.

"We don't have to whisper," Mordant said.

"I'd feel better if we did," Theo whispered.

"We won't be long, I promise," Ricki said. "Let's search the living room first."

Theo led the way with a flashlight. Once inside the room, Mordant turned the switch on a lamp. "Don't." A panicked Theo whisper-shouted this. "You'll expose us."

"Theo, you set up a legit showing," Ricki said. "Sneaking around with a flashlight is much more suspicious than turning on the lights."

"Fine," Theo grumbled. "But hurry."

Ricki and Mordant perused the room. Ricki noticed a clean, empty spot amid the Lalique sculptures on the side table. She pointed it out to Mordant. "When we saw Tomas carting something out of the house, I bet it was whatever used to be here."

"Agreed. And get this." Mordant handed Ricki a receipt he'd found under the table. "Someone who I'm guessing was Phyllis paid cash for a one-way ticket to Nicaragua. You know who does that?"

"Someone who doesn't want to leave a credit card trail that could trace them to Nicaragua. And since the lack of extradition treaty means Phyllis wasn't worried about the government, she must have been hiding her flight departure from other people who'd want to track her down."

"Yup."

Ricki continued to examine the room as she walked over to

a short stack of boxes. "These came from Mexico. You don't happen to have a box-cutter handy, do you?"

"Voila." Mordant reached into a pocket of his black jacket and whipped out a box-cutter. "A private eye never knows what they're gonna need."

He handed the box-cutter to Ricki, who cut opened a box, accompanied by an anxious squeak from Theo. "When I said I'd get you in here, I didn't mean for you to destroy the place," he hissed.

"Theo, I opened one box. I'll put it on the bottom of all the others and no one will ever know it happened on your watch." Ricki reached in the box and took out a bottle similar to the Futura bottles on the room's folding table. She looked into the box and saw it was packed tight with the product. She examined the bottle in her hand. "This is in Spanish. My Spanish isn't good enough to translate. I'll have to type into a free translator on my phone."

"Not necessary. I speak it." Mordant took the bottle and read its label. "El cuidado de la piel del mañana hoy."

"Does that mean what I think it does?"

"If you think it means 'Tomorrow's skincare today,' then yes."

Ricki sat back on her haunches and took this in. "Which was the tagline on Dr. Vernon's Futura skincare line."

"I believe we know the dirt Phyllis had on Dr. Vernon," Mordant said.

"The doctor was importing products from Mexico, relabeling them, and selling it as her own Futura line." Ricki finished his thought. "I'm sure when Phyllis figured out what Vernon was up to she used it to blackmail her. But I wonder if she meant for these boxes to be evidence she could take to the police if Vernon balked, or if she was planning to force the doctor to continue the line and cut her in on the profits."

"All questions for NOPD when we let them know what we discovered," Mordant said.

Theo nervously tapped his watch. "Tick-tock, people."

"Yes, sorry."

Ricki gave the room a once-over. Her eyes lighted on one of the cat photos on the fireplace mantel. Now that she'd met a few of the Peony Place residents, she recognized the person smiling with Sparkle in their arms. She picked up the photo. "Mordant—"

"I found a death threat."

This prompted another anxious squeak from Theo.

Photo still in hand but forgotten, Ricki went to Mordant, who was flat on the floor next to a tall display cabinet. He rose to his feet and handed Ricki a ragged piece of paper he'd uncrumpled. "It was stuck on a nail in the back of the cabinet. Whoever tossed it must have been aiming for the trash bin and missed."

Ricki read the note. "Give me my money or else. I mean it this time." She gave the paper back to Mordant. "It sounds like someone used 'Threatening Notes for Dummies' to write this."

Theo held up a hand. He put a finger to his lips and mimed shush. The three heard the sound of a key being inserted into a lock, then the front door opening. "Hide!" he hissed.

The three scrambled. "Here!"

Mordant pushed the other two under the folding table, then followed. He pulled boxes in front of the table to cover the hiding place and the three squished together. "Great, just great," Theo whisper-lamented. "My first showing could be my last."

"Wait," Ricki whispered. "We have a legitimate reason to be here. We shouldn't be hiding."

"Too late now," Mordant said, his low voice a rumble.

Footsteps came their way and they froze. Then the steps went off in another direction.

"Let's make a run for it."

Theo started to climb out from under the table. Mordant pulled him back. "We don't know where the person is."

The footsteps came their way again. "I know you're here," a male voice said. "I saw the light on. And didn't see anyone leave. Do yourself a favor and come out of wherever you are. Don't make me come get you."

Theo's eyes widened. His hands flapped. He pinched his nose with one hand, using the other to cover his mouth, and . . . sneezed.

A booted foot kicked boxes out of the way, exposing Ricki, Mordant, and Theo. House sitter and gig worker Tomas stood over them holding a butcher knife. Theo let out a strangled screech. Ricki held up her hands as if under arrest. "Don't hurt us. We're here to see the house."

"Really." Tomas's tone made it clear he didn't buy this. "Then why are you hiding under the table?"

Ricki gave up the pretense. "I'll tell you the truth if you promise not to hurt us."

Tomas lowered the knife. "I'm listening."

"We're trying to help NOPD solve your neighbor's murder because people I love are under suspicion and they didn't do it."

Tomas lowered the knife further. "That's too crazy for you to make up. Come on out."

The three crawled out from under the table and staggered to their feet. Face to face with Tomas, Ricki found him much less threatening. He still had a baby face, which put him in his early twenties. He wasn't much taller than her five-foot-three height and his slight build indicated he probably weighed less than her. He wore his longish medium brown hair in a top knot.

Ricki shook off a few dust bunnies that had attached themselves to her black leggings. "It would make me feel better if you let go of the knife entirely."

Tomas placed the knife on top of a box. "If you're wondering, I didn't kill Phyllis. Not that I didn't want to. But I didn't."

Mordant parked his gangly body on the arm of the sofa. "So, what's your story? Why are you in a dead woman's house? You have a key. But why are you still using it?"

Tomas shrugged. He leaned back against the fireplace mantel. "I guess it doesn't hurt to tell you what I told the police before they confirmed my alibi."

Hearing the word "alibi," Ricki crossed another suspect's name off the list she kept in her head.

"I grocery shopped for Phyllis," he continued. "A lot of time I did it for free because of her fibro thing."

"Fibro?" Ricki repeated, confused. "You mean like fibromyalgia? I thought she had a rare form of Lyme disease."

"She told me the fibro thing."

"Grifter," Mordant muttered.

"We got to talking and Phyllis had the idea of us going into business together. Like, me shopping for people in a more personal way than you get with apps. She said she knew someone who could build me a website and my own app, so I gave her the money."

"And there was no website or app."

"Phyllis said her connection died. She apologized and gave me a ring I could pawn to make up for the money." He scowled. "I don't have to tell you how that went down. When I found out the ring was fake, she swore she didn't know but I didn't buy that for a second. I got mad. I wrote her threats. When the police said she was murdered, I got scared that even with an alibi they'd find a way to nail me. So I've been coming back to see if she kept the letters so I can get rid of them. I haven't found them anywhere, so I guess I lucked out."

"Here." Mordant gave him the threatening note he found. "There are more in the trash bin."

"Oh. Thanks."

Tomas bent down and began going through the trash. Ricki remembered the photo she'd been holding before being forced to hide. She picked it up from where she'd dropped it and showed it to Tomas. "I recognized the man in this picture."

The gig worker checked out the photo. "Sparkle. Man, she loved that cat. I'm surprised she let Mr. Broussard hold him."

Ricki showed the photo of a smiling Art Broussard holding Sparkle to Mordant. They exchanged a knowing look. "From what I've been told, Phyllis got along with the Broussards," she said to Tomas. "Did you ever get the feeling there was more going on between her and Art?"

Before Tomas could answer, Theo, who'd disappeared during the conversation, appeared in the doorway. "Sorry if I missed anything. I took myself on a realtor's tour." Sirens whined nearby. He raised his voice to be heard over them. "This house has great bones. I have some real clients who might be interested—"

The sirens grew to an earsplitting level. Red lights flickered in the windows.

Ricki craned her neck but she couldn't see out the window. "What's going on? Did someone call an ambulance?"

Theo pulled the window curtain aside. He let out a yell. "It's the police!"

TWENTY-EIGHT

"Duck!" Theo hit the ground and combat-crawled back under the folding table.

"No one's shooting at us, Theo," Ricki retorted. Mordant flattened himself against a wall out of the window's eyeline. "Someone may have seen us and called the police."

"Reminder, we're here for a very legitimate house tour," Ricki said, sounding braver than she felt. "But just in case . . ." She flattened herself against the wall next to Mordant.

Tomas crouched down and peeked over the windowsill. "I think we're OK. The police are next door at the Broussards."

"Really?" Intrigued by the unexpected development, Ricki shimmied against the wall and dropped down next to Tomas. She peered over the window's edge. "I see a patrol car. And there's an ambulance, Theo. I wonder what's going on?"

"I'll find out," Tomas said. "I can sneak out the back door and up the side yard between here and the Sachs' house. If you give me your number, I'll text when y'all can come out the same way."

He and Ricki held their phones next to each other to exchange contact information, then Tomas scooted out of the room. Theo whimpered. "How many real estate agents have lost their license the day they got it? I'm guessing one. Me!"

"Please don't worry," Ricki said. "I promise we'll cover for you. We owe you for getting us into the house." She peeked over the windowsill again. "I have a theory, based on the Sparkle picture."

"So do I," Mordant said. "I bet we're thinking the same thing."

"Phyllis and Art were having an affair."

"We are," Mordant said. "I'll go next. Phyllis ended the affair . . ."

"Which is why there's only a one-way ticket to Nicaragua. Paid for in cash . . ."

"So Art wouldn't find out."

"But he did," Ricki said. "And furious, he killed her."

"Which is why the police are here. To arrest him."

"Exactly," Ricki said with a note of self-satisfaction.

"Then why is there an ambulance?" Theo asked from his hiding place.

"Good question," Ricki said, her bubble not burst but at least a bit deflated. Her phone buzzed. She checked it. "We can go find out. Tomas said we're clear."

The three made a stealthy escape through the house and the back door. They plastered themselves against the side of Phyllis's house to ensure no one saw them. "Pretend we're out for a walk," Ricki said to her cohorts.

Theo snorted. "Yeah, that'll work. We're dressed like cat burglars."

"No one will notice if we act casual. Come on." Ricki made a run for it. Mordant and Theo followed.

They reached the sidewalk and slowed to a nonchalant pace. "Hi there," Ricki said to Tomas when they reached him, calling up her minimal acting chops to act like they'd never met. "It's a beautiful night and my friends and I were out for a walk when we saw all this commotion. Is everything OK?"

"Doesn't look like it." Tomas motioned to a coroner's van pulling up behind the ambulance.

Ricki examined the scene more closely. She saw Melissa Sachs comforting a weeping Brenda Broussard while David conferred with a police officer. They separated and the officer headed to the coroner's van.

Ricki hurried to the contractor. "David, hi." She repeated her lie. "My friends and I were out for a walk—"

"You were, huh?"

Ricki ignored his skepticism. "We saw all the commotion at the Broussards. What happened? Are they all right?"

"Afraid not. Art Broussard passed away."

"*He died?*" The unexpected development stunned Ricki. "How?"

"He hasn't been well lately. He had diabetes and it caused a lot of complications."

"I overheard Brenda say something at the party last night about him losing a toe. She was also giving him grief—understandably—for eating things he shouldn't be eating."

"He drank more than he should have at the party, too. I heard the EMTs talking and apparently he forgot he'd given himself a dose of insulin tonight and accidentally gave himself a second one."

"My former boss had diabetes," Ricki said. An unwanted image of Barnes Lachlan came to mind. "Monitoring it incorrectly is dangerous."

"On top of Art's bad diet from last night, it turned out to be lethal."

Melissa gave Ricki a somber nod to acknowledge her, then wrapped a silver emergency blanket around a stunned, shivering Brenda. She led her now-widowed neighbor to David. "I told Brenda she could stay with us tonight," Melissa informed her husband. "It's too traumatic for her to be at her and Art's house."

"Of course," David said.

"I usually gave Art his shots but he wouldn't let me tonight. He was still mad at me from last night." Obviously in shock, Brenda sounded robotic. "He said he was tired of me always nagging him about his diet and could take care of himself. I should have argued more. I shouldn't have given up."

"This isn't on you," Melissa said, comforting her neighbor. "You did everything you could but at the end of the day, Art was gonna do what he was gonna do. Now, let's get you inside. I'll make you a cup of tea."

Melissa gently steered Brenda in the direction of the Sachs' home.

"I better check with the police," David said. "See what happens next."

"You're a good neighbor," Ricki said.

She returned to Mordant, Tomas, and Theo, and filled them in on what she'd learned about Art's cause of death. "She *was* on his case a lot," Tomas said. "I'd hear them from their driveway when they came and went from Art's doctor's appointments." His cell played Bachman Turner Overdrive's "Taking

Care of Business." "I gotta make groceries for a Tulane frat house munchies run. I'll see you around." Tomas left, crossing the street to his house sitting digs.

"Let's go before they bring out the body," Theo said. "That always creeps me out when I see it on the news."

The three started down the street to where Ricki had parked around the corner from Peony Place. "So," Mordant said, "there goes our theory about Art being the murderer."

"I feel terrible after seeing how upset his wife is." A light rain began to fall. Ricki wiped drops off her face. "I guess we're back to Dr. Vernon as the prime suspect. I'll make up a story to get Nina to Phyllis's and show her what we're talking about."

"Keep me out of it," Theo said. "The ink isn't even dry on my real estate license. Metaphorically speaking. It was emailed to me as an attachment. Anyway, I'm done taking risks."

"About that . . ." Ricki gave him a sheepish look. "I have one more teensy favor to ask."

The next morning, Nina snapped on latex gloves and removed a jar of moisturizer from one of the boxes in Phyllis's living room labeled with a Mexican return address. "How did you come across this?" she asked Ricki.

"Theo got his real estate license. I told him I'd be interested in running the estate sale when the time came, so he got me in here to do an inventory."

"Uh-huh."

"Estate sales would be a perfect side hustle for me," Ricki said, feeling defensive. "But, back to these products. I'm sure Dr. Vernon was passing them off as her own Futura line and Phyllis found out about it."

Nina picked up a bottle of cleanser from the folding table. "I believe your theory about Vernon selling under false pretenses may be right."

"And be a motive for murder." Ricki did her best not to sound smug.

"Unfortunately, that's where you hit an investigative roadblock. We've been able to confirm alibis for several members of the Crescent City Concierge team and Dr. Vernon was one of them. She was at a conference in Atlanta. Her stay there covers the window the medical examiner puts as Phyllis's time of death."

"Oh." Ricki didn't bother to mask her disappointment. "Maybe she flew back?" she suggested, hopeful but knowing it was a reach.

"Sorry. If it makes you feel better, we'll be all over her for the skincare scam."

"What about other patients or staff?" Ricki thought of Helene Mansieur. "Or spouses?"

"We're working on it. But we've still got the Bongle Bandit to deal with. There's also the report of a new gang of criminals, right in this neighborhood." Nina opened the photo on her cell phone and called up a picture from a security camera showing three people dressed in head-to-toe black creeping around the side of Phyllis's house: Ricki, Mordant, and Theo.

"Who reported us?" Ricki said, busted.

"A Mrs. Rancourt, who has more security cameras than a Mafia don."

Ricki curled her upper lip. "I hate that woman."

"I've only read the term 'battleax' in books, but she is definitely one come to life. However . . ." Nina fixed a look on Ricki. "If the officers on hand at the Broussards had caught you and your sleuthing buddies, they would have arrested you. And you would have deserved it. A woman was murdered, Ricki. This is dangerous stuff. People like me go through intense investigative training to solve crimes. You have impressive instincts, for sure."

"Thank you," Ricki said, slightly assuaged.

"But you also act before thinking sometimes, which we're trained not to do. I know we've had this conversation before—"

"We had it last night at the party."

"And there's no point in telling you to stop doing what you're doing—"

"I can't," Ricki said tearfully. "You and NOPD are doing the best you can and you're amazing at your job. But you have a caseload of cases to solve and politics on top of that, which put the Bongle Bandit above everything else. Meanwhile, Virgil's show could go under and my parents don't know whether to stay in New Orleans or go. It's crazy-making."

"I get it. I really do. I'll shut up now." Nina texted a message. "The Crime Scene Unit is on its way to pick up the skincare line." Her phone dinged. "Oh, and Sam is back from Domilise's with our po'boys." Nina gestured to the hallway with her hand. "After you."

The women left the house. Ricki got in her car. She saw Nina watching to make sure she drove away. Ricki waved and u-turned to drive away from Peony Place. The minute she was out of sight from Nina, she pulled over and parked. Dr. Vernon might have an alibi but Nina hadn't mentioned someone else connected to Crescent City Concierge Care had one.

Ricki texted Josepha, who was there at work. Can you get me Helene Mansieur's address? I have an idea.

TWENTY-NINE

osepha came through with the Mansieur's address. The next morning, Ricki stopped by Nutmeg on the way to her destination. In addition to its many gift items, it carried a line of elegant invitations for the Big Easy's wide range of fancy events. She found shop owner Guidry and asked, "Do you have a spare invitation? Something I can write on. I only need one."

"Sure. Our supplier always sends samples to entice us into buying a new line. Follow moi."

Guidry led her to the shop's stockroom. He opened a file cabinet and took out a five-by-seven-inch invitation on thick card stock. He handed it to Ricki. "How's this?"

The edges of the ivory invitation were bordered with gold fleur de lis. Calligraphy lettering left space for the hostess to write in the essentials of her event. "Beautiful," Ricki said. "How much is it?"

"Free. We ordered the line, so the supplier owes us."

"Awesome. Can I fill it out here? I need drop it off on my way to Bon Vee."

"Absolutely." Guidry rummaged through a drawer in the stockroom desk and located a black gel pen. "Here you go. I'll leave you to it."

Guidry returned to the shop sales floor. Ricki quickly but carefully filled in the necessary details. She left the stockroom, thanking Guidry on her way out.

"Not a problem. On another subject, did you ever find a gift for Virgil?"

"No, and to be honest," Ricki admitted, "I haven't thought about that in days. I'm a terrible girlfriend."

Guidry dismissed this. "Please. I've met a few of his past girlfriends and chère, you could not be more of a step up in every possible way."

"I'm flattered." *And also a little disturbed,* Ricki thought. *What exactly were the kind of women Virgil used to date?*

She left Nutmeg and drove to the address Josepha had supplied. Shortly after, she pulled up in front of an impressive turn-of-the-twentieth-century Romanesque-style limestone house with a red-tiled roof and limestone columns supporting a copper awning over the front door. Ricki parked on the street in front of the house. She got out of the car and used the sideview mirror to check her outfit. To give the appearance of being a soignée Uptown type—or at least Uptown-adjacent—she'd dressed in her most conservative outfit of a camel-colored 1960s pencil skirt with a saddle brown cardigan over a Peter Pan-collared ivory silk top from the same era. Chunky ankle boots prevented the look from veering into a mid-century caricature.

Ricki tucked a loose curl behind her ear. She took a breath to steady her nerves and proceeded up the path to the front door. She rang the doorbell. After a moment, a woman on the other side of the door said, "Hello?"

Unsure if the speaker was her target, Ricki resorted to the name-dropping guaranteed to open upscale doors. "Hi, I'm Ricki, Eugenia Charbonnet Felice's cousin, and I have an invitation for Helene Mansieur from Eugenia."

"Oh," the woman said, sounding delighted. She opened the door. It was Helene, casually dressed in jeans, white sneakers, and a pink polo shirt. Ricki suddenly felt ridiculous in her cosplay outfit. "Hi, Ricki. We met at my husband's office. And I saw you at the party the other night, although we never got to talk. Come in."

Ricki followed Helene into the room's two-story foyer. Ricki marveled at the ornate glass dome shedding light from above. "Wow. Gorgeous."

"Isn't it? It's why we bought the house. Can I get you a cup of tea? A sweet tea? A lemonade?"

"A lemonade would be nice. Thank you."

Helene deposited Ricki in the home's living room, which with its mix of beiges, creams, traditional, and antique furnishings, brought to mind every other tasteful New Orleans living

room she'd ever been in. From her viewpoint on the room's
bouclé-upholstered rolled-arm sofa, she swiveled to explore the
room. She did a double-take at the painting above the fireplace.
A nude woman closely resembling Helene reclined on what
appeared to be the exact couch where Ricki sat.

"Here we go."

Ricki whipped around as her hostess came into the room
and set down a tray with a plate of cookies, a pitcher, and two
glasses of lemonade on the cocktail ottoman, upholstered in
creamy leather. Helene took a seat opposite Ricki. Positioned
under the portrait, the resemblance was unmistakable.

Helene reached for a glass of lemonade. Ricki did the same.
"This is delicious," Ricki said after a sip. "It tastes homemade."

"It is. We have a tree in the backyard and more lemons than
what I know what to do with. I'll send you home with a bag
of them. So, tell me about this party. Is it a fundraiser? I can
donate right now."

Ricki plunged ahead. Her goal was to shock Helene with
the realization that Ricki—and others—knew her true identity.
"I'd like to invite you to a tea party for my mother, who's in
town for the holidays. She worked at Charity Hospital and
apparently you have a connection to it too. My landlady Kitty
Kat Rousseau recognized you at Olivia's party. She's the nurse
who treated your hand at Charity Hospital."

She watched for Helene's reaction . . . which turned out to
be the exact opposite of what she expected. To Ricki's amaze-
ment, Helene burst out laughing. "She is? Oh my goodness,
that is *hilarious*." She held up her left hand to show Ricki the
scar on the side of it. "Did she tell you how this happened?"

"No," Ricki lied.

"It's a wild story. You might want a hard lemonade."

I wish I had one now, Ricki thought as the plot she felt so
sure of upended.

Helene leaned back against her chair, completely at ease, as
opposed to Ricki, who was doing everything in her power not
to hide how mortified she felt. "I won't go into details but there
was a period in my life where I worked as a paid escort. I mostly

did exactly that—escorted men to various events where they needed a date. Sometimes with closeted gay men, poor guys, I served as a beard. Occasionally, the line blurred and the relationship became . . . frisky." Helene winked. "Like it did with Damian Arvois at Charity. He was single at the time, so we fell into a brief, casual relationship. He dared me to get romantic in an operating room and I took him up on it." She chuckled at the memory, to Ricki's acute discomfort. "I brought a candle for mood lighting, but when I lit it, it set off an alarm and I burned my hand rushing to put it out before security came down on us."

"I promise I won't tell anyone about your past," Ricki blurted, suddenly paranoid Helene might think she'd revealed too much.

"Aw, chère, that's so sweet but don't worry, I'm upfront about it myself." She gestured to the portrait above her. "I kinda have to be when this is front and center, huh? Jeremy had it commissioned as a sixtieth birthday present to himself. We met when he came into the menswear shop I'd saved enough money to open on Magazine Street. We got to talking, then dating, then married. He knows all about my 'past,' as you put it, and doesn't give a rat's backside about it. I'm his third wife. His kids are grown and flown. Two sons. One's in Atlanta, the other's in Chicago."

"I'm so glad Dr. Mansieur supports you," Ricki said. Instead of considering Helene a murder suspect, Ricki found herself rooting for her. "I hope none of his patients have an issue with your past . . . work."

"If they do, we haven't heard about it. Crescent City Concierge is a one-of-a-kind medical practice. Patients who want to remain patients have a vested interest in keeping their opinions to themselves or risk getting booted from the practice and . . ." Helene mimed a horrified expression, ". . . having to go to a *regular* doctor."

She shuddered theatrically, earning a laugh from Ricki. "There is someone who could have tried to use it against you," Ricki said, taking a final stab at connecting Helene's past to the present. "Phyllis Gibbs. She worked at Charity when you had your . . . accident."

"That scam artist," Helene said with a sneer. "She nosed around but I shut her down. I didn't trust her for a minute. Between us, Jeremy was on the verge of firing her." Her expression darkened. "But someone had a much bigger problem with her than we did, didn't they? You could say a 'killer' of a problem."

"I guess so." Ricki swallowed a gulp of lemonade. A chunk of lemon irritated her throat and she coughed.

"Your glass is almost empty." Helene refilled it. "Enough about me. The tea party sounds lovely. I'd love to see the nurse who treated my hand again. I'll never forget how kind she was. And it would be nice to socialize with 'average' people." Helene mocked the word "average" with air quotes. "I can't tell you how boring it is to clink champagne glasses with snobs I wouldn't say boo to if I didn't have to for Jeremy's sake. When is the tea party?"

"All the information is here." Ricki took out the fake invitation she'd made and gave it to Helene.

"Thanks." The doctor's wife read the invitation. "I'm free on Wednesday. Consider this my RSVP."

Ricki finished her drink and Helene sent her off with a grocery bag full of lemons. She'd just finished buckling her seat belt when Josepha called. "I'm dying to know, how did it go with Helene?"

"I doubt she murdered Phyllis," Ricki said, "I have a ridiculous amount of lemons. And we're having a tea party."

THIRTY

When Ricki got to Miss Vee's, the shop glowed with holiday lights and the tree twinkled with tinsel from the 1960s Ricki had bought at an estate sale. Rosemary Clooney crooned classic tunes through a Bluetooth speaker. None of this dispelled the gloom emanating from Olivia, who'd opened the shop for her cousin.

Ricki deposited her grocery bag on top of the shop desk. "I'd offer you lemons but you're already in a sour mood."

"Not funny," a glum Olivia responded.

"You're right. I'm sorry. It's not the time for dumb jokes. Have you talked to Lizette?"

"No."

Olivia's brusque tone sent the message not to push her. Ricki changed the subject. "I do have to unload at least half this bag, so it's a free lemon with each purchase for the first however many customers."

She went to a shelf marked "Entertaining" and removed two cookbooks dedicated to tea parties. Now that the fake event had become a reality, Ricki found herself looking forward to it. "I'm hosting a Ladies Only tea party on Wednesday," she said to Olivia. "Want to come?"

"I'm not in the mood to socialize, especially with a bunch of old ladies."

"I'm not even thirty yet, so ouch. Chalking it off to your bad mood." She handed Olivia one of the books. "Get your mind off your troubles by flagging every lemon recipe in the book."

Olivia grunted an unenthusiastic response but turned to the index and began locating said recipes. She had her head down, so she didn't see Lizette enter the shop. But Ricki did. She cleared her throat and Olivia looked up. She froze when she saw her friend.

"You ghosted me," Lizette said, sounding more plaintive than accusatory.

"When you find out your best friend stabbed you in the back, you kinda have to," Olivia said, her tone ice-cold. "I'm not a fan of toxic relationships."

"Livs, I swear I had no idea I was next up for queen. I mean, come on. Look at me." Lizette held out her arms like she was being frisked. She was dressed in black from her combat boots to half her hair, which was dyed fifty percent pitch-black and fifty percent platinum blonde. She'd even traded her nose piercing for a black stud. "Does this look like a person who wants to wear a rhinestone crown? I'm still in shock I'm on the court at all. I blame my gran, who I'm sure scared the guys on the krewe into including me."

"Having met her grandmother Mrs. Rancourt, I can believe this," Ricki said to Olivia.

Lizette pulled her cell phone from her leggings pocket. "I wrote an email telling the krewe I'm quitting the court. I wanted to check with you before I sent it."

"You don't have to," Olivia said, thawing. "If you want to be queen, go for it. As long as we stay BFFs."

She ran from behind the desk and hugged her friend. Lizette held up her phone. "Email sent."

"I don't want to be on the court without you. I'm quitting too." Olivia darted back to the shop desk and grabbed her own phone.

"I texted the other girls we're quitting," Lizette said.

"I got the text. Just emailed my resignation." Both girls' phones dinged multiple time. They scanned them. "The rest of the court wants to quit too," Olivia said.

"Yaas." Lizette raised a fist. "Girl power!"

Olivia held up a fist in solidarity. "Whoo-hoo!"

"Haven't your parents already ordered your court dresses?" Ricki asked.

The girls dropped their arms. "Oh. Right." Olivia pondered this. Then her face lit up. "I know. We'll do our own krewe. The Krewe of BFFs."

"Awww . . ."

Lizette and Olivia hugged again. Ricki returned to thumbing through cookbooks for tea party recipes while the girls chattered away about their new krewe. Ricki let them enjoy the moment, knowing their euphoria would be short-lived once the parents and krewe adults got involved.

Having put a date on the fake tea party invitation she'd given Helene, Ricki was stuck with it. Josepha arranged to have Wednesday afternoon off. Fortunately, Kitty Kat was between hospice patients, so she was available. Eugenia would also be attending. Now that Helene was deemed an improbable murder suspect, the Bon Vee board president decided to put her muscle behind turning the doctor's wife into a museum donor. Her enthusiasm for the party proved a big help to Ricki. Eugenia closed off the mansion conservatory to tours for the morning and arranged for one of her posh eatery connections to cater the tea with recipes culled from Ricki's cookbooks.

Ricki decided to check in with Nina on the off chance there were developments in the search for Phyllis's killer. She didn't get a response to her text and guessed why when she received an alert from OhNo!La that the Bongle Bandit had struck again, this time at the Gucci store in the French Quarter. The reminder of the bandit triggered the hint of a memory for Ricki but it disappeared before she could recall it.

The day of the tea party coincided with the last morning of filming for Virgil's show, *Réveillon: A Delicious Dining Tradition*. Ricki closed Miss Vee's early to join the impromptu party in the Bon Vee kitchen. She arrived at the exact moment director Patrick announced, "Cut! That's a wrap," to applause from the small show crew. Luis clapped loudest of all. Ricki sidled up to her father, who said in a low voice, "I'm grateful for the job and Virgil's the best, but I'm not sorry it's over. I won't have to deal with Patrick anymore."

"I thought he got better," Ricki said.

Luis responded with a skeptical expression. "I'll be having a 'Come to Jesus' talk with that young man." He furrowed his brow in a frown. "If he wants a career in this business, he'd be wise to listen."

Luis joined his fellow crew members, who were pouring champagne gifted to them by Virgil. Ricki went to the chef. "Congratulations," she said, kissing him on the cheek. "You look happier and more relaxed than you have since—"

"This whole dang thing started." Virgil finished her sentence and gave her an impish grin. "Relaxed, relieved . . . and yes, even excited. The editor in L.A. is happy. He already cut promos for Food Plus, which are airing on their most popular shows. Patrick ended up doing a decent job. Thanks to your father."

"Really?" Ricki's gaze wandered over to her father. She recognized his favorite playlist coming out of his portable Bluetooth speaker and watched with affection as he attempted to teach one of the young production assistants how to salsa.

"Luis made sure we had all the coverage we needed," Virgil said. "Some of it he did on the down-low so Patrick's ego wasn't bruised. I owe him."

"No you don't. That's my dad." Ricki was filled with pride for him. "The man who gives a thousand percent. Even if he has to do it 'on the down-low.'"

Someone clinked a glass with a utensil, setting off a chain reaction. "Attention, everyone," Patrick called to the crew. Everyone silenced. "Um . . ." he glanced down at the floor, then raised his head. "I know I've been a little tough to deal with on this shoot."

"A little?"

The blurt from one of the production assistants got a big laugh. Even Patrick chuckled. "I want to thank everyone for being so patient with me on my first big gig," he said to the crew. "I hope it's the first of many times we get to work together. A toast to a great crew . . ." He raised his glass in Virgil's direction. "And a great leader."

Everyone cheered. Virgil raised his glass in return. "Thanks. Seconding everything Patrick said about y'all and adding one more shout-out." He turned to Luis. "To the best dang camera operator in the business: Luis James-Diaz!" He let out a whoop that the whole crew echoed . . . even Patrick. Luis's bronze skin shaded red with embarrassment but his daughter could tell he was proud to be acknowledged.

Theo stuck his head in the doorway. "Can I join the party?" He smiled and puffed out his chest. "I've got something to celebrate too. I scored my first listing as a real-estate agent. Just signed the contract."

"Theo, that's fantastic," Ricki said, happy for her cousin.

"Great news. Definitely come join the celebration."

Virgil motioned to him. Theo came in and the men fist bumped.

"So, what's the listing?" Ricki asked.

"Brenda Broussard. Poor woman just lost her husband and she can't face being in the house without him."

"That's so sad," Ricki said.

"But it's also a testament to the power of their love."

Virgil delivered this with meaning, his eyes on Ricki with an expression that made her heart flutter. *I have got to come up with a decent Christmas present for this man!*

Ricki left the celebrants and started for the conservatory and the tea party. By the time she arrived, the guests were already there, along with Cookie and Zellah, who hovered over a small brown box on a café table not set for dining. "We've been waiting for you," Cookie said with a broad smile.

"What's going on?" Ricki asked.

"We're doing what authors call an unboxing," Zellah said. "Of ARCs for our community cookbook."

"ARCs?" Josepha repeated, puzzled.

"It stands for Advanced Reader Copies," Ricki explained to her mother and the other guests, channeling her past as a rare book specialist. "They're uncorrected versions of a book that publishers send out in advance to press outlets for early reviews."

"Exactly." Former children's librarian Cookie gave an approving nod. "Eugenia OK'd us making twenty-five ARCs. There are copies for each of us to proof, copies to send to local media outlets and influencers—"

"And we gift each of our special guests with a rare advance copy of what I know will be a big seller at Miss Vee's Vintage Cookbook and Kitchenware Shop in the new year," Eugenia explained. She indicated Helene with a bow of her head.

"Eugenia, you don't have to fawn all over me," Helene said, laughing. "I'd love to donate to Bon Vee and help it grow, so chill."

Eugenia released a sigh of relief. "As Ricki would say, awesome. Now, let's crack open that box."

Cookie filmed with her phone as Zellah used a box-cutter to open the box. She pushed aside the flaps and extracted a copy of *New Year, New Recipes from Bon Vee: A Culinary House Museum Cookbook*. The golden spiral binding of the culinary house museum's first cookbook sparkled and the cover featured an exquisite pen-and-ink rendering by Zellah of the Bon Vee façade. A sticker on the cover marked it as an "Advanced Reader Edition."

Zellah handed the cookbook to Ricki, who caught her breath at the result of her inspiration. "It's gorgeous."

The other women echoed agreement.

Ricki carefully placed her copy at a place setting on the table set for tea. She went to the box and gently removed six copies. "A complimentary copy for each of you." She passed out the cookbooks.

"Thank you, chère." Kitty Kat caressed the cover of her copy. "It's truly a thing of beauty."

Josepha clutched her copy to her chest. Her eyes shone. "I'm so proud of you."

"It was the definition of a group effort." Ricki placed an affectionate arm around each of her friends. "I couldn't have done it without these two or Eugenia or Theo, who'd be here but he's celebrating his first listing. Brenda Broussard signed him as the agent for her house. She's too bereft about her husband's death to live there anymore."

"Yay Theo, yay to all of us," Cookie said. "Let's eat. I'm starving."

Zellah gave her the side eye. "You're always starving."

Cookie shrugged. "Blame the city. Too much good food." She took in the buffet. "Crawfish mini quiche? *Yum*."

The women filled plates with sandwiches and assorted savories, then sat down. Pots of tea were passed and cups topped off. Helene opted for a sweet tea. Her phone alerted her to a text. She read it, then said, "Josepha, when you go to Crescent Care tomorrow, it's going to be an extremely busy day. The partners just let Dr. Vernon go."

Ricki almost choked on her mini quiche. Josepha maintained her cool. "They did?" she asked, all innocence. "Why?"

"She was selling a product line under false pretenses. Fraud. She's facing possible criminal charges for it. You're lucky you're not at the practice today. The staff is alerting all her patients. But the partners are bringing in a dermatologist who graduated first in her class at Tulane Medical. They lured her away from a concierge practice in Dallas. She starts tomorrow."

"Such a surprise about Dr. Vernon," Josepha said. "I never would have guessed." She popped a cucumber sandwich into her mouth as Ricki managed not to do a spit take.

"I know. A total shock to the other doctors. Oh, thank you." Helene flashed a smile to Eugenia, who had refilled her tea glass. "By the way, they're extremely grateful to you for filling in at the practice. They rave about you."

"That's lovely to hear. Although from what I hear through the office grapevine, the bar may have been set medium to low by the poor woman who came before me. The one who was murdered. Phyllis something."

Ricki's mouth, full of a caramel petits fours, dropped open. She snapped it shut. *Brava, mama*, she thought, impressed by how offhanded Josepha made the fraught subject sound

Helene nodded vigorously. "*So* much to unpack there. You just reminded me of something. Ricki, you mentioned Brenda Broussard. She and her husband Art were Jeremy's patients." She hesitated. "I don't know if I should say anything else. I wouldn't want to violate the Hippocratic oath."

"Only applies to doctors, not their wives, so you're in the clear." Cookie had no idea if this was true but she loved all gossip. "Go on."

"To be honest, I was surprised to hear Brenda was bereft about Art's death. I don't think they were getting along very well recently. If at all. Jeremy got me a new car, an EV. All electric. I'd only had it a few days and was in the VIP parking lot waiting to pick him up for dinner. I was playing around with the car—you know, shiny new toy and all that—when Brenda Broussard zoomed into the parking lot. She got out of her car and started pacing back and forth, stomping around, furious." Helene made an angry face. She formed her hands into fists and stomped up and down with her legs to illustrate Brenda's state. "Phyllis, the woman you've replaced, came out and Brenda just lit into her." Helene jumped to her feet and began acting out the scene. "'You SOB, you're having an affair with my husband! Don't you dare deny it! I thought something was going on between you two and I got into his phone. I saw the filthy, disgusting texts!'"

"Whoa, you're good," Cookie said, rapt. "Did you ever act?"

"Minored in Theatre in college." Pleased with herself, Helene sat down.

Ricki's heart raced. "When was this?" she asked in as nonchalant a tone as she could muster.

"Let me think. Hmm . . . About a month or two ago? Phyllis died a few weeks later." What she was implying dawned on her. "Oh no. Oh no. Do you think Brenda killed her? Oh no. I should have told the police what I saw. I didn't put it together until now. But I saw Brenda and Art at your granddaughter's party and they seemed fine. Like your average couple. If they'd been acting tense or hostile I would have remembered the confrontation and called the police."

"You did nothing wrong," Eugenia assured her, backed up by the other women. "Ricki's friends with the detective on the case—"

"Again, not sure if 'friends' is the right word," Ricki said as she quickly typed a message on her phone.

"Whatever you want to call it, you have a relationship with Nina and should let her know about this."

Ricki held up her cell phone. "I just did." She held up her teacup as if to toast. "Ladies, I think we just solved the murder of Phyllis Gibbs."

THIRTY-ONE

The room buzzed while the women waited for Nina's response. "I can't wait for some of Jeremy's stuck-up patients to learn I took one of them down." Helene flashed a devilish grin and rubbed her hands together in anticipation.

The mood changed when Nina finally responded. Thx. Will bring her in for questioning.

"That's it?" Eugenia grumbled. "How disappointing. Remind me not to put her on any more of my guest lists."

"There's not much more she can do," Ricki said, realizing she'd simply sent Nina more speculation. "We have one murder on our minds. NOPD has a long list of them, plus other crimes—especially the Bongle Bandit. I'll give her a couple of days and then follow up. In the meantime, let's enjoy our party."

Conversation resumed on a more superfluous level. It took a herculean effort on Ricki's part to stay engaged as Brenda's prime suspect status cemented in her mind. *The jilted spouse is so on point*, she thought while absent-mindedly agreeing with the others that the Roosevelt Hotel's holiday light display ranked on par with the ones at the White House.

The tea party ended a success, with Helene welcomed to the Bon Vee executive board and a promise of another get-together before the holidays ended and Josepha returned to Puerto Vallarta. Everyone except Ricki seemed to forget about Brenda and the most significant moment of the party. But with nothing to do except wait for an update from Nina, she joined the exchange of goodbyes before hurrying off to open Miss Vee's for the last tours of the day.

Chatting with customers and helping them fill their Miss Vee tote bags with holiday gifts provided a refreshing distraction for Ricki. She even got into the holiday spirit, joining an impromptu chorus of "Deck the Halls" prompted by an a cappella group of high-school students seeking gifts for their moms. She took down their contact information as a much more pleasant alternative to the competitive and creepy carolers fired by Eugenia.

Ricki was locking up for the night when Zellah texted an invitation to stop by the café and help herself to leftovers. With her empty refrigerator in mind, Ricki took her friend up on the offer. She was deciding between a roast beef and turkey-cheddar po'boy when Theo hurried over. "You mind if I grab the roast beef?" he asked, hastily shoving it into his briefcase, along with a pecan bar.

"Too late for me to say no," Ricki responded dryly, reaching for the remaining po'boy.

"Sorry. I have an emergency meeting with my new client. She's flying out tomorrow and is leaving the house sale in my hands. I have a lot to do before she goes."

Ricki stopped midair. "Wait, what? Are you talking about Brenda Broussard?"

"Yup." Theo added a bag of Zapp's Voodoo Potato Chips to his haul, oblivious to the concerned look Ricki and Zellah exchanged.

"Where is she going?" Ricki asked.

"Somewhere in Central America. Nicaragua, maybe? Didn't have time to get the deets. Gotta go. See you tomorrow." Theo jogged off.

"Nina has to do something," Ricki said, typing like mad on her cell phone as she spoke. "The U.S. doesn't have an extradition with Nicaragua."

"I wouldn't put money on her getting back to you fast. I just got an alert from OhNo!La. 'Bongle Bandit Burgles Buddy's Toys.'"

Ricki released a string of frustrated profanities. "Great. Another tongue-twisting robbery from New Orleans' most wanted criminal." She leaned over the counter to watch the video alert on Zellah's phone. A reporter for a local TV station held a microphone up to an infuriated woman holding the hand of a young boy in front of the popular shop. "What kind of monster robs a toy store at the holidays?" the woman vented.

"And dressed like a character I grew up with. I still have my Mr. Bongle plushie. I was gonna give him to my son Dylan." The boy at her side tried to look sad but it was obvious he was getting a kick out of being on camera. "But how can I do that now? It's outrageous. And NOPD isn't doing a thing about it." She scowled at the camera. "Shame on the police. Shame, shame, shame." The video went on to show not only the NOPD police chief but also the mayor, jointly vowing to throw everything in the city's arsenal at catching the reviled cartoon criminal.

The video ended. "By the time this resolves, Brenda Broussard will be on a beach in Nicaragua with a mojito in each hand," Ricki said, feeling a mixture of glum and despair.

"Mojitos are Cuban, but I get your point."

"No." Ricki slammed a fist on the café counter. "Ow." She rubbed her hand.

"Yeah, that's gonna hurt."

Ricki jumped off the counter stool. "Text Mordant to meet me at Brenda Broussard's house. I have a plan."

When Ricki got to Peony Place, she spied Mordant running toward her from the opposite direction. He reached her as she got out of the car. "I have the hearse today, so I had to park on another street," he said, panting. "I tried to tone down my costume so I look like a potential homebuyer."

Ricki gave his outfit of black high-waisted pants, white button-down shirt, and hobnail boots a once-over. "You look like a waiter at old-timey themed restaurant but it's better than an undertaker, so we'll go with it."

"Does Theo know we're coming?"

Ricki showed Mordant the screen of her phone, which was plastered with angry emojis and the words NO! FORGET IT! followed by a countless number of exclamation marks. "He does."

The two quickly walked up the path to the Broussard's redbrick Georgian colonial. Ricki rang the doorbell. An infuriated Theo yanked open the door. Ricki responded with open arms and a big smile. "Theo, hi! Thanks so much for arranging a showing at the last minute."

"If you screw this up for me, the next murder will be yours," he hissed as she and Mordant blew past him into the hallway.

"I already love this house," Ricki said loudly. She said to Theo in a much lower voice, "Where's Brenda?"

"All over the place," he whispered back. "She's packing. Making sure she's got everything she wants or needs to take with her."

"Noted." She turned to Mordant. "Honey, we have to keep the tour brief. Why don't you take a look upstairs and I'll check out the layout on this floor?"

"Sounds good . . . honey." Mordant was already halfway up the stairs thanks to his long legs.

With Theo on her heels, Ricki strolled through the living room and study to the right of the front door. French doors opened to a flagstone patio. She stepped outside and studied the garden . . . which featured a colorful profusion of delphinium and larkspur. She glanced around to make sure no one saw her and snapped a few photos.

She re-entered the house, passing through a first-floor bedroom and then the dining room to the living room. As opposed to Phyllis's clutter, the Broussard's home was almost obsessively neat. The knick-knack count was low, with photos and a spare amount of them arranged purposefully. The home's splashes of color came from the one design touch there was plenty of: needlepoint. Couches sprouted multiple finely stitched pillows while framed canvases decorated the walls of every room, including the center hall.

She visited the kitchen next. Her pulse jumped up when she saw Brenda pulling items out of the freezer. She greeted the homeowner with her friendliest smile. "Brenda, hi. We met at my cousin Eugenia's party the other night."

Brenda glanced at Ricki, then returned to her task. "Yes, I remember." Devoid of makeup, dressed in jeans and a T-shirt with her color-treated hair held back by a plastic headband, she looked younger than Ricki remembered but tense. Even though she was working through whatever was in the freezer, sweat dripped down her forehead.

"My fiancé and I are house-hunting." Ricki blithely shared

the lie that now came naturally to her. "When I heard Theo was the agent on your house, we begged him to be the first buyers to see it."

"They did, they really did," Theo, who had popped up behind her, said too emphatically.

Ricki shot him a warning glance, then continued. "Your garden is gorgeous. I love all the delphinium and larkspur."

"The garden was Art's baby. I wouldn't know a larkspur from a lark."

"Oh." The casual and sincere response wasn't what Ricki expected. She gestured to the trash can Brenda had filled with frozen breads and muffins. "But you must have been the family baker."

"That was Art's thing too. He made all of this junk."

Ricki's eyes widened at this second unexpected development. "Really? He did all the family baking?"

"Some people love baking, some love cooking. I'm more of a cook, although my main hobby is needlepoint. Since Art enjoyed baking, we balanced each other out in the kitchen."

"Nice." Ricki did her best to appear nonchalant as she checked out the plastic-wrapped loaves and muffins in the trash can. "These look delicious. Are any of them zucchini bread? It's my favorite."

"No. Doesn't matter. They're only good for the garbage now."

Brenda lifted the trash can and carried it out the side door. Theo made wild gestures to Ricki indicating she should hurry and wrap things up. He instantly dropped his arms when Brenda came back inside. "So, Ricki, great house, huh? Why don't you and Mordant go home and think about it?" Theo asked this in a stiff tone that was testament to his lack of acting talent.

"I haven't seen the whole place yet," Ricki said with a benign expression. Theo clenched his teeth.

"The refrigerator is empty," Brenda said to Theo. "I'm going to finish packing."

She left the kitchen. Theo craned his neck to make sure she was gone, then mouthed to Ricki, "Hurry!"

Ricki gave a quick nod, then yanked open the side door and

scurried outside to the garbage can where Brenda had deposited the frozen baked goods. She reached into the can and pulled out the one frozen loaf wrapped in tin foil and not plastic wrap. She opened the flashlight app and held it up to the loaf, half of which was missing. The light illuminated flecks of green. "Zucchini," Ricki murmured. She hadn't intuited Brenda was lying when the widow said she preferred cooking to baking. Meaning if Art was responsible for the zucchini bread, he was also guilty for Phyllis's murder.

She turned off the flashlight and activated voice texting. "Nina, it's Ricki." She spoke in a low, urgent voice. "I'm at the Broussards on Peony Place. Brenda Broussard didn't kill Phyllis, her husband Art did. I have half a loaf of zucchini bread that may prove it. I'm sure they were having an affair that went off the rails. We need to meet."

The voice text finished, Ricki stuck the phone in her leggings pocket and returned to the kitchen with the zucchini loaf surreptitiously tucked under her arm. She zipped through the kitchen to the center hall and called to the others. "Theo? Mordant? I'm done. I'm ready to leave." Neither responded. "Guys? Hello?" Mordant finally appeared in the door frame separating the living room from the center hall. "Oh, good. Where's Theo? He's not with you?"

"He is not," Brenda's voice came from behind Mordant. She peeked out from behind his back.

Ricki sensed something was very wrong and fought to remain calm. "I've got an early day tomorrow so Mordant and I need to get going. I love your house but we'd need to update the kitchen and bathrooms, which puts it out of our price range. But I'm sure it will sell fast. Best of luck in your new life." She cupped her hand toward Mordant. "Come, sweetie."

"Oh, how I wish I could," Mordant, extra doleful, said.

He took a step forward, nudged by Brenda. As the two moved into the entry hall, Ricki saw that Brenda held a gun to a needlepoint pillow against Mordant's back.

"I caught your fiancé, if that's what he is, which I doubt, poking around my late husband's diabetes equipment in our bathroom medicine cabinet," Brenda said.

Ricki flashed on the night of Art's death. The theory being expounded was that the dentist had accidentally given himself a second dose of insulin, which proved fatal. Hearing this had bothered her but she couldn't put her finger on why. Now she knew. She thought of her former boss, Barnes Lachlan. Even when his life and career were blowing up and the Feds were descending on him, he never missed a beat of monitoring his disease. She couldn't imagine him making a deadly mistake with his treatment. And she doubted Art Broussard did either.

She forced herself to focus on the current dire situation. "Mordant, honey, I told you not to do that," she scolded with fake annoyance. "I'm so sorry, Brenda. He's very nosy. It's a problem in our relationship. He didn't mean anything by it."

"He tried the same lie on me," Brenda said. "I didn't believe it from him either."

Ricki's heart pounded as she desperately ran through possible ways to de-escalate the situation. "Brenda, I know you didn't kill Phyllis. You definitely don't need the gun."

"I disagree."

"I'd hate to see you ruin the pillow," Ricki said, flailing. "It's stunning. You must have put so much work into it."

"I have plenty more. This one was never my favorite. It'll do a nice job muffling the sound if I have to shoot."

"You said 'if.' That's promising."

"Why couldn't you leave me alone?" Brenda sounded plaintive. "All I want to do is get out of this country and start a new life."

"At the moment, that sounds really appealing to me," Mordant said.

"Shut up." Anger supplanted Brenda's other emotions. "I never wanted to kill anyone else. But if I let you go, you'll turn me in."

Ricki banked the "anyone else" for a future conversation with Nina, if she and Mordant managed to make it out of Peony Place alive. "I have a better idea. Why don't you lock us up somewhere? I'm assuming that's what you did with Theo."

"He's in our bedroom closet. I could put you in with him. Or the basement."

The split second Brenda took to debate the options gave Ricki the opportunity she needed to distract her. "The police!" she yelled, pointing to a window behind Brenda.

Mordant's captor instinctively turned her head. Ricki threw the frozen loaf at her. Unfortunately, it hit Brenda's shoulder and not her arm but struck with enough force to elicit a yowl of pain. Brenda reached to it with the hand holding the gun. The pillow dropped. Mordant grabbed Ricki's hand and they bolted out the front door.

"Help!"

Ricki continued screaming. The Sachs' front door flew open and David ran outside. Tomas, who'd just pulled into the driveway, leaped out of his car. Brenda burst out of her house and began shooting wildly. Everyone hit the ground. A bullet shot through Renate Rancourt's living-room window.

A roar came from inside the Broussard house. Theo stormed out clutching one of Brenda's framed needlepoint canvases. Fueled by fury, he brought it down on Brenda's head. Shattered glass flew in all directions as she slumped to the ground.

Theo grabbed the gun she'd dropped and trained it on her. "First thing I'm telling whoever buys this place," he said, panting from exertion and the adrenalin rush, "is to change out all the old hardware on the closet doors. It doesn't hold at all."

The others slowly rose to their feet. An unmarked police car turned onto Peony Place and drove down the street until it parked in front of the Broussards. Sam and Nina got out. Nina surveyed the scene. "Well . . . this is a thing."

Across the street, the Rancourt front door opened. Renate Rancourt appeared on the threshold in her wheelchair. She shook a fist at the tableau on the Broussard lawn. "Whoever put a bullet through my front window, you're paying for it!"

THIRTY-TWO

It took local news crews mere minutes to crowd Peony Place with their vans. Nina forbade Ricki, Mordant, and Theo from talking to the press until after she and Sam interviewed them, so the reporters hit up the street's residents for interviews. The trio still wound up on camera due to being referenced as crime-stopping heroes by Tomas and the Sachs, among other interviewees. This resulted in a slew of WTF?! texts from the Bon Vee Three's friends who'd received push alerts about the police action from a variety of sources. They promised to meet with everyone at the Bayou Backyard post-debrief at NOPD's Sixth Division.

By the time Ricki, Mordant, and Theo reached the BB it was nine o'clock, and from the looks of things the gang had already been partying a while. A waitress was piling dirty plates onto a tray while Ky delivered a fresh batch of drink pitchers. "One pitcher's Pimm's Cup, just for you," he told Ricki. "I thought you'd prefer your favorite cocktail to white wine tonight."

"Thanks," she said, touched he remembered her favorite drink. "After tonight, I may call dibs on the whole pitcher."

"I'll bring another one as insurance," Ky said with a laugh. "I'll bring out another platter of appetizers, too."

"Awesome. I haven't eaten since lunch."

Ricki squeezed into a spot between Virgil and Olivia, who had finally turned twenty-one in late October. Lizette sat on the other side of her friend. Virgil poured her a drink. She gratefully accepted it, along with the hand he placed on her thigh. "This has been a night," she said. "I'm not kidding when I say I was so scared I thought I'd pass out."

"And you weren't supposedly locked in a closet," Theo said, pouring himself a mug of beer.

"And didn't have a gun stuck in your back," Mordant pointed out.

"Poor baby." Zellah gave his back a soothing rub.

"Right now I'm feeling like it was worth it," Mordant said with a dreamy expression as she rubbed.

"Long night, you almost died, we get it, now spill," an impatient Cookie barked from the other side of the table.

"I want to wait until my parents get here. I texted them but haven't heard back." She checked her phone. "Still nothing. I'll wait a little longer."

"No!" her friends chorused.

"Whoa." Ricki held up her hands in a gesture of surrender. "Fine, I'll catch them up later." She took a sip of her drink, then began. "I've learned not to be amazed by what people will say without a lawyer present." She shook her head, bemused. "Brenda was blabbering away trying to defend herself while Nina was putting her in handcuffs. Brenda knew Art and Phyllis were having an affair but I think her marriage had become one of convenience, so she didn't care at first. Her attitude changed when she found out they were going to use the money raised for Phyllis's supposed Lyme disease to run off together to Nicaragua. She was so angry she might have killed one or both of them, except . . ."

Mordant picked up the story. "Phyllis decided to take off without Art. His illness got worse as he got older and she didn't want to end up being a nurse *and* a purse. According to Brenda, he went ballistic and confronted Phyllis when he got wise to what she was up to. He threatened to reveal her fake health scam and she retaliated by threatening to take him down with her. He pretended to back off and make peace with a loaf of her favorite zucchini bread. Which was laced with enough plant poison to knock her off."

Zellah furrowed her brow. "Something doesn't make sense to me. If this Arthur Broussard murdered Phyllis, why did his wife go nuts and try to shoot y'all?"

"Because Art's death wasn't an accident," Ricki said. "She gave him the fatal insulin overdose."

"When she caught me checking out the medicine cabinet, she got scared I suspected her," Mordant said. "Which I did. But I should have been more careful. Noted for the future."

"But why did she kill him?" Zellah wondered. "Was she mad he was going to run away on her? Panicked because he'd murdered Phyllis?"

"According to Brenda, Art had set her up to take the fall if the police figured out the poisonous plants came from their yard." Ricki's explanation met with a sea of perplexed faces. "I found the killer loaf in the garbage after Brenda cleaned out her freezer. Art had saved it. He was old-timey sexist and thought that if the police came calling they would buy Brenda as the jealous, vengeful baker sooner than they'd buy a man who liked to garden and bake. Brenda still insists Art's death was an accident, by the way. But the police don't buy it. The police think she got to him before he could get to her. They found syringes in the trash and Nina's sure Brenda's prints will be on the most recent one used."

Cookie shuddered. "When I win the lottery, remind me not to spend it on a house on Peony Place."

Theo poured himself a second beer. "I'd say I hope other buyers don't feel the same way but it's not my problem. Needless to say, I'm not Brenda's listing agent anymore."

"I'm sorry, Theo." Ricki felt bad for costing him his first listing. "But between Phyllis, the Broussards, and Mrs. Rancourt, I don't think it's the most pleasant street to live on." Remembering she was talking about Lizette's grandmother, Ricki quickly added, "No offense, Lizette."

"None taken." Lizette flashed an impish grin. "Olivia and I have news too."

"That's why we were already here celebrating," Olivia said. "The Gaia court is back on."

Lizette gave her an affectionate pat on the shoulder. "And this one's back to being queen."

"That's great," Ricki said, adding, "I think? I've lost track where you stand on the whole court thing, Liv."

Olivia acknowledged this with a rueful nod. "Yeah, that's on me. But I'm a hundred percent excited now."

Ricki refreshed her drink. "So, what happened?"

"When I quit as queen, the whole court quit with me," Olivia said. "It was the nicest thing ever. I get emotional thinking about it." She squeezed her eyes shut and shook her hands. "Not gonna cry, not gonna cry."

"It's OK if you do," Lizette said, adding for the benefit of the others, "I'm a psych major. I encourage people to have all the feels."

Virgil choked back a laugh and Ricki kicked him lightly under the table.

"The guys in charge of the krewe started investigating to see who was behind the campaign to get rid of me and . . ." Olivia stopped. She cast a hesitant glance at Lizette.

"I'll finish the story," Lizette said. "I'm the one who . . . what do they say in mysteries? Broke the case? Cracked the case?"

"Either's fine," Ricki said.

"The whole anti-Olivia movement was because of my effing, pardon my language, grandmother," Lizette said. "You know, Mrs. Rancourt. But it wasn't personal to Olivia. Gram would have pulled her sh— her stuff on whoever was queen. She freaked out that I broke the family chain of Gaia court queens. I would have been fourth gen. Penelope Vogelspack told me her dad has been trying to get my grandmother to switch from her long-time law firm to his for years. She finally did and I heard my dad arguing with her about it and thought it was weird, so I told him what Penny told me. And Mr. Vogelspack got busted. It turns out he and my grandmother made a deal. She'd give him her business if he got rid of Olivia and installed me as queen so there was no break in the Rancourt chain."

Zellah chortled. "That's some serious Uptowner chicanery. I love it."

"Gaia was gonna kick Lizette and Penny off the court but I wouldn't let them," Olivia said. "They shouldn't be punished for the adults' stupid behavior."

"That's super mature," Ricki said, impressed. "You'll make a wonderful queen . . ." she made a mock bow. "Your highness."

Olivia groaned and made a face. "Ugh. People better not do that at the Mardi Gras ball."

Theo let out a joyous shout, startling everyone. "You're not gonna believe this. I'm a meme! I'm 'Real Estate Man.'"

He showed off his phone, scrolling through multiple images of him bonking Brenda on the head with the framed needle-point with various cartoony tags like the one he'd mentioned. A number of comments lauded his courage. "Tomas took the pics and posted them to his socials. A couple of ladies said I was hot." Theo delivered with a swagger. "Unfortunately they're out-of-state followers. Except for one guy. I'm pretty sure it's the barista from the coffee shop near me. I could never tell if he was being polite or flirty. Now I know."

"Good for you," Ricki said. "You earned your hero title. I hope it translates into new clients."

"It already has," Theo said, exultant. "I just got a text from Helene Mansieur. She wants to meet with me. She and her doctor husband are considering selling their house and down-sizing to one of the Four Seasons condos." Theo hooked his thumbs under his arms and struck a cocky pose. "And I know who can talk them into it: Real Estate Man!"

Theo shot out his arms like Superman and pretended to fly, to everyone's amusement.

Ricki's phone buzzed with a text alert. "It must be my parents." She checked to see the sender. "Darn, it's not. It's from Nina."

"Does Nina say anything about me and how heroic I was?" Theo asked, ever hopeful.

"I doubt it," Cookie said, "but I'm sure the words 'restraining order' are in there somewhere." This earned her a dirty look from Theo and laughter from the others.

"Nothing about you good or bad," Ricki said. She read the text out loud: Nice work. Now do us a solid and catch the Bongle Bandit.

This garnered more laughs. Ricki joined in, then stopped. Her friends and family fell into casual conversation. Suddenly Ricki cried out, "That's it!"

Her outburst startled the others. Cookie clutched her chest. "Give me a heart attack why dontcha."

"Something tied to the Bongle Bandit has been floating around in my head and I finally remembered what. Lady said there was no way the bandit could be from New Orleans.

Edgar, the caroler who got into a fight with Larry, another caroler, isn't from the city. Maybe he's the bandit."

"Not being from here isn't a lot to go on," Mordant said.

"True," Ricki admitted. "Still, I never completely trusted the carolers. They were way too cheerful. It felt forced to me."

"That could be because they got tired of singing all those carols ad nauseum and had to fake it sometimes," Cookie said.

"I guess. Sorry about that. Too much amateur detecting on my part. I'm officially off the clock."

She drained her Pimm's Cup and was about to refill it when her phone rang. She traded her cup for her phone. "It's Mom. Finally." She answered the call. "Mom, hi. Where are you guys?"

"I don't know. I mean, I know where I am. I don't . . ."

Josepha let out a sound that was half gasp, half sob. Ricki had never heard her mother sound so distraught. Alarm coursed through her veins. "Mom, what's going on? Where's Dad?"

"I don't know." Josepha's voice broke. "He had a post-mortem meeting with Patrick and never came home. I've been trying to reach him but he's not responding and his location feature is turned off. I think something's happened to him. Something bad."

THIRTY-THREE

The minute Ricki told everyone Luis was missing, the group sprang into action. Ricki and her friends now huddled around a Bayou Backyard picnic table where Virgil had spread out a paper map of the New Orleans metro area that the BB kept on hand for tourists "The police can only cover so much ground," Virgil said. "We can split up and take sections of the city."

"I got Nina's permission for all of us to put her on speed dial with the proviso we delete the number the minute Dad is safe," Ricki said. "That means you, Theo."

"Real Estate Man" grunted reluctant agreement.

Virgil began sectioning off the city. A few frat boys had stopped their game of cornhole and wandered over, sensing the fraught situation. "Oh, hey, Mateo," Olivia said, recognizing the lanky, dark-haired leader of the group.

"Hey." Mateo eyed the map with curiosity. "Whassup?"

Olivia filled him and his fraternity brothers in. Intrigued, they stepped in for a closer look at the map. "Who's got the Bywater?" a frat brother asked. "You gotta search that big old abandoned building on the river."

One of his frat brothers scoffed. "The old naval base? Dude, no. That place is Crime Activity Central. Way too obvious."

"There's this big train yard out by where my family lives in Jefferson," Mateo said. "Lotta train cars are parked there. Some are old and fancy and being fixed up. When I was in high school, we used to sneak on to some of the cars and get high. It's pretty huge and only one guard. Not much he can do."

"Jefferson." A snippet of the only exchange Ricki ever had with Patrick came back to her. "Patrick grew up there."

"Then he'd know about the train yard," Mateo said. "It's like, a thing."

"Mordant, you section off the rest of the city," Virgil said. "Ricki and I are heading to the train yard."

"I'll come with you," Mateo said. "I know it."

"Me too," Olivia jumped in.

Virgil and Ricki hesitated, then Virgil said, "We'll do it because it'll get us there faster. But you two never leave the car. You got it?"

The intensity in his voice got through to the twenty-somethings, who swore agreement.

Virgil's hybrid SUV raced along Airline Drive. "Next left," Mateo said. Virgil followed the student's directions, turning onto Tom Benson Way, then Stable Drive. Dozens of train cars sat lined up on tracks, some freight, others antique passenger cars in various states of restoration.

"This is a maze," Ricki said, disheartened.

"The guard house is up ahead," Mateo said. "Maybe he can help us. Like, let us know if he's seen anything suspicious."

"Good idea," Olivia said, impressed.

Virgil kept driving until they reached a double-wide trailer. He parked and told the others, "Ricki and I will go inside. You two stay here and don't move."

"I know the guard, he's been here forever," Mateo said. "He's actually a nice guy. He never called the cops on us."

"Maybe Mateo should come," Ricki said. "We don't know how the guard will react to you and me barging in on a dark night."

"Point taken. Mateo, you're in."

"No way am I staying in the car alone," Olivia declared.

All four got out of the SUV, shutting their doors as quietly as possible. They took the four steps up to the trailer door. Mateo gave it a gentle knock. "Harris, hey. Hello?" There was no answer. "Maybe he's patrolling. We can leave him a note."

He tried the door. It opened and they stepped inside. Olivia gasped and clutched Ricki.

An elderly man in a security uniform lay on the floor. He groaned.

The four dropped to the floor by his side. Virgil and Mateo

helped him to a sitting position. He pulled away from them. "Are you with the other guy?"

"No, and what other guy?" Virgil asked.

"The one who cold-cocked me when I wouldn't give him keys to an old Pullman sleeper car."

"I know that car," Mateo said, excited. "It's cool."

The older man peered at Mateo. "I remember you. You're one of the kids I was always chasing off."

"Yeah," Mateo said, sheepish. "Sorry about that."

"Why would he want to hide in that car?" Ricki wondered.

"It's attached to a freight train pulling out tonight," the guard said. "Rich people rent it for parties. It's going to Phoenix."

"Plenty of open space on the way for Patrick to push your dad off the train and no one to find the body," Virgil said, his tone grim. "You kids stay here with Harris. Call the police."

"Where's the sleeper car?" Ricki asked.

"Farthest end of the yard," Harris said.

"I know where it is," Mateo said. "I'll take you."

Ricki and Virgil didn't protest. It made sense. Luckily, Olivia didn't balk at being left with Harris. She was busy tending to the bump on the back of his head when the others left.

Virgil, Ricki, and Mateo made their way past the rows of silent, empty trains, their eyes gradually adjusting to dark. "We're almost at the sleeper car," Mateo whispered. "It's on the other side of the turntable they use to turn the engines around."

They were in sight of the car when Virgil pulled up short. "There," he whispered.

Ahead of them, Ricki saw Patrick holding a gun to her father's back as they emerged from the train tracks and started across the turntable.

"He's got a gun?" Ricki muttered. "First Brenda, now him. There are way too many guns in this state."

"We can talk politics after we rescue your father," Virgil said.

"I can't alert Nina, my phone will light up and Patrick will see us."

"You may not have to. Listen."

Ricki heard police sirens, their distant wail growing louder by the minute. She saw Patrick register the sound. He turned and their eyes met. Ricki stood still, paralyzed with fear. Suddenly Luis let out a roar. He became a whirling dervish, his meditative low-impact tai chi movements morphing into their original intent of self-defense. A high kick to Patrick's arm sent the kidnapper's gun flying. Virgil grabbed the gun while Luis used a few more moves to take Patrick down and pin him to the ground.

"Oh man, that was awesome," Mateo said, entranced.

"We forget tai chi began as a Chinese martial art," Ricki said as they ran to her father. "Dad, are you OK?"

"I'm better than OK." Luis planted a foot in Patrick's back and raised his arms like a triumphant prize fighter. "I just caught the Bongle Bandit."

By the time the gang once again gathered at the Bayou Backyard, it was one in the morning. Nina, who got the honor of booking Patrick, delivered Luis to a hero's welcome. Eugenia even showed up to make sure granddaughter Olivia hadn't experienced another trauma like the close call with a kidnapping she'd endured on Halloween.

"Can you stick around tonight?" Ricki asked Nina. "I'd like to treat you to a drink. Or ten."

Nina checked the time on her phone. "It's 12:01 a.m. Technically it's tomorrow morning, so I'm off duty. Not only can I join the festivities, I can take you up on those ten drinks."

Nina inserted herself on the bench next to Ricki, who poured her a mug of beer. "Abita Amber."

"A favorite." Nina took the mug. "Thanks." She put two fingers of her free hand in her mouth and emitted an ear-shattering whistle that got everyone's attention. She held the mug up to Luis. "To the man who saved Christmas for me. And New Orleans."

"I guess my fifteen minutes are over," Theo said with a theatrical sigh as everyone clamored to hear Luis's story.

"How did you figure out Patrick was the Bongle Bandit?" Cookie asked.

"I wish I could say I did, but I didn't," Luis admitted. "I

kept a list of all the times I covered for Patrick on the shooting. Plenty you didn't know about, Virgil."

"I had a feeling," the chef said. "But I got the impression you wanted to handle it yourself."

"I did. I showed Patrick the list when we met. Originally, I was gonna report him to the union for contract violations but I decided to talk to him first. If he owned his behavior and promised to change, I wouldn't say anything, depending on how his next job went. But it turned out a lot of the times on my list lined up with Bongle Bandit burglaries. That's what he thought I was confronting him with. By the time we realized we were talking about two different things, it was too late for me. He'd outed himself as the bandit."

"I was way off on this one," Ricki said. "My friend Lady at Good Neighbor Thrift said no local would besmirch the name of the Bongle Bandit, so I ruled out Patrick when I found out he was a metro NOLA native. I thought the bandit was one of our creepy carolers."

Nina snorted. "Oh, that foursome of thieves. We picked them up this afternoon. They were lifting items from homes where they'd been hired to sing at private parties."

"Yes! I knew it," Ricki said, pleased with herself. "I'm relieved I still have decent instincts."

"Back to our bandit," Nina said. "Sam and I dug up the real reason Flynn lost his job at the news station. Corporation HR departments are so terrified of lawsuits you practically need a warrant to get anything out of them these days. It does help when you wake up the head of the department in the middle of the night and their defenses are down."

"So, what's his story?" Zellah asked.

"I'm gonna take a guess and say gambling debts," Mordant said.

"Well done," Nina said. She gave him an approving thumbs-up. "Flynn may have been doing it on his own time, but no newsroom is gonna be on board with an employee cutting deals with gang-connected loan sharks."

"I'm just relieved it's all over," Josepha said, clinging tightly to Luis's hand.

"And now I know I can use my tai chi as a martial art," Luis said. "I always wondered."

"I hope you never have to again," Ricki said, squeezing her father's other hand.

"We owe a thank-you to another person at this table." Virgil used his beer mug to indicate Mateo. "Without you, buddy, Luis might be lying in a patch of dirt between here and Phoenix."

"Whatevs." Mateo shrugged and smiled shyly. "Glad I could help."

"Mateo, I was thinking, would you like to be a duke in the Krewe of Gaia court?" Olivia asked.

"Sounds cool." Mateo pushed a chunk of his shoulder-length hair that had fallen over his eyes out of the way. He took a rubber band out of his jeans pocket and pulled his hair into a top knot. "But are you sure you want a Hispanic first-gen scholarship student?"

Olivia folded her arms in front of her chest. "My court," she declared. "My rules."

Mateo's smile faded, replaced by worry. "I won't have to cut my hair or anything?"

"Nah. Lizette is talking about getting a face tattoo."

Eugenia choked on her Martini. "I'm beginning to fear next year's Mardi Gras," the older woman said once she got her breath back.

"Relax. It's months away." Ricki patted her on the back. "Just close your eyes and think of Christmas."

THIRTY-FOUR

The Saturday night prior to Christmas, Virgil invited friends and family to a *Delicious Dining Tradition* watch party at Bon Vee, while enjoying their own Réveillon dinner courtesy of the chef. The show earned a standing ovation for Virgil, who reacted with both embarrassment and pride. Ricki refused to let him dismiss the accolades as an expected reaction from loved ones. Reviews and ratings the next day confirmed their enthusiasm.

On Sunday, Ricki retrieved Red Beans from Kitty Kat. "I expect you to behave," she told the kitten as she carried her into the house. Red Beans responded by immediately chasing Princess and her Lamby into the closet. Taking this as a win, Red Beans pushed her luck and batted Lamby out of Princess's paws. The German shepherd shot up to her full height and let out the kind of growl that made the breed a popular choice as guard dogs. She followed the growl with a cacophony of angry barks. Red Beans released what Ricki swore sounded like a terrified *Eep!* She dropped Lamby and took off, leaping her way to the top of the cat tree. Princess stopped barking and retrieved her favorite toy. She rested her head on Lamby and closed her eyes to nap. "I'll leave this in your hands, alpha girl," Ricki said to Princess, petting her smooth fur.

Ricki picked up her car keys and headed out to pick up her parents. It was time to introduce them to a spot that had become dear to her heart. Circumstances had precluded this so far in their visit. But with Virgil's show in the can, Luis's schedule was wide open. So was Josepha's. She'd given her notice at Crescent City Concierge Care, admitting to the real motivation behind her taking the job: digging up dirt on Phyllis. The response to her subterfuge was unexpected. "Why didn't you tell us this in the first place?" Delia demanded. "None of us liked her. We would've been happy to help!"

As Ricki drove her parents to Dispersed of Judah Cemetery, the tone was somber. She led Josepha and Luis through the hallowed grounds to a simple above-ground tomb. Carved into its front was a name and date: Benjamin David Fine, 1931–55. A Star of David was the tomb's only ornamentation. Ricki had told her parents Mordant had tracked down her great-grandfather as soon as she'd learned of his discovery. They'd insisted on paying homage to him by making a pilgrimage to his resting place.

The three closed their eyes for a moment of prayer, then opened them. Josepha and Luis simultaneously began crossing themselves, dropping their hands when they realized what they were doing. "Lo siento," Luis said, abashed.

Josepha echoed his apology. "It's instinctual for us. We'd never want to be disrespectful of his religion."

"I'm sure he would understand, and appreciate you showed him respect in your own faith." Ricki placed a hand on the tomb. She was silent, deep in thought. After a moment, she spoke. "For the longest time, I've been obsessed with finding my birth family. But after everything we've been through . . ." Ricki paused, her emotions welling up. "I have my connection to my great-grandfather and grandmother Genevieve. I have Eugenia. Theo. Olivia. All the Charbonnets. For better or worse, and some of the distant relatives are definitely for the worse. But most of all, I have you. So I don't need to search anymore."

The tears came. A river of them.

"Baby girl." Josepha, also weeping, held out her arms.

"Ricki sandwich!" Luis cried out. He threw his arms around Ricki from one side and Josepha from the other, with Ricki in the middle. The family held tight to each other, their tears commingling.

Josepha pulled away. She wiped her cheeks with the back of her hand. "But you shouldn't stop searching, baby. You've got every right to want to know your birth roots. It's necessary for when you have your own kids, and notice I said 'when', not 'if.' You may have health questions only your birth family can answer."

"That's true." Ricki sniffled. Luis dug a tissue out of his pants pocket and gave it to his daughter. "I'll think about picking it up again in the new year. Right now, I want to focus on our time together. We can go now."

"First . . ."

Josepha laid a hand on the tomb. Luis and Ricki followed suit. After a moment of silence, they headed back to the car.

On the walk back, they passed a crypt whose front appeared carved with a letter. "Is that a recipe?" Josepha squinted to see.

"It is." Ricki checked it out. "I thought it might be the one the carolers fought over for our cookbook but it's not." They continued toward the car. "It's pretty cool, isn't it? There are recipes like this scattered around cemeteries across the country."

"Now that would make one interesting cookbook," Luis said.

Ricki stopped in her tracks. Her face lit up. "Dad, you just gave me a fantastic idea. Thank you."

Luis shrugged. "No idea what I did, but if you're happy, I'm happy." He affectionately ruffled Ricki's mop of curls and hopped in the car.

Ricki spent the next two days begging favors from her friends to help her bring idea to fruition. She finally finished on Christmas Eve and passed out, waking up on Christmas morning.

The James-Diazes, which now included Virgil, joined the Charbonnet-Felices for a luncheon at Bon Vee catered by Commander's Palace. After spending the day with their own families, the Bon Vee staff showed up for champagne and dessert. The white lights and golden ornaments decorating the front parlor's stately Christmas tree cast a glow on the celebrants.

While everyone enjoyed a second and in some cases third round of champagne, Ricki led Virgil into her shop for privacy. She clutched a gift-wrapped shirt box in her hands. She was about to hand it to him when she was beset by an attack of insecurity. "This is super rudimentary. I didn't have the idea until a couple of days ago. Zellah and Cookie helped me pull it together, but it's still very basic and—"

Virgil put a finger to her lips. "Stop apologizing. Gimme."

He winked and held out his hands. Ricki handed him the box. He unwrapped it and a wide grin spread across his face. "This is awesome, as a California friend of mine would say." He held up a handmade, spiral-bound cookbook. The cover featured the recipe Ricki had seen on the gravestone in the Dispersed of Judah cemetery, beautifully illustrated by Zellah.

"It's a collection of recipes people have used to pay homage to their loved ones at their resting places," Ricki, flooded with relief, explained. "I found a few in the New Orleans area and Cookie helped me research the rest. They're from all over the world. When the recipe was in a foreign language, I put photos of the gravestones on the front of the page and translations on the back."

Virgil thumbed through the cookbook, beaming. "This is incredible. And you know what? It'd be a great theme for my next cooking show."

"There's going to be another one?" Ricki asked, thrilled for her love.

Virgil gave a proud nod. "*Réveillon* is such a hit that Food Plus is already working up a contract for my next project."

"That's fantastic," Ricki gushed. She threw her arms around Virgil.

"My turn to gift you." Virgil separated from Ricki. He reached into his blazer interior pocket and pulled out an envelope. "Here."

Ricki opened the envelope and took out a document. "This looks like an itinerary."

"It is. You've immersed yourself in my world. Now it's time for you to show me yours. I bought us a long weekend in Los Angeles, with first-class airfare, an ocean-view hotel room in Santa Monica, and a rental convertible EV. I figure that's as L.A. as it gets."

"It is," Ricki said laughing. "I'm going to start a list of all my favorite places to take you. There's an awesome hike in the valley. And one of our favorite restaurants in East L.A. Oh, and we have to go to the Huntington Gardens in San Marino."

Brimming with enthusiasm, she added, "It's the perfect present, Virgil. Thank you."

"Merry Christmas, chère." Virgil placed a finger under Ricki's chin and lifted her lips to his. "There's one more gift for you. Not from me. From Mordant. Hold on."

He took out his cell phone and typed a text. The shop door opened and Mordant popped his head into the shop. "I've been waiting in the hallway for you to give me the high sign."

"The floor's yours," Virgil said.

Mordant stepped inside. He appeared a combination of excited and nervous. "I have news. Big news." He took a breath and then said. "Ricki . . . I've found your birth mother."

Ricki gaped at him. She felt lightheaded and swayed. Virgil steadied her. "Easy, chère. You need to sit down?"

She shook her head. She opened her mouth, but nothing came out. She tried again. "Wha . . . how?"

"I wish I could say it was because I'm a brilliant investigator," Mordant said. "But I don't get any credit for it. When was the last time you checked your ancestry site?"

"I have no idea. I've been too busy. Plus, I kind of gave up."

"Since I have your log-in info, I check it regularly."

Mordant opened an app on his phone and passed the phone to Ricki. She read what was on the screen. "The name. It's familiar." Ricki hurried to the shop desk. She opened a drawer and pulled out receipts. She landed on one. She read it, then held it up with a shaking hand. "Here. This is her."

"She knows about you and is very eager to meet," Mordant said.

Ricki put a hand to her heart to quell its rapid racing. "Yes, yes. I would love that. Tonight. Now."

"She doesn't want to wait either," her P.I. friend said.

Mordant parked his hearse in front of a lovely Victorian home on Race Street in the Lower Garden District. "I'll wait here."

Ricki got out of the car. She walked across the sidewalk and up the home's front steps. She took a beat to calm herself, then rang the doorbell. The door instantly opened, revealing Beth

Norris, the customer from New York who'd been so kind when Ricki experienced her post-mask skin disaster.

There was a moment of silence. Then the women burst into tears and fell into each other's arms. "I had no idea it was you when I was at your shop," Beth said through her tears. "My kids, they're twins, and they just started college. I waited until now to tell them I'd given up a baby at sixteen. They're the ones who gave me the courage to look for you."

"My half-siblings," Ricki said through her own tears.

"They bought me a DNA kit for my birthday in November," Beth said. "I got the test results back yesterday. That's when the results must have shown up on your family tree and your friend Mordant saw them. I can't believe we found each other."

"Same." Ricki clung to her birth mother. Over Beth's shoulder, she saw Mordant had gotten out of the hearse. He was leaning against it, watching the reunion of Ricki's literal lifetime. He wiped a tear from his eye.

"We have so much to talk about I don't even know where to begin," Beth said.

Ricki thought of all the questions she'd accumulated over the years, so many she'd written them down in a journal, ready for the day when she finally found her birth parents. She made a decision.

"Talking can wait." She let go of Beth. "It's Christmas. I'm bringing you back to Bon Vee. Everyone is waiting to meet you. My family. Your family."

Ricki looked into Beth's eyes, the same shade of hazel as her own. "Our family."

RECIPES FOR A RÉVEILLON DINNER

Thanks to Virgil Morel, you too can create a Réveillon dinner. ☺.

Kidding aside, the recipes I chose for *Crescent City Christmas Chaos* are all inspired and adapted from Louisiana-themed vintage cookbooks in my personal collection. The cookbooks include *To a King's Taste: Recipes Collected by The National Society of the Colonial Dames of America in the State of Louisiana* (1955 ed.); *The Second Ford Treasury of Favorite Recipes from Famous Eating Places*; compiled by Nancy Kennedy (1954); *The Art of Creole Cookery*; William I. Kaufman, Sister Mary Ursula Cooper, O.P. (1962 ed.); *The New Orleans Restaurant Cookbook: Revised and Updated Edition*; written and illustrated by Deirdre Stanforth (1976); *Louisiana Legacy*; Thibodaux Service League, Inc. (1982); *The Encyclopedia of Cajun & Creole Cuisine*; Chef John D. Folse, Lafitte's Landing Restaurant (1983 ed.)

I've arranged the recipes in order of a Réveillon meal: first a soup, then an appetizer, followed by a main course with two vegetable side dishes, and finally a traditional New Orleans dessert of bread pudding, with a twist courtesy of yours truly. I've also included a "lagniappe"—that's a Louisiana term meaning "a little something extra." In this case, it's a recipe for Little Rice Cakes, also known as Calas, a Big Easy treat popular in the nineteenth century.

In my study of vintage cookbooks, I've noticed there's often an absence of herbs and spices in books published prior to the 1960s. When I adapt a recipe, I try to stick to the original ingredients as closely as possible, but I encourage you to play with seasonings.

THE RECIPES
Almond Soup

This is one of the strangest recipes I've ever adapted. It's less of a soup and more of a porridge. When it cools, it's so thick you can eat it with a fork!

If you do decide to be adventurous and give it a go, experiment by adding Cajun seasoning. You can also try halving the amount of almonds, and/or adding more milk to reduce the thickness of the "soup."

You know what, now that I think about it, in its porridge consistency this would make an interesting savory breakfast dish.

Ingredients:

1 lb. chopped almonds, finely chopped (I used a food processor)
¼ cup butter
¾ cup flour
2 pints whole milk
Salt and pepper to taste
Worcestershire sauce to taste
1 jigger sherry
2 stalks chopped celery
2 small or 1 large shallot, chopped
½ pint whipped cream, unsweetened

Directions:

Melt the butter in a Dutch oven over medium-low heat. Add the celery and shallots and cook until soft and wilted. Add the flour, salt, pepper, Worcestershire sauce, milk, and sherry. Stir constantly for ten or fifteen minutes, making sure the flour is integrated and doesn't clump. Remove from heat and add almonds. Serve with a dollop of whipped cream on top.

Servings: 6–8 (or more, if the serving size is small, like a half-cup)

Shrimp Au Gratin

Ingredients:

2 lbs. cleaned and peeled raw shrimp
Dash of lemon juice
½ cup butter
1 cup flour
1 tsp. salt
¼ tsp. black pepper
3 egg yolks, beaten
2 T. sherry wine
3 T. grated parmesan cheese, divided
Breadcrumbs to cover the shrimp, about ½ a cup to ¾ cup

Directions:

NOTE: Make sure you have all your ingredients ready to go, because things progress fast with this recipe.

Place the shrimp in a large saucepan with a quart of water and a dash of lemon juice. Bring to a boil. When the shrimp turn pink, use a slotted spoon to remove them and put them in a bowl. Keep boiling the water for about five minutes.

In a large skillet or sauté pan, melt the butter, then add the flour and stir until smooth. Add four cups of the shrimp stock, stirring constantly. (I use a whisk to break up the clumps.) Stir in the salt, pepper, beaten yolks, wine, and two tablespoons of the cheese, then add the shrimp.

Transfer the mixture to a buttered casserole dish and top with the third tablespoon of cheese and the breadcrumbs.

Bake at 350–375 degrees for around 15 minutes.

Servings: 6–8

Chicken Creole

Ingredients:

3 ½ to 4 lb. chicken, in pieces
¼ cup (4 T.) butter (Note: the original recipe called for 2 tablespoons of butter, but the chicken was sticking to the pot, so I added 2 additional tablespoons of butter)
1 cup sliced onions
1 cup cooked or canned tomatoes
2 T. flour
2 cloves minced garlic
1 tsp. dried thyme leaves
2 tsp. minced parsley
2 bay leaves
3 cups seeded and chopped green peppers
2 celery stalks, chopped
1 cup boiling water (Note: the sauce in this recipe is soupy, so if you'd prefer it thicker, start by adding less water and then add more if you think you need it)
1 ½ tsp. salt
¼ tsp. black pepper

Directions:

Rub the chicken with the salt and pepper. Melt the butter in a large sauté pan or Dutch oven (which is what I used). Brown the chicken for about five minutes. Remove the chicken to a plate.

Add the sliced onions and brown them. Add the flour and stir until it browns. Add tomatoes, garlic, thyme, parsley, celery, and bay leaves. Cover the pan and simmer over low heat for about five minutes, stirring from time to time. Add the chicken back to the mixture and stir to coat the chicken.

Add the green peppers and boiling water and simmer until the chicken is tender, stirring occasionally and turning the chicken pieces over at least once to cook thoroughly. To make sure the chicken is done, I cut deep into the thickest breast and confirm it's no longer raw or pink.

Serve over a half-cup or cup of cooked white rice. Put a bottle of Tabasco sauce out on the table so guests who'd like to add a little heat can season to taste.

Servings: 4–6

Spinach Dunbar

Ingredients:

4 bunches fresh spinach (or 1 ½ lbs. frozen spinach)
1 quart water
¾ tsp. baking soda
¾ tsp. salt
1 half-cup stick butter
1 tsp. flour
¼ can evaporated milk
Salt and pepper to taste
1 hard-boiled egg, riced

Directions:

If using fresh spinach, boil in water with baking soda and salt for 8–10 minutes. Drain the spinach and chop fine. (If using frozen spinach, cook according to the directions on the package.)

Melt the butter in a saucepan and slowly stir in the flour. Gradually blend in the milk, then add the spinach. Season to taste and garnish with riced egg.

Servings: 6–8

Champignons Chablis

Ingredients:

1 lb. medium-size fresh mushrooms
1 tsp. sweet basil
1 tsp. marjoram
1 tsp. minced chives
½ cup melted butter
⅓ cup chicken bouillon
⅓ cup Chablis or other white wine
¾ tsp. salt
Dash of black pepper
Dash of sherry

Directions:

Preheat oven to 350 degrees.

Wash and dry the mushrooms and trim the ends if necessary.
Arrange them in a one-quart casserole dish.

Mix the remaining ingredients and pour over the mushrooms.
Cover the casserole dish and bake for 20–25 minutes.

This recipe creates a delicious broth. I recommend serving
the mushrooms, along with the broth, over rice.

Servings: 4

Bread Pudding With
Rum Sauce

IMPORTANT NOTE! This recipe makes a huge amount of filling. I wound up using both an 11" x 17" baking dish and a 9" x 13" baking dish.

Ingredients:

For the bread pudding:
2 loaves day-old French bread
6 eggs, beaten
2 cups sugar
2 T. cinnamon
2 T. nutmeg
2 T. vanilla extract
¼ lb. butter
½ gallon whole milk
1 can evaporated milk
1 small can crushed pineapple
4 bananas, sliced

For the rum sauce:
¼ cup butter
¾ cup packed brown sugar
¼ tsp. cinnamon
Dash of ground nutmeg
Dash of ground cloves
¼ cup heavy whipping cream
¼ cup rum

Directions for the bread pudding:

Preheat the oven to 350 degrees.

Melt the butter in a large saucepan over medium heat. Add the evaporated milk, the sugar, and ½ gallon of whole milk. Stir to combine and continue to heat until the mixture is hot. Remove from heat and let cool.

Break the French bread into chunks or slices, if it's baguettes, and place in a large bowl. Once the milk mixture has cooled, whisk in the beaten eggs, nutmeg, cinnamon, and vanilla extract. Add the can of pineapple and mix well. Pour the mixture over the bread and let it soak until the bread is soft. Add the bananas, mixing well to combine.

Pour the mix into both baking dishes, distributing evenly. Take turns making each for approximately an hour.

While the bread is baking, make the rum sauce.

Directions for the rum sauce:

Melt the butter in a large skillet, then stir in the brown sugar, cinnamon, cloves, and nutmeg. When the mixture starts bubbling, add the heavy cream and quickly stir to combine, otherwise it will harden. Once the cream is incorporated, stir in the rum. The sauce will be extremely hot, so let it cool a bit before serving.

Serve the sauce on the side or on top of the bread pudding.

Servings: a lot!

"Lagniappe"—A Little Something Extra
Little Rice Cakes (Aka Calas)

Little Rice Cakes are also known as "Calas," a treat sold during the nineteenth century from baskets or bowls "Calas women" carried on their heads. The cakes were often served with apple jelly or Louisiana orange marmalade as a tasty addition to a chicken or ham dinner. To my mind, the Little Rice Cakes, which are like beignets with rice as an added ingredient, would also make a great breakfast treat—probably a better one than the Almond "Soup" porridge!

Ingredients:

1 cup cooked cold white rice
3 whole eggs
½ cup granulated sugar
½ tsp. salt
Pinch of nutmeg
1 cup flour
3 tsp. baking powder
Vegetable oil for frying
Powdered sugar or cinnamon-sugar

Directions:

Beat the eggs until fluffy. Add the rice, sugar, salt, flour, and nutmeg and beat well.

Heat up about half an inch of vegetable oil in a large sauté or frying pan. (Once the oil is hot, lower the temperature so that it doesn't splatter and burn you.)

Drop the batter into the oil by hefty, rounded tablespoons.

Fry the rice cakes on one side until the batter bubbles a bit and hardens around the edges, then use a spatula or slotted spoon to flip each one. Fry until the cakes are puffy and golden brown. Remove them from the oil and drain on paper towels. Sprinkle with powdered sugar or cinnamon-sugar and serve immediately.

Servings: approximately 20

Acknowledgments

Profuse thanks to everyone at Severn House for making the publication of my fourth Vintage Cookbook Mystery such a great experience. Additional thanks to my wonderful agent Doug Grad for the fantastic publisher matchmaking.

Special thanks to Nicole Vickers for her beta reads of both *French Quarter Fright Night* and *Crescent City Christmas Chaos*. I'm so grateful to you, Nicole! I also have to thank my old college pal Frank Moon for always sending me the most interesting articles, especially the one about recipes written on gravestones. You can thank him for that particular subplot in this book, lol. Keep 'em coming, Frank!

Huge love and thanks for my fellow blogmates at Chicks on the Case, my group mates at the Cozy Mystery Crew Facebook page, and my Fearless Foursome. And a shout-out to my NOLA crew! Your support and insight inspires me, as does our beloved Crescent City.

As always, a ton of love and gratitude to my husband Jerry and daughter Eliza for their patience and endless support. I truly couldn't do this writing thing without you. And to my late mom and dad, two voracious readers who passed on their passion for books to all three of their children. I will miss you both forever.